A Soldier's Dilemma

A Soldier's Dilemma

Brig Baqir Shameem (Retd)

Published by
PRABHAT PRAKASHAN PVT. LTD.
4/19 Asaf Ali Road,
New Delhi-110 002 (INDIA)
e-mail: prabhatbooks@gmail.com

ISBN 978-93-5521-905-3
A SOLDIER'S DILEMMA
by Brig Baqir Shameem (Retd)

Edition
First, 2023

Paperback Price
₹ 400.00 (Rupees Four Hundred only)

Printed at
R-Tech Offset Printers, Delhi

To

Nilofar my eternal partner

Acknowledgement

My sincere thanks to Mr Soumendra Padhi, movie director whose maiden film Budhia Singh : Born to Run was awarded National and International awards. It has been over two years since we have associated ourselves in crafting the novel. His valuable inputs through discussions and pointers on the pages sent to him, have been extremely valuable to me to evaluate and create.

Many thanks and gratitude to my wife and the children for their love and care.

Preamble

Urmila wiped the sweat from her forehead with the hem of her sari and sat down on the bed to rest awhile. It was humid and even with the air conditioning she could feel the moisture spread all over her body. It further accentuated as she got up and exerted herself to assemble and pack the household goods in suitcases and container boxes.

"Mommy! I do not want to go to Hyderabad, I want to stay here in Gauhati," she heard her daughter Hina say as she entered the room.

"Fine with me! You stay alone here! Papa and me are going," Urmila teased her.

"You know that I cannot stay alone! I want you both to stay here! Please! I do not want to leave my friends!" Hina pleaded.

"Tell them to come with you!" She smiled and said.

"No! I will not! They will not leave their mummy and papa!" Hina replied curtly.

"Then you will have to leave them!" Urmila said, looking towards her.

"Oh mummy! You are so cruel!" Hina called out and stamped her feet in frustration.

"Really? Let us ask your father if he feels the same!" She said and got up. Hina followed her to the next room where Brijesh was clearing his table and placing various articles in a box.

"Papa, please do not go! I do not mind staying here, even if you come very late from your office! Sometimes when I do not meet you, mummy forces me to go and sleep!" Hina looked at Brijesh and pleaded.

"You know Hina! After lots of hard work your Papa has got this job in DRDO (Defence Research and Development Organisation). They have very strict office timings from 9 to 5. I will be back home by 5.30 in the evening everyday! We can go out and enjoy after that!" Brijesh patted her head and told her.

"Fine! Then I will go with you to Hyderabad," Hina smiled and replied

"Have you packed your bags?" Brijesh asked her

"Yes, Mummy helped me to put all my clothes and toys in my suitcase. I am not taking my books. I do not require them. I want new books for my new class in Hyderabad!" Hina replied.

"Yes you are a big girl now! You are going to study in first grade," Urmila said and pinched her cheeks.

"Mummy! Do not do that! I told you many times that I do not like it! My cheeks will become hard!" Hina shouted in frustration.

Urmila pulled her closer and planted kisses on both her cheeks!

"Now they will remain soft!" She said and laughed.

"Mummy! Behave yourself, I do not like it!" Hina retorted, showing her annoyance.

"Why are you irritating my sweetheart? Come here beti let me wipe your cheeks," Brijesh told her, removing a kerchief from his pocket.

Hina ran towards Brijesh who held her by the shoulders, bent down and planted kisses on her cheeks!

"Papa! You are as bad as mummy! I will never talk to you both!" She shouted and ran away towards her room.

With smiles on their faces they sat on the same sofa, close to one another. Brijesh held Urmila's face in his hands and kissed her lovingly. Brimming with emotion, Urmila held him tightly and responded with equal gusto.

"I saw you! I saw you!" They heard Hina clapping and shouting out loud. Disentangling themselves, they got up with a start and looked towards her.

"Go and sleep now. We have an early morning train to catch. Good night!" Brijesh told Hina opening the door to her room.

With the lights off Brijesh and Urmila resumed their compassionate copulation with greater intensity and vigor and stopped when they were tired. In the next room Hina had closed her eyes the moment she lay on her bed and soon was in deep slumber.

Brijesh had decided to travel by train primarily due to the large numbers of domestic baggage that had accumulated over the past years. It had also cost him a handsome amount to book them on the train. He had ruled out sending the baggage and the scooter by road transport due to the prevailing insurgency situation in the region. There were innumerable incidents of attacks by insurgents on individual vehicles and convoys. The recent raid and assault on a train too had unnerved him. He could have traveled by air, however, the financial implications deterred him as he had to meet the fare from his pocket. Having no other choice he chose the cheaper option fully aware of the probable risks.

They left for the station early in the morning and boarded the train well in time.

"Papa, when will we reach Hyderabad?" Hina asked him. They were seated in a first class air conditioned compartment. A young Assamese boy was their companion for the journey.

"Now let me see! The train is starting in another ten minutes, that is at 6.30 in the morning. It will reach Secunderabad railway station after three days at 4.20 in the morning. It is a long journey." Brijesh looked into the train time table book and informed her.

"Three days? What am I going to do! I have no friends to play!" Hina said feeling depressed.

"Cheer up! Here are some toys and comics to keep busy," Urmila told her and gave her a bag.

Hina took the bag and looked into it for some time then closed its zipper.

"I am feeling bored! Uncle, my name is Hina! What is yours?" She asked the Assamese person sitting next to her.

"My name is Ajoy! Nice to meet you Hina!" he replied with a smile.

"Will you play with me Ajoy uncle?" She asked him.

"Sure! What will we play?" Ajoy asked her

Hina unzipped the bag and took out a pack of cards from it.

"Do you know how to play slapjack?" She asked Ajoy.

"No! But you can teach me!" He replied with enthusiasm.

"Ok! Now listen to me very carefully," she said and explained to him the method to play the game.

"I got it! Let us play," Ajoy said looking at Brijesh and Urmila who smiled and nodded.

Hina dealt the cards. Ajoy picked up his pack and they commenced playing in earnestness.

The train had left the station and kept accelerating until it reached its cruising speed. Both Brijesh and Urmila were engrossed in reading books of their interest; Brijesh was absorbed in the latest developments in missile technology while Urmila was enjoying the latest Eve's weekly magazine. Tired of playing, Hina packed the cards and kept them in her bag. She took out a comic from it and started reading it. Ajoy closed his eyes and fell asleep. It was now nearly three and a half hours since the train had left Gauhati and was approaching Bongaigaon, a small town in the Kokrajhar district.

The train driver applied the brakes when he noticed a large boulder between the rails at some distance. The moment the train screeched to halt a few feet short of the obstacle, a dozen armed men emerged from the undergrowth and boarded the train whose doors were opened by passengers from within.

A few minutes later they heard the loud banging on the doors of their adjoining compartments. Out of curiosity Ajoy got up and as he opened the door, he was pushed back by an armed militant whose face was covered with a piece of cloth.

"We are here only to collect taxes from you for entering our beloved Motherland! Place all the cash and jewelry in this kerchief and hand it over to me," he told them pointing his pistol towards Ajoy. The rest sat stunned with their eyes glued towards the intruder.

"They are lying in the suitcases under the seat. We have to take them out," Brijesh told him.

Hina kept looking at the militant with awe and fear written all over her face! Urmila removed the gold chain rings and earrings from her person and put them on the kerchief. Ajoy who lay on the floor from the fall kept his eyes on the militant. A loud noise from the next compartment distracted the insurgent who turned his head to look behind. Ajoy raising his leg kicked the assailant's arm that held the pistol, which flew out from his hand and landed in Hina's lap.

Before Ajoy could get up the assailant pounced on him, grabbed his head and raised it and banged it several times on the floor. Ajoy blacked out and lay lifeless.

When the assailant was attacking Ajoy, Brijesh shouted out to Hina who was sitting across. She was holding the pistol in her hand with the nose of the barrel pointing towards her stomach.

"Throw the pistol to me Hina!" Throw it now!" He cried out. Filled with fear and in agony, she held on to the pistol with greater firmness. Tears streamed from her eyes and her voice choked, she looked at him helplessly. Brijesh leaned forward towards her to grab the pistol from her. The assailant heaved up and pushed him away. He fell on Urmila who bore the impact and sat still on her seat. The rebel snatched the pistol from Hina and standing erect held the upper berth seat with his left hand to steady himself.

"So you want the pistol? You will now get its bullet!" The assailant said facing Brijesh and fired as the train jerked.

Brijesh noticed the smoke coming out from the nozzle of the pistol and heard a loud sound but did not feel the impact of the bullet. Bewildered, he waited in anticipation for another bullet, however, to his astonishment he noticed the rebel go down yelling with agonising pain.

Ajoy who had recovered had landed a forceful kick on the rebel's groin. He quickly got up, stood on his feet, removed the pistol from the rebel's hand and fired at his head. A part of the brain spurted out and landed on the seat close to Hina. She closed her eyes and shrieked loudly. Her shrieks grew louder when she noticed blood gushing out from the rebel's head.

She jumped up, looked towards Brijesh and then sideways at Urmila. Stunned and dumbfounded, she sank down on her seat and fainted. Alarmed, Brijesh looked at her then at Urmila. His heart sank and he felt the floor falling apart from under his feet!

The bullet meant for him had hit Urmila on her temple killing her instantly. Blood oozed out from her wound as she sat limp and lifeless!

□

1

His parents who resided in Delhi, had rushed to comfort and console him as soon as they heard the tragic news. They remained close to Brijesh, comforting and soothing him to prevent him from falling apart during the agonising period. His office bosses left him alone to sort out his affairs and told him to attend only when normalcy returns to his life.

Urmila was cremated at the Hyderabad crematorium in front of the relatives, who had come from all over the country.

Grief stricken, Hina had not spoken a word since the incident and remained aloof, with eyes hazy and a deep remorseful demeanor. She took no interest in her surroundings, slept less and only nibbled her food after repeated persuasions.

Brijesh took her to the doctor at the first opportunity. After carrying out various investigations he spoke to him with their results a week later in his office in the hospital.

"Hina is suffering from selective muting. It is a social and mental problem arising from an anxiety disorder. She will remain quiet, shy, with a fear of being embarrassed in public and wanting to be let alone," he said.

"For how long will this continue?" Brijesh asked him.

"The speech impediment is temporary, and will last only for a few weeks. You have to have someone with whom she can talk with ease. A new person could also join in. Be patient with her, she may communicate only with gestures initially then gradually speak a few words in whispers. Expose her to as many outdoor activities preferably sports and entertainment. These will stimulate her and soon restore her to partial normalcy," the doctor elaborated.

"Why partial? Why not complete it?" Brijesh asked him.

"You mentioned to me the tragic incident she has witnessed. This is the main reason for her trauma. She will recover completely when she overcomes the guilt and self blame. Only when she is convinced that she could not have averted the tragedy and once she realises that it was not due to her inaction and helplessness that her mother died, that will be the day when her recovery will be total!" The doctor replied.

"Any medicines?" Brijesh asked him.

"Yes, I have prescribed these for the time being. Do bring her for a regular checkup every month," he said, getting up and shaking his hands.

Hina joined her school, Brijesh dropped and picked her everyday. She made friends with a few girls from her class. They did not make fun of her when she communicated with them through gestures with her hands, eyes and head nods. Her teachers too kept a strict vigil to ensure that she was not troubled by anyone.

It was in the evenings when she was in the park with her Grandma that she enjoyed most! Her granny helped her on the merry go round, the see saw swings and ladders. Very often her father too joined her. He pushed the swing hard which thrilled her with delight as she sailed higher and higher. He ignored her grandma's protestations and kept on pushing the swing to hear her laugh and shriek out loudly. The sound of her voice was music to his ears.

After six months she started speaking, initially in whispers and gradually raising her voice during contentious arguments. All of them were overjoyed when at a family gathering she recited a poem that she had learned in her school.

Her swimming lessons started a year later and she loved to be in the pool. During one such lesson she found herself struggling to keep her head above the water and kept splashing fervently with her arms to keep afloat. The teacher and the lifeguard were nowhere in sight. When she shrieked out loudly, the water entered her mouth. Soon she began to cough and splutter. From the corner of her eye she noticed a person fully clothed jump into the swimming pool. He grabbed her and lifted her above his shoulders.

The lifeguard, alerted by her shrieking, reached and helped in carrying her to the pool deck where he lay her down, and applied pressure on her chest with his hands. With a few pushes and presses from him when she coughed, the water emptied from her stomach and poured out through her mouth.

She looked up and noticed her father who was fully drenched in his office clothes and shoes. It was he who had jumped into the pool to rescue her. She smiled on noticing him smile filled with relief.

"You should not have entered the deep end. You have a lot to learn," he said, bending down and planting a kiss on her forehead. She sat up quickly and hugged him tightly, encircling her hands around his neck.

Over the next years both Brijesh and his parents noticed the welcome changes in Hina, though at intervals bouts of stillness seized her wherein she remained aloof and uncommunicative. The frequency of such seizures reduced as the days passed on.

She had entered tenth class when her father took her to the equestrian academy. For fourteen years old, she picked up riding quickly and was allowed to ride a full bred horse. Her instructor called her 'shahswar', a cavalier! During a practice session, her horse from a slow trot suddenly galloped without any warning. Caught unawares, she found herself ejected from the saddle and fell forward. She desperately clung onto the horse's neck. Sensing her helplessness the horse sped faster and faster, shaking his neck vigorously in annoyance. Her legs lost their grip and when she was about to fall she felt her father's strong arm around her waist trying to pull her away from her saddle. She leaned forward, steadied herself, returned to the saddle, held the reins in both hands and gripped the horse firmly with her thighs. Her father removed his hand from her and in a loud voice shouted out 'bravo well done!'

"That was great beti! I loved your confidence," she heard her father's soothing voice as she alighted from the horse.

She had entered her final school year and though she continued to participate in outdoor activities her major time was spent in preparing for the School Board examination. When the results came out, she was surprised to find herself among the top ten students in the list. Brijesh and his parents were thrilled and presented her a unique gift contained in a rather large bag. Hina unzipped it, took out the contents, placed them on the floor and was pleasantly surprised.

"Oh my God! The entire Ski kit! I love the skis, they look so strong and yet they are light! You have left out nothing, apparel gloves, snow boots, helmet, goggles, bindings and so many tools and accessories! Thank you my Dada and Dadi, I love you!" She said as she put each item back into the bag.

"You deserve everything and the best!" Her Dadi said, hugging her.

When she joined the college, Brijesh sent her for mountaineering training to the School in Sonamarg where she also imbibed trekking skills. It was in her second year at the college that she joined the Three Peaks Expedition organised every year by Adventure Consultants of a private Company. It offered her an opportunity to participate in a journey that covered a lot of terrain and enabled them to make multiple ascents on moderately high peaks.

The initial journey was not that easy as she climbed the two peaks using crampons, ice axes and fixed ropes. However, it was a stunning view of the surrounding Himalayan peaks and of Everest that took her breath away. In the area she also saw Cho Oyu, Nuptse, Lhotse, Makalu, Ama Dablam and many more smaller peaks which were quite awe inspiring.

She was on her way to the Island Peak, the highest of the Three Peaks, referred to by the local Sherpa people as Imja Tse, an 'Island in a glacial sea.' It was the last exciting and popular peak which had snow and ice on the upper sections. She was enthusiastic and hurried forward to catch up with the leading Sherpa.

"Take it easy Hina! Conserve your energy!" She heard her father as she passed him.

She looked back, smiled and slowed down. This season, she had an advantage over her father as she had recently returned from advance training at the Sonamarg Mountain Climbing School.

The course was sponsored by her College as an encouragement package for girls.

Her climb to the Island Peak 5806 m (19049 ft) summit commenced with the Sherpa and an equally enthusiastic boy, Shailesh, who took the lead. A rope connected them as they trudged in a single file. Whenever the Sherpa stopped, she looked back towards her father who was following them. It took them nearly an hour to reach the summit where they halted to enjoy the view.

She counted herself blessed as her eyes savored the mind boggling panoramic view around the upper reaches of the Khumbu and Imja Khola Valley systems. Looking up she noticed the Lobuche East peak and found it challenging.

"You want to climb Lobuche? You have to be very careful. The ascent is at a fairly steep angle on long snowy and icy slope." The Sherpa told her when she took a step forward in the direction of the peak.

"I want to give it a try," she requested.

"I too want to try," Shailesh said.

The Sherpa reconnected the rope and both of them commenced the ascent. The mountain was more alpine in nature and she also found herself exposed to high wind. Her ax often slid as it hit the hard ice. Gradually with deep concentration and body control, in small steps she reached the top of the peak, with Shailesh following her. Looking below she could clearly see her party and recognised her father among them. She waved and they waved back at her.

A sudden strong gust of wind hit her, making her lose her balance. She steadied herself but saw Shailesh plunge down into the deep gorge. As the rope connecting them pulled her towards him, she swirled, hung in the air for a moment and landed on the snow at the edge of the peak. She looked down and fear gripped her! The ground below was nowhere in sight. Shailesh who was connected to her with the rope was dangling below her freely.

She realised that if her foot slipped a few inches more she would fall further down into the abyss. Anxiety and agony gripped her! She turned her face and saw her father looking towards her and shouting at her with his hands cupped around his mouth.

She felt the same helplessness and fear fill in her! In the fateful train long back, she had kept silent and looked stupefied at her father who was asking her to throw the pistol towards him. The same scene appeared to be repeating. She continued to slide downwards as the strain on the rope increased with Shailesh dragging her down.

Shaking her head forcefully and shirking the dreadful dismal thoughts from her mind, with utmost determination, she retrieved the additional axe from her trouser pocket. Holding the axe in her left hand and bending down she struck on the hard ice. She continued striking the axes alternatively with both hands and inched her way upwards gradually, pulling up Shailesh. This continued until she felt the tenseness in the rope slacken. Shailesh had found the icy ground to plant his feet and no longer was floating. She slid her body over the ridge, stood up and started to walk towards Shailesh. Gripping his hand she pulled him up over the ridge. They lay down on the ice, breathing heavily.

The descent towards the rest of the party members who were anxiously observing them took her another half an hour. As she met her father she felt her energy draining out of her body and sat down on the ice to rest. Brijesh sat next to her and encircled his arm around her shoulders.

"Beti I am very happy and proud! You were great!" He said.

"Thank you Papa! Please listen to me Papa! My past is no more with me! It has left me forever! Papa, I fear it no more!" She stated, seriously, looking into his eyes.

Brijesh hugged her and looked up thanking the Almighty!

□

2

"The missiles rising in the sky in quick succession that you see on the screen have been fired from Abdul Kalam Island. These are Ashwin interceptor missiles which will collide in midair with missiles coming from the opposite direction and fired from a submarine," the Commentator explained to the audience watching the film in the auditorium.

On the screen when the two missiles collided, the audience gasped and clapped.

"Besides India the three other countries that have this capability are, USA, Russia and Israel. An enemy missile heading towards our mainland could be carrying nuclear, WMD or conventional bombs. From trials so far it is observed that when intercepted the missiles with WMD and conventional bombs get ignited in midair and the falling debris from these missiles can cause major casualties and collateral damage to the areas on which they fall. However, when missiles with nuclear bombs collide, the impact of their collision does not trigger a nuclear explosion as normally the bombs do not explode in midair. Due to the impact the debris from these bombs could be in the form of plutonium or Uranium and may cause some radiation which can be cleaned up," the narrator said and paused.

"You all are watching this movie because you all are part of the team that is going to help in the preparation of launching pads for our missiles to shoot down enemy missiles in their country when launched by them. Your team leaders will guide you and assist you in this task," he said and finished the narration.

On the screen debris of the missile falls over the sea water. The screen goes blank and the lights come on in the hall. The audience leaves the hall which soon empties.

"Sir the Managing Director (MD) would like to see you now," the secretary came over to tell Brijesh who after leaving the auditorium was sitting in the visitors room.

Brijesh thanked her, entered the spacious room and noticed his boss Maj Gen CV Raman, MD Bharat Dynamics Ltd (BDL), browsing through a file. He greeted him and stood in front of the large desk behind which his boss sat occupying the executive chair.

"Please sit down Brijesh. How are you keeping? Hopefully everything is fine here in the office and at home," Raman said with a smile.

"Everything is fine here and at home Sir, thanks to the Almighty," Brijesh replied.

"Yes by and large we are doing good work here, though I wish some of our colleagues would hasten up a bit with their projects. However, I do not want to put any pressure on anyone. I know that they are doing their best," Raman said.

Brijesh was aware that his boss, a reasonable and decent person, had a very professional approach towards the staff of BDL.

"I really appreciate the amount of effort put in by you in writing the report on Operation Indradhanush (Rainbow), it is very comprehensive," Raman said and got up.

He moved towards the large digital screen on the wall and Brijesh followed him. Raman pressed a button and the Indian map appeared on the screen.

"Your report says that we have so far identified on the ground the locations of our future missile launching pads in Gujarat, Rajasthan, Punjab, Jammu and Kashmir to counter and destroy the missiles launched by Pakistan from their forward missile pads in Skardu, Mardan, Sargodha, Multan, Jacocabad and Mirpur Khas," Raman said pointing out the locations on the map.

"Yes sir," Brijesh replied.

"I am certain that our proposed launch pads will destroy any enemy missile in their territory as soon as they leave their silos,"

Raman confirmed. Brijesh nodded his head in agreement and Raman continued.

"Our team here at BDL is examining these locations to formalise instructions for constructing and erecting the launching pads with the assistance from our army. Once the Government gives the go ahead the work will commence. You state in the report that you and your team are now ready to commence the ground identification of the sites along our Eastern borders with China?" he asked.

"Yes Sir! The team is ready to move any day now. However, there are a few hiccups that we could face as we progress along the Chinese border," Brijesh informed him.

"What are these?" Raman asked.

"We are concentrating our efforts in the North East presently. In this region there are basically two areas of concern where our work could be held up and also disturbed. I do not know if Nepal will agree to locate the missile pads on its soil; presently the political relationship does not seem to favor even approaching them with a request. However, in future as cordiality returns we could take the initiative to forward our proposal to them," Brijesh said, indicating on the map with the pointer.

"Yes you do have a point there. I will take it up with the Ministry," Raman said.

"The second issue is of working in areas where insurgency is still active to a certain extent. These are Mizoram, Manipur, and Nagaland. Although we do not have a common border with China in these states we are identifying locations in the vicinity of our border with Myanmar. Here we have to rely heavily on the army for our protection as the insurgents living in camps in the Myanmar forests may interfere," Brijesh emphasised.

"Yes we have to be very careful in these areas. Be rest assured the State Police force will protect you and our Army will always be ready on call," Raman said and smiled.

"Why the State police Sir? Why not the Army?" Brijesh queried.

"We have to keep it low key, hence all administrative and security arrangements are given to the State Governments. They are not aware of the real purpose of our Operation and neither will we tell them. Any association directly with the Army will arouse suspicion not only within our people but with our enemies too," Raman replied.

They returned to their seats and drank tea poured into the cups by Raman, from the flask placed on the side table.

"If you permit, my team can leave for Arunachal by the 16th of this month. I will catch up with them in a fortnight later," Brijesh requested.

"Yes you all have a long journey to undertake starting from Arunachal, Nagaland, Manipur and Mizoram. Go ahead, you have a week to tie up loose ends before your team leaves," Raman said.

"Thank you Sir! Hopefully we will soon have the launch pads ready and our missiles in position! I am really thankful to our satellites for providing us round the clock cover all along our border to give us real time warning of enemy missiles that leaves its pad from across the border," Brijesh said.

"Let us do our bit for Op Indradhanush. We must ensure that this is kept TOP SECRET at all costs. Your operational cover must always remain safe and secure. To the outside world you and your team are employees of ISRO (Indian Space Research Organisation) and you are mapping and collating the border areas for underground water for developing wells for drinking water. You and your team are NOT from BDL and have no connection with them. You will continue to have your offices in ISRO premises as a part of their National Remote Sensing Centre (NRSC) and work from there without compromising details of the Project with the Head of ISRO and his staff. This cover should never be disclosed to anyone at any cost. Our entire effort will fail if our neighbors even have a whiff of our main objective," Raman emphasised.

"We will guard Op Indradhanush with all our might and never disclose it to anyone under any circumstances," Brijesh assured him.

"By the way, what about golf this Sunday?" Raman asked him and smiled.

"Sorry Sir, I stopped playing golf quite long back. My holidays and spare time are now reserved for my daughter." Brijesh replied, looking away from him.

"Yes Brijesh, I realise and understand your situation; Urmila left all of us when she was so young. A tremendous loss not only to you but to all of us. Give my love to Hina. She is a lovely and wonderful person," Raman said, got up, held Brijesh's hand and shook it warmly.

Satisfied with the meeting he had with his boss, Brijesh returned to his office at ISRO and scheduled a conference with his subordinates for the next day. He left the office an hour later after he was satisfied with the contents of the detailed agenda for the meeting that he had written and stored in his computer.

"Why are you not following the normal route?' He asked the driver when the car took a right turn.

"Sir, Hina didi (sister) has asked me to get your blood pressure tablets. We are going to the medical shop," the driver replied.

Brijesh smiled and kept silent; he was certain that Hina had given the money to the driver, who stopped the car, brought the medicine from the shop and gave it to him for verification.

"Yes these are the tablets, let us go," Brijesh told the driver

His thoughts raced back to the tragic day when he had lost his wife, Hina was not even five years old. Losing her mother had devastated her and it took his and his parents total devotion and perseverance for a considerable period to restore tranquility and serenity into her life. It was not that, Hina had ignored him and leaned on her mother alone, the opposite was more truthful. He had always endeavored to be very close to her and stole her affection to the extent that Urmila frequently remonstrated that he was pampering her.

As they reached the house he felt happy when he saw Hina's scooter parked on the berm near the garage entrance. The driver parked the car, he got down from it and entered the house through the door opening into the garage. He found Hina seated in the living room and in conversation with a middle aged person.

"Papa, you are a bit late today! Meet uncle Gopal who is here at my request," Hina said, getting up from her seat.

"Good evening Sir!" Gopal said and extended his hand towards Brijesh.

"Good evening Gopalji! Very glad to meet you! Please be seated," Brijesh said, occupying the sofa next to Hina's.

"Gopal has a very big and famous boutique. I normally buy my clothes from his shop. He is also a fashion designer and has held many fashion shows to display the dresses he designs," Hina said introducing Gopal.

"Oh that is wonderful! Go ahead and discuss it with him. I will freshen up and join you very soon," Brijesh said getting up.

"No Papa please stay! Gopal uncle is here to take your measurements for the suits to be stitched for you," Hina said.

"But Beta,why call him here, when I can go to his boutique?" Brijesh questioned her.

"Papa, when did you last get your suit stitched? When Mama was alive and that was many many years ago! You do not have any good suits now, all are worn out," Hina pleaded.

"That is not good, Brijeshji. You are a very important person, you meet so many high officials! You should wear good clothes," Gopal said.

"I feel guilty that you have left your boutique and have come to take my measurements in my house," Brijesh said.

"I am here because I love my daughter Renu as much as you love Hina! She is Hina's classmate and her very close friend. She told me about your reluctance to go to a shop to give measurements for your clothes," Gopal said with a smile.

"Yes Papa, you gave me no other choice! Renu was delighted with my proposal, more so this has also offered an opportunity for you both to meet," Hina said.

Brijesh smiled and stood up allowing Gopal to take the measurements with the tape while Hina noted them in a pocket book as he spoke out.

"Renu will bring the suit for trial tomorrow evening and will mark alterations if any on it. Thereafter, give me two days to have it stitched and delivered to you," Gopal said.

"Thank you very much uncle! Please stay back for dinner. It won't take long. You and Papa can chat as I warm up a few dishes," Hina said.

"Beti I would love to, but my people at the shop require my

presence now. I got a call from them. Will certainly drop in soon with Renu," Gopal said and got up.

Brijesh shook his hand warmly and thanked him. Hina escorted him to his car and hugged him before he sat inside the vehicle.

After their dinner, they went to their respective rooms; Brijesh changed and sat down to read the latest article on the guided missile system, Hina who had a tiring day read her emails on her mobile and soon fell asleep.

In her dream she heard herself laughing and splashing water in the swimming pool as her parents encouraged her to swim; pressing her little legs and pushing the water sideways with her small hands she managed to stay afloat. They were all in their swimsuits with her mom looking very pretty in her colorful one piece. Her mom was nearly as tall as her father and also slim; she loved watching her swim and wade through the water with graceful strokes. Her father matched her in skill and as they raced but he always allowed her to win. She smiled and waved at them. In a flash her dream wavered, she found herself sitting in the train, the man forcing himself into the compartment, holding the pistol, blood oozing out from her mother's temple!

She got up with a start with sweat all over her face and her heartbeat racing exponentially; with heavy breathing and loud murmur she got out of the bed, headed towards the kitchen and poured a glass of water from the flask. She sat down on the stool and sipped the water slowly as her nerves calmed down.

"It is nearly three years since you last had this nightmare!" Brijesh said. He had heard her walking into the kitchen and stood close to her with his hands on her shoulders. She looked at him and held his hand.

"I am alive beti only for you! I know you miss your mother and so do I! We have to spend the rest of our lives together without her. You are the only one whom I live for!" He said pressing her hand.

Hina got up and hugged him resting her head on his shoulders with tears flowing down from her eyes.

"Papa please forgive me! I just cannot explain how all of a sudden this nightmare flared up! Please do not worry, I am fine!

No longer afraid! You are everything to me, you are my mentor and my God! My entire life is yours! I will never allow any harm to even touch you!" She said, wiping her tears.

"Now, now beti! Let us not get too sentimental! We will always remain for each other! Go to your bed and rest. Get some sleep, tomorrow we have a busy day," Brijesh said.

She wiped her eyes and left, hugging him. He returned to his room, lay on his bed and closed his eyes, heartbroken and depressed.

The next evening Renu came in her car with Brijesh's suit for trial. He was alone and greeted her warmly.

"Very sorry uncle I got so late! The tailor handed over the suit only half an hour back and Papa insisted that I should meet you with it today only. On the phone Hina too insisted that I should bring it immediately. I hope I have not disturbed you?" Renu queried.

"No issues beti! Thanks for coming, now I know how sweet and pretty you are!" Brijesh replied with a smile.

"Not as pretty as your real daughter, uncle!" Renu remarked playfully.

Brijesh wore the suit and it fitted his body perfectly, showing no wrinkles or sagging or tightening, absolutely made to order. Renu gave him a broad smile when Brijesh handed over the suit to her. She put it in her bag and left wishing him goodbye.

"Renu brought the suit for trial, her dad is really fast! Something urgent has come up. I have to catch an early flight to Delhi tomorrow to attend a few meetings." Brijesh told Hina when she entered the house after her evening run.

"When will you be back?" She asked him.

"I really do not know. My return flight has not been booked. I will call you up as soon as I know," Brijesh replied.

"OK Papa! Enjoy your stay in Delhi and have no worries about this place." she said and sighed audibly.

"Any problem Beti? I can postpone my visit if you want," Brijesh said looking at her.

"No problem Papa! I am a bit tired and I think I will hit the bed early today," she said, hugged him and left.

Next morning, Brijesh left her while she was asleep and called her up later on his mobile, when he had reached Delhi. He spoke to her everyday on the mobile phone, however, Hina did not ask him his arrival schedule nor did he tell her.

"When is uncle returning? Any news from him?" Renu asked her on the third day, in the college dining hall during their lunch break. Hina smiled and shrugged her shoulders and kept eating from her plate.

"Looks like he has forgotten! How sad!" Renu remarked.

"I know my father very well. He will never forget, he loves me very much!" Hina said with a smile.

"Yes I know and the whole world knows that you and your father are inseparables! Both are extremely devoted to one another and love each other immensely," Renu remarked.

"Yes today what I am is because of my father! He took care of me from the day I was born," Hina sighed and said. She looked down to hide her moistened eyes.

"When I was nine years old, I remember I got very sick with high fever and was shivering immensely. The doctor, who was my father's friend, came to my house to examine me and gave the medicine from his bag he carried with him. I felt better after an hour or so but the body temperature remained high. Throughout the night I kept tossing and turning in my bed. My father sat in a chair next to me placing wet cloth on my forehead for the temperature to recede. He did not move from his seat until my temperature was normal, which happened in the early hours of the morning. After a short nap he left for the office. I dressed up and without his knowledge went to the school to write the final exam paper. He returned early from the office and finding me absent, rushed to the school and waited for me to finish the exam," Hina narrated with gratitude reflecting in her words.

"Did he scold you?" Renu inquired.

"No! On the contrary asked me whether the exam paper was tough or easy," Hina smiled and said. They finished their lunch and got up to empty their plates in the trash can.

She returned home from college on her scooter and after washing changed into a casual dress. The maid served her a cup of tea and homemade cookies. She sat on the sofa resting her head on the backrest and closed her eyes. Her conversation with Renu during the lunch hour flooded her mind with the past memories, which kept flashing in her mind. Several incidents from past years kept appearing as a slideshow. Her near death experiences in the swimming pool and later on the mountain peak, the outings with her Dadi in the park, the wayward horse and many more, revisited her.

"Didi (sister) your tea is getting cold, should I warm it?" She heard the maid saying and sat up with a start.

'No there is no need, I will drink it as it is," she told her with a sigh and picked up the cup to sip from it. She felt lonely and missed her father.

The next day when she arrived at the college she was greeted by most of her classmates with hugs and kisses.

"Happy Birthday Hina! So when and where are we meeting for the party?" Renu asked her.

"Mmm. I will tell you by this evening," she replied.

The lessons in class kept her engrossed and busy. She was fond of transcribing copious notes as the teacher spoke, however today she felt tired and putting her notebook and pen away listened attentively. As the class was about to end for the lunch break she was distracted when she noticed a smartly dressed courier boy open the classroom door and wave his hand, inviting the attention of her teacher. Who noticed him and nodded his head. The boy came forward and handed an envelope to the teacher who tore it open read the letter and smiled.

"Go bring it in," the teacher told the boy and looked towards Hina.

"Please stand up Hina," she said and read the letter loudly when Hina stood up.

"My dearest beti, Happy Birthday! Sorry I cannot join you and your friends, however, my best wishes and love are forever with you. Please give my best wishes to your teacher and your classmates. Your Papa."

Her entire class gasped out loud and after a moment clapped and thumped their desks.

"Hold it! We have the cake to cut and lunch packets to consume," the teacher said, as the boy placed the cake on the teacher's table and with the assistance from the students deposited the lunch packets on every desk.

"Come around my table for the cake cutting!" The teacher called out.

They gathered around Hina as she cut the cake and gave a piece to her teacher. Holding each other's hand and singing loudly in unison, her classmates wished Hina happy birthday.

"Thank you everyone! I really am stumped! I really cannot ask for a better party! You folks are great and so is my father!" Hina cried out loudly. Her friends clapped whistled and lifted her on their shoulder.

"This is not the first time he has surprised me!" Hina said when she found her feet on the ground.

"Tell us about it!" A student shouted out loudly.

"Oh! That was long back when I was in the eighth class! I had finished my lunch during the recess and we were discussing whether we should burn the Diwali crackers the next day or have a silent Diwali by lighting diyas (earthen lamps) and candles only. I saw my father advancing towards us with a bag in his hand. He asked us all to close in and took out paper plates from the bag. He then removed sweet packets from the bag and gave it to me to distribute it to everyone," Hina said and paused.

"We sat down with him and enjoyed the sweets leaving not a small bit behind. I request all of you to enjoy the cake and the lunch packet," Hina said and laughed.

"Three cheers for Hina's Papa!" One student shouted out loud and the rest joined him.

"Three cheers to Papa! I love you!" Hina said and clapped.

She was pleasantly surprised when she arrived at her house in the afternoon. She saw the driver removing her father's suitcase from the car dicky. Parking her scooter, she ran and entered the room to find her father sitting on the sofa and sipping water from a glass.

"Oh Papa! Thank you very much! It was wonderful! Everyone enjoyed it!" She said and hugged him.

"Happy birthday Beti! I am glad that you celebrated your birthday with your close friends," Brijesh told her.

"I missed you Papa!" She said.

"I am here with you now and I have a pleasant surprise for you!" He said getting up. He held her hand and took her towards the guest room.

Hina stood at the entrance stunned with disbelief, when she found her grandparents relaxing on the bed. They looked up towards her, got up immediately and stood with open inviting arms. Hina ran towards them and circled both with her arms hugging each vigorously.

"Dada! Dadi! What a surprise! It is unbelievable that you are here! Thank you very much!" She cried with tears of joy rolling down her eyes.

"They had planned to be here later, on my suggestion they agreed to surprise you on your birthday," Brijesh told her.

"Oh Papa! Thank you, I am so happy!" Hina said.

"Beti you are our most precious gem! We both love you very much! Happy birthday! God bless you," Dadi said, kissing her on her cheek.

"Happy Birthday! Beti you are the best and I love you!" Dada said, hugging her.

"Look in that bag! A birthday gift from your Dada and Dadi!" Brijesh said pointing at the black bag on the carpet.

Hina unzipped it, took out the contents, placing them on the floor with admiration and pleasure.

"Oh my God, the entire Ski equipment! Thank you so much! The earlier one was damaged and I needed a new one badly. Thank you my Dada and Dadi I love you!" She said after emptying the bag.

"You deserve everything and the best," Dadi told her.

"Yes, now you can out race any skier and enjoy skiing with your father as much as you want," Dada told her.

Hina sat with Dadi holding her hands and inquired about her health. She was thrilled to learn that her Dadi had completely recovered from a recent bout of dengue fever.

"I have invited a few guests for dinner tonight. Get ready they will be arriving shortly," Brijesh told Hina.

"Oh Papa! Another party? I knew you would never forget my birthday! Thank you very much!" Hina said and got up.

She left the room with Brijesh and headed towards the kitchen. She was surprised to find that the dinner arrangements were through the caterers, who had taken over the kitchen and were busy organising the place and warming up the dishes.

Brijesh and Hina were ready before the guests started arriving. Hina's face lit up when she noticed that her father was wearing the new suit which Renu had handed over to her a day back.

"You look smart and dashing in the suit! You should be wearing it when you go out to an official meeting or party. Not at home Papa!" Hina exclaimed.

"To me this is the best occasion to wear it!" He smiled and replied.

The guests arrived and soon the hall was filled with chatter and laughter; the elder ladies occupied the chairs and sofas while the younger lot preferred to stand holding their drinks in their hands. Hina felt relaxed and cozy in the company of her close friends from the colony and a few of her classmates.

"My father never forgets," she told Renu with a smile.

"Yes! I was completely surprised when he rang me after I reached home and asked me to come to the party and to also bring a few of our friends. You are very lucky you have a great father who cares for you so much!" Renu said.

With loud music and full throat voices the invitees sang the birthday song. After Hina had cut the cake, Brijesh and his parents in turn placed the pieces in her mouth. She too fed small slices to them and to Renu. Brijesh had invited his boss, whom he escorted to the buffet table and offered him a plate. They picked up the delicious cuisine from the dishes laid out and sat down to eat.

Hina stood nibbling from her plate and chatting with a classmate, and was soon joined by a young lady with charming looks and a smart slim figure.

"Happy Birthday Hina! I am Malini, General Raman's daughter," she said, shaking her hand.

"Thank you very much! I am extremely happy to meet you and many thanks for attending the function," Hina told her in her pleasant voice.

"I am glad that I came to this young and vibrant gathering," Malini replied.

"I have not seen you earlier. Are you visiting uncle?" Hina asked her.

"Yes, this year I decided to spend my annual leave with my parents. Normally I choose a hill station where they join me," Malini replied.

"I hope I am not too inquisitive! Where do you work?" Hina enquired.

"Oh! I am Capt Malini Raman from the Corps of Signals Indian Army," she said.

"You are an engineer?" Hina asked her.

"Yes. I graduated in Computer Science from IIT," she replied.

"Are you comfortable living and working with all the soldiers around you? Don't you feel scared sometimes?" Renu, who was standing near them, asked her.

"I am much more safe and comfortable with my soldiers and officers than, I think, I would be with the workers and bosses in the corporate world," she smiled and said.

"Where are you posted now?" Hina asked her.

"I am with my unit at Udhampur," Malini replied.

"Oh, so close to Gulmarg, my favorite ski resort!" Hina exclaimed.

"You are into skiing? I started skiing last season," Malini told her.

"Yes me and my father have been skiing for past three years or so. Every winter we ski at a resort depending on the condition of the ice on the slopes. Last year we went to Kufri and stayed there for fifteen days," Hina told her.

"That is really great! What are your plans for this year?" Malini asked her.

"No plans so far. Papa is preoccupied with his Project. He has no time for skiing," Hina replied.

"Do you want to go to Gulmarg this season? I can arrange it and join you," Malini suggested.

"I will have to ask Papa. I do not mind, I will graduate next month and then I am free," Hina said.

"What are you graduating in?" Malini queried.

"In Telecommunication Engineering. An Officer from the army visited us and gave us a presentation in which he mentioned that the Corps of Signal requires telecom engineers," Hina said.

"That is right. It is the right Corps for girls, if they wish to join the army. Do let me know if you decide to visit Gulmarg," Malini said and handed over her business card.

Later after the party when she mentioned it to Brijesh, he was glad that Malini had invited her to Udhampur to stay with her. He told her that he was keen for her to have an exposure to army life.

Three months after her graduation Hina joined Malini at Udhampur. She was impressed with the meticulousness and pleasing arrangements in her room in the Officers mess. The relaxed mess life with everything always on call kept her at ease and happy.

Malini introduced her to the officers and also took her to eat with jawans in their langar. She also took her to her workplace and explained the tasks that her unit in general and she in particular were performing. Hina was excited when she observed that she was familiar with some of the technical details which she had learnt in her curriculum in college.

They drove down to Gulmarg in the unit Jonga and stayed in the officers' mess of the Battalion stationed there. The very next day after their arrival, at Malini's request an officer from the Battalion accompanied them to an outpost close to the Pakistan border. To Hina it was a thrilling experience to be with the soldiers at such high altitudes and spend the day with them. She had heard many stories, but now she was with the brave men guarding the borders under very difficult conditions.

They spent the next fortnight skiing everyday and enjoying every moment. It was a unique adventure which she would savor for quite some time. Days passed quickly and she had to bid goodbye to Malini reluctantly.

Brijesh who was present at Hyderabad for official work met her at the airport and found her in high spirits.

"I missed you Papa!" She said hugging him.

"I missed you too! You look happy and relaxed and that I treasure most!" He said.

They were travelling over the flyover and finding no cars ahead the driver pressed the accelerator.

"Papa, I am going to ask your permission for something. Please do not hesitate to refuse it if you consider it unsuitable," Hina said, holding her father's hand.

"Go ahead Beti and ask," Brijesh smiled and said.

"Papa, I want to join the Army!" Hina said in a timid voice

Brijesh looked at her with surprise. He paused for a while, smiled and patted her on her arm.

"You have my permission! However, please also speak to Dada and Dadi before you finally make up your mind," he said. Hina let out a sigh, grasped her father's hands and pressed them softly.

"But I will be very far away from you for most of the time. Will you not miss me?" she asked, teasing him.

"In any case, this is bound to happen one day, when you get married!" Brijesh replied and smiled.

"Thank you Papa! I will seek Dada's and Dadi's permission," Hina leaned and planted a kiss on his cheeks.

She spoke to her grandparents the next day when she escorted them to the temple. After they had paid their obeisance to the deity she broached the subject.

"Dadi I am going to finish my studies soon and I want to do something with which you all will really be proud!" Hina said enthusiastically, as they were coming down the temple stairs.

"I will be filled with pride if you get married soon and give me a grandson!" Dadi told her.

"I will Dadi! But much later! I am only 21 years old and would like to do something more useful before I get married," Hina told her.

"What is on your mind beta?" Her Dada asked her.

"I want to join the Army!" She said in a soft tone and looked at them.

"What? Never! Never! You are talking like a fool!" Her Dadi cried out, flinging her arms sideways.

"Are you sure you want to do this? You will not repent later?" Her Dada asked her with a worried look.

"No Dada! I will not repent! Papa is with me and he has given his permission," Hina said emphatically.

"You have my permission too! Beta may God bless you." Dada said and placed his hand on her head.

"But... "Dadi was cut short by Dada when she tried to protest.

"No buts! Our Army requires girls like her. She is going to guard our country!" Dada said, stopping any further discussion.

□

3

She entered the room, walked up to the desk and saluted the person sitting in the chair across the table.

"At ease and take your seat," said Colonel Somnath Pathania, Deputy Director in Military Intelligence Directorate at Sena Bhavan, New Delhi. As she sat down, he looked at the file in front of him lying on the table and read it out loud.

"Captain (Capt) Hina Rathore you reported to this office from HQ Western Comd three months back. You did very well on your basic course at the MI School in Pune and that is the reason you are here in the Military Intelligence branch. You have outstanding reports from your superiors in the units you have served." He stopped reading, put the file aside and looked at her.

"Thank you, Sir," she said in a steady voice.

"Capt Hina, what is your problem? You do not like what you are doing now?" He asked. Hina felt alarmed and surprised at his question.

"I have no problem with what I am doing Sir!" She replied in a firm voice.

"I have this letter from Army HQ giving their approval to your joining the Special Action Group (SAG)! Are you sure you want to go there? Of course your final acceptance by the SAG depends on you successfully passing their grueling training tests," he reminded her.

"Yes Sir, I had applied from my last Unit and I want to serve with the SAG!" She replied.

"Why? I hope you are aware of what you are getting into?"

He asked with a frown on his forehead. She paused and looked down, aware that this was not the first time she had to answer this question.

"Sir I joined the Army to serve my Nation to the best of my capabilities. By Joining the SAG I am confident that I will meet this commitment. I have sufficient knowledge about it. Our neighbor in Hyderabad has a son who finished his stint in SAG last year, through him I have gained sufficient information," she replied.

"What does your father do? Do you have any relatives in the Defense Forces?" He asked her.

"My father Shri Brijesh Singh Rathore is a scientist and works in Indian Space Research Organisation (ISRO). He is posted in Hyderabad though presently he is in Nagaland on a Project. I do not have any other close relatives in the Defense Forces," she replied quietly.

"I suppose you have your father's blessings?" He posed.

"Yes Sir. He had given his permission before I applied," she replied

He got up from his chair and came around the table and shook her hand.

"I wish you all the best. If at any instant you require any assistance do not hesitate to ask us," he said.

"Thank you, Sir," she said and left the room after saluting him.

A week later she joined the National Security Guard (NSG) Center at Manesar, Gurgaon. She drove in her car the 40 Km distance from her Government flat in Palam to the NSG Campus.

Early next morning she stood with her batch in the open ground to listen to the training instructor.

"The first three months of training will decide whether you are in a condition to enter advanced level. In the next ninety days you all will go through physical fitness training which has 26 elements ranging from the normal jumping from heights to cross country obstacle courses. We will gauge your performance when you are under stress especially during martial arts and live target shooting, which is at the end of an obstacle cross country run," the burly instructor addressed the fifty trainees who stood facing him in three lines at the obstacle course ground.

To Hina most of the course regime and curriculum was a repetition of the training imparted to her in the Officers Training School at Chennai. However the martial arts and the cross country obstacle course did stretch her physical and mental boundaries.

"A pressure point is a specific area on the human body where a nerve lies close to its surface and is supported by bone or muscle mass. Direct pressure to a pressure point may cause extreme pain, stunning effect or sensation, disorientation, loss of consciousness and even death!" The martial arts instructor told the group and asked for a volunteer trainee to step forward.

Hina came forward and stood facing him and he commenced to demonstrate the techniques on her. He pressed his thumb and fingers on various parts of her body which included spots between her eyebrows, center of the temple, throat, eyes, ears, nose, chin and the back of the neck. As he did not apply any pressure on these points she did not feel the sensation which she was supposed to.

"Remember you are to apply this technique only in self defense against your enemy and not against your wife or husband!" He said amidst an outburst of laughter from his students.

Over 20 trainees dropped out towards the end of the three month period. Most due to injuries during the rigorous rugged and challenging cross country obstacle course. A few missed hitting the target at the firing range.

During a weeks break Hina made a trip to her flat and stayed there meeting friends and acquaintances. She had been speaking to her father earlier on her cell phone off and on. She now had the leisure and sufficient time to speak at length with her grandparents too. She rejoined the school fresh and relaxed, ready for the final phase of the training.

"You all have survived the basic training and that is the reason you are now with me for the next nine months to see you go through advance combat training. You will be fighting with knives, demolishing targets with bombs and explosives, shooting the enemy in quick reflex actions and rapidly learning the techniques to maintain surveillance to gather intelligence. It will be tough and dangerous as you will face situations with live ammunition. Only the brave and the brawny will survive!

My best wishes to you," the Deputy Commandant of the School addressed the trainees.

Each passing day had surprises for Hina and by the time she fully grasped, adapted and accepted the challenges, the training period had reached its last month. On the firing range they were drilled only to take head shots and two at one go. For proper neutralisation of the target in the battle inoculation program they had to stand right next to the target, while one of their partners shot at it with live ammunition. As they did not wear the kavach or the bullet proof vest during this drill, they therefore had to be absolutely precise and accurate when shooting the target.

She was fascinated with the combat room shoot in which candidates enter a dark room, adjust their vision to the darkness and shoot at a target within three seconds using torchlight or a compatible laser image intensifier. Similar training was also conducted under makeshift discotheque strobe lights.

Her skills were tested and honed at an electronic combat shooting range which was divided into 11 zones and spread over 400 metres. She had to cover the distance in 6.30 minutes and fire at 29 dynamic targets of all kinds, all along the way with the target exposure time between two and three seconds. The faster she engaged the various targets the more points she scored. It was not only on non reactive targets that she scored but also shot her rival, visible on the screen in the adjoining room, who was shooting at her on the screen from his room. She neutralised her opponent more than he did. Her response time and accuracy under near field conditions were better than her opponents.

Though she often experienced extreme measure of fatigue during high stress, dreadful and scaring situations, she faced them with alacrity, aplomb and dexterity. At the end of her training she found herself rejuvenated recharged with full confidence in herself and her abilities. When the nine month period ended, only 11 trainees survived the ordeal, she was listed among the top five!

"You have succeeded in becoming commandos who in anonymity and without any glamour serve the Nation to thwart all attempts by our enemy's subversive terrorist activities on our sacred soil. We have full faith in you and you too should never lose or doubt your own potency and competence. We wish you good hunting!" With these words the Commandant concluded his address at their final passing out parade.

A month after rest and recuperation she joined her unit 51 SAG at Gurgaon. Within three days of her arrival she was tasked to participate in live confrontation with terrorists. With her team she flew from Palam airport to Pathankot airfield in an AN 12 aircraft.

"This being your first mission you will work under me before you can command your platoon," Major Sardul her senior told her before they boarded the aircraft.

Their mission was to exterminate the five terrorists who had infiltrated and struck Durgi Police Station located close to the border in Gurdaspur district of Punjab. The police station had been destroyed and fatal casualties were reported.

"The situation on the ground is tense. The terrorists after attacking the police station, killed the policemen and are attempting to flee back to their country. The BSF Company has successfully blocked their exit routes across the border and is engaged in a fierce battle with them. Exact details are blurred however it appears that the terrorists have rounded up men and women and are holding them as hostages," Major Sardul Singh spoke to the platoon which consisted of five hit teams each having four combatants and one technical soldier.

From Pathankot airfield the platoon was ferried in two choppers to the BSF out post at Dugri. The men were taken in buses from the helipad to join the BSF troops engaged with the enemy. One chopper remained on call at the helipad.

"So far it is a stalemate, though we have managed to restrict their movement towards the border. They are holed up in two double storey buildings and fire at us when we approach them. When we return their fire, the young children, men and women whom they are holding as hostages are pushed in front of the windows and openings," Mukesh Kumar the Deputy Commandant informed Sardul as they stood on the terrace of a building opposite the terrorist locations.

"How many are they in each building?" Sardul asked.

"In the white building there are three and in the grey there are two, five in all," Mukesh replied.

"How do you communicate with them?" Sardul asked him.

"Through my mobile phone. They have sent their mobile numbers through an old man whom they released." he replied.

"What are their demands?" Sardul asked him.

"Before sunset, they want a safe passage to the border in a bus in which they will carry ten hostages, who will be released after they have reached their destination," he replied.

"And if we do not agree?" He asked.

"They will kill all the 18 men, women and children, destroy the buildings and commit suicide," Mukesh replied.

"Are they well armed?" He asked.

"Yes. They have semi automatic rifles, machine guns, hand grenades and sufficient ammunition," he replied. Sardul looked at his watch and stepped closer towards him.

"We hardly have five hours before the sun goes down. Thank you Mukesh! I will step in now with my men. You and your men should be ready to help as soon as we call up." Sardul said, shaking his hand.

Sardul beckoned Hina, pinpointed the buildings to her and communicated the information he had gathered from Mukesh.

"I want you to take stock of the situation and come out with your plan to flush the insurgents out with minimum collateral damage to the hostages and our property. We do not have much time, therefore we have to do it quickly," he directed her.

Hina heard him with rapt concentration absorbing every word that he uttered. She called her Hit team commanders and conferred with them for fifteen minutes. Alone, in her notepad she made short notes on the probable options for execution and called up the team leaders again for detailed discussion. Finally satisfied, she approached Sardul.

She outlined her plan to Sardul who accepted and modified it with minor suggestions. Returning to the Hit team commanders, she issued executive orders to them. When satisfied that her Hit team members were positioned facing the buildings, she lifted her hand indicating the firing to commence. Two men from each team fired five shots with their rifles towards the windows and openings in the two buildings and stopped.

Soon they noticed civilian faces peeping at them from these openings. When she found the windows fully blocked by the hostages, Hina signaled the other two men from each Hit team, who got up and ran towards the buildings.

"Hina come back! You do not have to go!" Sardul shouted, when he saw her following the men.

His voice was drowned by the noise of another volley of rapid covering fire from the Hit teams. However, the bullets were now soaring over the building roof well away from the windows and entrances.

Hina and her team had reached the building entrance and headed for the stairwell. She led them as they climbed the stairs with stealth and caution. Nearing the second floor landing, she observed a man holding a gun positioned at the room entrance with his face turned towards the stairs. She raised her hand and the team members sank down onto the floor. She fixed the silencer in her pistol and crawled a few feet to have a better view. On reaching the spot she saw him in the same location, though now he had leaned forward and was looking suspiciously down into the stairwell.

She stood up quickly, and in one action aimed and fired from her pistol. The noiseless bullet hit the person's head, his body sank on the floor and he lay dead.

She asked the man behind her to move forward and followed him to the entrance door which was open. Cautioning her man to take position at the entrance, she crawled ahead, sat down and peeped inside the room. The walls facing her and to her right had windows in front of which young boys and girls stood crying hysterically. Along the walls were stacked wooden crates and boxes with sundry items placed on them.

In the center were a group of men and women of all ages; some sitting, some lying and others reclining. She noticed one commonality among them, they looked forlorn, dejected and tired. Above the din of the rifle firing from outside, she heard the conversation between the two terrorists who were not very far from her.

"Not one bullet has hit a person standing behind the window, no window pane has shattered either. There appears to be something weird going on," the first person said.

"Yes there is certainly something very weird happening! The firing has been going on for nearly 10 minutes and no one was wounded or killed? Very strange indeed! I think they are trying to enter the building. The firing is mere subterfuge to divert our attention," the second person said.

"I also think they are trying to enter the building. Go check with Abdul he is at the entrance door," the first person said.

The second person turned and advanced towards the door and halted suddenly.

"Who is that?" He shouted on noticing Hina, who was late in moving away from her position.

He fired his revolver, the bullet missed her as she had dived on hearing him. The soldier behind her fired back at the terrorist, his bullet hit him on the head killing him instantly.

The firing and the commotion alerted the hostages in the room who stood up shouting and yelling. The lone terrorist panicked, lost his cool and fired at random, killing a man. He grabbed a girl and put his pistol on her head.

"Sit down, otherwise I will kill all of you!" He shouted at the hostages.

They all sat down and barring the sound of the rifle fire from outside there was no other noise from the room.

"Do not fire, leave the girl. Keep your weapon on the ground and surrender yourself! Both your men are dead! You will live if you surrender," Hina called out to him.

"I will not surrender! I do not fear death! I will kill everyone in the room before I kill myself. Get me the vehicle, I will leave with these people and free them when I cross the border. Call your higher officer, I only speak to men, not to whores like you!" the man said.

"Don't you have sisters and mother and aunties? They are all women, are they whores too?" Hina shouted back.

The man fumed and called out a few filthy slang words. He hit the girl on the head with the butt of his revolver. The girl shrieked out loud in pain, slumped down and lay unconscious on the floor.

"I will kill this one!" He said, picking up another girl and pointed his revolver over her head.

"Wait, I am coming to talk to you! Here I see my rifle is on the ground! I am coming unarmed! You can take me as a hostage!" The Hit team leader spoke out and entered the room with his hands raised.

Hina had positioned herself behind the team leader and remained crouched behind him when he was speaking to the terrorist.

"Sit down and raise your hands higher," the terrorist said and advanced towards the soldier.

As the soldier bent to sit, Hina got up and fired her pistol over his head. The bullet pierced the terrorist's skull, killing him immediately.

They carried the bodies of the dead man and the wounded girl down the stairs to the waiting ambulance.

The team from the other room too had finished their operation with success. They had rescued all the men and killed the two terrorists in the encounter. However, one member of the Hit team was seriously injured and succumbed while undergoing first aid treatment. The operation ended with nineteen hostages rescued alive and one dead.

By sunset the choppers had lifted Hina and her team to Pathankot air field and in two hours the AN 12 aircraft ferried them to Palam airport.

"The Director General (DG) NSG and the Inspector General (IG) SAG are waiting in the VIP lounge to meet the team," a NCO saluted and told Sardul as they alighted from the plane.

They assembled in the lounge where refreshments were laid out on the table and the two senior officers greeted them with smiles.

"You boys have carried out your task with the usual clinical efficiency and professional maturity. I am happy that we have succeeded with minimum harm to ourselves and killed all the terrorists with least collateral damage. I do extend my deep sympathy and commiseration to the family of Nk Narender Kumar who was killed in action. I am proud of you all! Very well done! Let us now have some refreshments!" Shashi Damodar Kulkarni DG NSG said addressing the team members.

They moved towards the tables laid with heavy snacks, tea and coffee.

"Capt Hina, can I have a word with you please?" Maj Gen Rakesh Malhotra IG, SAG, asked her.

Hina put her plate on the table and moved towards him.

"No, please bring your plate and keep eating," he said.

She picked up the plate filled with snacks and came near Rakesh and found him conversing with Shashi.

"Ah Hina! From the reports I have received you lead your team with perfection. Your own courage and determination were of the highest standard! Well done Capt, you make us all very proud and honored!" Shashi said and shook her hand.

"Thank you Sir," Hina said.

"You have done very well Hina. Keep it up," Rakesh told her and shook her hand.

"Thank you Sir," Hina said.

"I have a disturbing piece of news for you, Hina," Rakesh said, shaking his head. Hina looked at him holding her breath, her heart beating faster than normal.

"Your Dad Brijesh has been missing for the past one week," he murmured and encircled his hand around her shoulders.

□

4

Unlike normal Military Operations rooms, where daily briefings and routine discussions on situation reports from various agencies and organisations were sieved and discussed, plans made and instructions formulated, this room was different in many aspects. Considering the need for extreme privacy and secrecy, the room was located ten feet below ground level, the walls were thick and sound proof, preventing any sound wave to enter or exit the room.

At the press of a button, the lone screen on a wall displayed stored information as and when required by those entitled and authorised to avail this facility. Other walls were totally bare, however sensors were embedded in them to capture any unauthorised electronic equipment that may have entered the room.

There were six comfortable cushioned chairs placed in a semi circle in front of the screen. Kept on a corner table, the lone telephone was the only means of communication with the outside world, once the thick steel doors were closed from inside.

This was the room where all Top Secret meetings were held by Suresh Mathur the National Security Advisor (NSA) to the Government of India! Today, an important meeting convened by the NSA was in progress in this room.

"Brijesh Singh Rathore, 49 years old, Senior Scientist in ISRO, was working close to Tuensang in Nagaland with his team for the past three months. It appears he has been kidnapped. He was heading the team from National Remote Sensing Centre (NRSC) to prepare groundwater prospect maps. These maps are useful in locating water for drinking and sanitation. They were working on a time bound Project under the Ministry of Science and Technology Government of India," Kamlesh Kumar the ISRO Director said to his audience consisting of Suresh Mathur NSA, Bhupinder Singh director Research and Analysis Wing (RAW) and Unnikrishnan the Intelligence Bureau Director (IB).

"Are you sure this was their primary task? I really fail to understand as to why someone should kidnap a person who is preparing maps to locate underground water? They can always get a water diviner for this purpose," Bhupinder asked.

"My hunch is that the kidnappers are assuming that Brijesh and his team were conducting some secretive project and they wanted to know about it," Kamlesh stated.

"I second that. The kidnappers are possibly in league with the Chinese and Pakistani agents and at their behest they have undertaken this criminal act," Unnikrishnan emphasised.

"Are these foreign countries under the impression that we are establishing some kind of ground stations to provide Telemetry Tracking and Command (TTC) support to our satellites and launch vehicle missions, which they see as a danger to their activities in this region?" Bhupinder remarked. They all looked towards Suresh who had remained silent so far. He shook his head and spoke.

"Could this be the reason for them to kill eleven team members and leave the rest in seriously wounded condition? No, the enemy has obviously a whiff of our Top Secret project with which Brijesh and his team are associated. Kamlesh has given you the cover up version. He too has been kept in the dark. Only a few of us, such as the Prime Minister (PM), his scientific advisor, directors DRDO and BDL and I are aware of its details; purely on a need to know basis. Therefore, Brijesh's kidnapping is a security threat to our Nation! We have to find him immediately!" Suresh said showing grave seriousness. The gravity of the situation struck those present and alerted them.

"Unni, any idea who is behind it?" Suresh asked director IB.

"Since the very first day of kidnapping, my boys have been working on it. From the preliminary reports that I have received, it appears that the kidnapping and killing was committed by Kiyanelie's men. The Naga rebel chief has sleeper cells in and around Tuensang," Unnikrishnan replied.

"What then are our sleeper cells and operatives doing in this area? They should have known that Brijesh and his team are vulnerable and should have kept their eyes and ears open. They should have given us some timely information to preempt the insurgents from acting as they did," Suresh told Unnikrishnan, who looked away feeling perturbed.

"Yes there has been a slip up! We did have an inkling on the insurgents activities. As they are based in Myanmar, to further scrutinise our information, we sent it to RAW to have it verified by their agents operating in that area. So far we have received no reply," Unnikrishnan replied.

Suresh looked at Bhupinder who took out a piece of paper and handed it to him.

"This is a message from my agent from that area. It says that an operative located near Kiyanelies camp in Myanmar is on his way to Tuensang bringing a top secret message for us. He is likely to reach there in a few hours and will speak with me through our secure phone line," Bhupinder stated.

Both Suresh and Unnikrishnan felt relieved though worry and apprehension still clouded their minds.

"The Prime Minister is keen that we do something before the media sensationalises the issue. We discussed a few options. One possible action is an immediate surgical strike across the border. Unfortunately, the insurgents have camouflaged their camp so well that our drones or satellites cannot pick up anything worthwhile. There is hardly any radio or telephone communication coming out from them which can give us information. We really know very little about them. We need to send someone urgently in the camp not only to spy on them but also to place devices in their buildings for our satellites and drones to capture and store activities and movements," Suresh explained.

"I think we could send in a small group immediately, primarily for human intelligence and for positioning our sensors in the camp premises to assist the satellites and the drones," Bhupinder said.

"I will go with that. Let us not task the Army for the time being but send a few of our SAG boys from NSG. I requested Shashi Damodar Kulkarni, DG NSG to meet us. We can call him now, he is with the Assistant Director waiting in his room," Suresh said, picked up the phone and spoke.

A few minutes later the door opened, a middle aged police officer with a protruding waistline and gawky ambling stance entered the room and greeted those present.

"Please sit down Shashi. You know Bhupinder and Unnikrishnan they may perhaps be your batch mates and therefore need no further introduction. Kamlesh is the director of ISRO. I am sorry to have called you here at such a short notice. You will soon realise that the reason you are here is extremely serious and urgent. We are discussing recent killings and kidnapping by rebel Naga insurgents and we need your help," Suresh said to him.

"I am at your disposal Sir! It is my duty to serve the Nation against its enemies!" Shashi replied confidently.

"You have served in Nagaland, tell us everything you know about Kiyanelie (picture and brief biodata appeared on the screen) the Naga rebel leader. I have been told by my research team that you are very friendly with him?" Suresh asked.

Shashi felt alarmed on hearing Kiyanelies name from Suresh. Considering the prevalent status of the insurgent leader, he had abandoned all ties and connections with him. He had not spoken to him for the past year or so. He realised that he had to tread cautiously and distance himself from the insurgent leader as much as possible.

"I have known Kiyanelie since we were together in college in Shillong. We were roommates and classmates and we graduated in political science. Together we prepared for the civil services examination, I passed and he did not. Thereafter, over the years we kept in touch with each other but I have not spoken to him for the past one year," Shashi said.

"You must have met him during your tenure in Nagaland as Commandant CRPF Battalion?" Suresh asked.

Shashi felt uneasy realising that Suresh was now treading on delicate ground.

"Yes, I did personally meet him once, but spoke to him on the phone regularly during my tenure with my Battalion in Nagaland," he replied.

"As a result of which, I have learnt that during your tenure the CRPF Battalion suffered no casualties from raids or ambushes from the insurgents," Suresh stated.

"Yes Sir, the insurgents did not trouble our Battalion, we were lucky," Shashi said with a smile.

"It is evident that Kiyanelie is not only your college friend as also your well wisher! Is it possible for you to speak to him now and get information from him, without mentioning us?" Suresh asked.

Shashi scratched his head and thought for a while. This was a good opening for him to extricate himself honorably from the predicament.

"Yes Sir! I can give it a try," he said.

"Gentlemen let us move to my office from where Shashi can call up Kiyanelie on his mobile phone," Suresh said and got up. They left the room and reached the ground floor by the elevator.

Suresh instructed his secretary and the peon to keep all messages and persons away from him for the next hour. As they settled in their chairs, Suresh looked at Shashi and nodded.

"Please ask him if he knows anything about the kidnapping of Brijesh Singh Rathore, and the murder of men of his team who were working at Tuensang. If he says yes, then get the details. If no, then do small talk and hang up," Suresh told him.

Shashi nodded and dialed the number from his cell phone which had an application installed to prevent eavesdropping. He heard it ring through the speaker which he kept open for everyone to listen in.

"Hullo, who is it?" He heard a female voice at the other end.

"My name is Shashi. Can I speak to Kiyanelie please?" Shashi replied.

"Please hold on," she said. After a pause they heard a male voice.

"Yes! Who is this?" Shahi recognised Kiyanelie's voice.

"Kiyna it is me, Sashi!" He said.

"Shashi ! Bless you man! Hearing you after so long! Where are you speaking from?" Kiyanelie spoke in an excited voice.

"I am in my office. Sorry I did not ring up earlier. My wife has been reminding me regularly to call you. Today I decided I must listen to her," Shashi replied.

"I know Usha has a soft corner for me! Tell her I am still a bachelor," Kiyanelie said and laughed.

"I will do that! I have seen your latest pictures in the newspapers and magazines and you have not changed a bit! You still have your good looks and the handsome fine figure! I am sure the girls there are madly in love with you!" Shashi teased him.

"Yes they are, but no juice left in me my friend!" He said and guffawed loudly.

"Kiyna I am a bit worried! This incident in Kurseong is creating a major problem. Everyone is talking about the Brijesh kidnapping and the killing of his team men. Do you know who has done it?" Shashi asked him.

"Oh that! Do not worry, I am not involved with it! I do not do such small and stupid things," he replied immediately with a tinge of annoyance.

"Thank God! That is a big relief! Any idea who did it?" Shashi persisted.

Kiyanelie paused for some time giving hope to them that they were on the verge of getting the information.

"No I do not know! Nor am I interested to find out. I do not want to make enemies by making inquiries. I may end up being called a spy in the service of your Government!" He said and laughed.

"OK! Before I forget you should know that Madhu has not married. She is still waiting, hopefully, for someone!" Shashi said, teasing him.

He waited for his response for sometime while others looked at him questioningly. He changed the topic quickly and continued speaking for the next three minutes or so on issues relating to their past and ended the call by telling him that he had a visitor in his room who had just stepped in.

"Do you trust your friend?" Suresh asked Shashi when he

finished the call.

"Yes, I do. So far he has given me no reason not to trust him," Shashi replied.

"What do you make of the conversation?" Suresh asked the other three sitting across the table.

"I cannot make out much from this short telephonic conversation, it is very difficult to judge," Bhupinder said.

"I agree, I really cannot comment. Maybe if we send the recording to an expert we may get a better opinion," Unnikrishnan stated.

"I have taped it on the office recorder and it will be sent to our experts." Suresh said, agreeing with him.

"Shashi, we are entrusting you with a very heavy responsibility. Your SAG has to perform certain very important and difficult tasks. You will get written instructions today in the next few hours. Please organise your requirements for the mentioned tasks and give it top priority! You can ring me up directly at any time. Here is my contact number," Suresh said and gave him his card.

"Wish you all the best," Suresh got up and shook his hand. Shashi left the room after shaking hands with others.

Bhupinder felt his cell phone vibrate in the pant's pocket. Removing it, he got up and proceeded towards the far corner of the room. He held the phone close to his ears and listened carefully to the voice at the other end.

"Sit down please. Let us discuss it a little longer. Bhupinder, you look worried, any problem?" Suresh asked him when he saw the worried look on Bhupinder's face as he approached him.

"My office rang me just now. Our operative who was located near Kiyanelie's camp and was on his way with top secret information was ambushed and murdered. His jeep was ambushed near Tuensang," Bhupinder said, showing disgust and frustration.

□

5

She sat waiting for the announcements to end and for the plane to taxi to the runway for the take off. She preferred the direct flight to Imphal, as the flying time from Delhi was less by an hour from the one stop via Gauhati, where the long layover and change of aircraft were the other irritants. She stretched her legs and arms to relax, which caused her to touch the passenger sitting next to her, who immediately pressed her shoulder with his. She leaned away from him towards the aisle and sat upright.

"I am sorry to have caused you inconvenience," she said and looked sideways at him.

"No problem! The pleasure is entirely mine! It is a very rare opportunity for me to sit next to a beautiful lady during an air flight! I am Shyam Sunder on a business trip to Kohima," he said.

"Hina Rathore, I am going to meet a friend in Imphal," she said, trying to keep the conversation short.

The man was in his late forties and signs of good life were evident in his opulence and flashy dress. Soft flesh under his chin and around his waist hung prominently.

"In Imphal, I too, have many friends. The Home Minister of Manipur is my college mate, I always stay with him," he said.

She nodded and kept quiet. The announcements had ceased and the plane was on its way to the runway.

"You know the funny thing! I prayed before entering the aircraft, 'Oh God please make me sit next to a beautiful lady for a change'! He has at last heard me!" Shyam said and laughed.

"So what is so great about it?" Hina asked him scornfully.

"Oh! It all depends on the lady! I am game!" He said.

"Are you married?" She looked at him and inquired.

"Yes," he said, looking away.

"Any Children?" She asked.

"Yes two brats," he mumbled softly.

"Don't you think you should grow up?' She looked at him contemptuously and asked.

He kept silent and did not attempt to make any further conversation. The plane was well on its way and soon the air hostesses served meals and beverages on payment.

"Apple juice and non veg meal for me," Shyam told the hostess.

"Anything for you?" The hostess asked Hina with a smile.

"No thank you. I am good," she replied.

"Try out their non veg meal, it is very tasty!" Shyam interjected looking towards Hina.

Hina shook her head and kept quiet. He finished his meal and got up to go to the toilet. Hina left her seat and stood aside in the aisle to let him pass and as he squeezed past her she felt his hand pinching her buttock. Startled, she looked back and found him smiling.

"I am very grown up sweetie!" He said with a smirk, looking back at her.

Hina perturbed, paced the aisle with dismal thoughts. Her instant reaction was to inform the air hostess and ask for a seat change. Looking around she did not see any vacant chair. A complaint by her to the cabin crew would lead to delays. Inquiries, statements, recordings by the officials would be a lengthy process which would dislocate her schedule completely. She was also wary of the media who would blow up the incident instantly. She decided to ignore it completely.

She kept her distance when he returned and occupied his seat and kept standing in the corridor until the announcement by the pilot instructed the passengers to remain in their seats as they were likely to face turbulence. She returned to her seat and fastened her seat belt. Another thirty minutes remained for the aircraft to land and without looking at him she sat back and closed her eyes.

"You know most women take the buttock pinching in Western countries as a compliment! I hope you took it too!" Shyam said, looking at her.

She did not respond and her eyes remained closed, hoping that it would keep him quiet. After a while she was startled and opened her eyes. She felt his fingers probing her crotch. She stood up immediately and looked at him with disgust and pity.

"OK Mr Shyam Sunder, you asked for it! Have a very sound and deep sleep!" She said and turned towards him.

Placing both the thumbs under his flabby chin she found the pressure point under his wisdom teeth and pressed them moderately. The initial look of lust in his eyes soon turned into wide disbelief filled with fear and horror! His head went down sideways with a slight whimper from his mouth as his body slumped on the seat. For the rest of the journey she sat relaxed feeling unconcerned and detached.

After leaving the aircraft when she moved towards the luggage collection point she noticed a flurry of activities. A doctor in an electric cart followed by another cart with a stretcher and oxygen cylinders, all of them speeding towards the aerobridge.

"What happened?" An inquisitive passenger asked a steward walking with him.

"Oh that! A passenger has fainted probably from a heart attack?" The steward replied.

"Any name?" He asked.

"I think he is Shyam Sunder, a frequent flier on this airline," the steward said.

Hina shrugged her shoulders, she was not aware that he had a weak heart, she wished that for his children's sake he survives.

She placed her luggage on the trolley and proceeded towards the exit and noticed a man in army uniform holding a placard with her name on it. She walked towards him and showed him her identity card. He stepped back and gave her a smart salute which she acknowledged by returning with equal alacrity.

"Madam, I am Havildar (Hav) Puran Bahadur Gurung. I am to take you in the jeep to Divisional (Div) Headquarters (HQ) at Zakhama," he said and took the luggage trolley from her.

As they walked towards the vehicle she silently thanked her immediate boss, Maj Gen Rakesh, IG SAG who had called up the GOC on phone for arrangements for her stay in Nagaland.

When Puran was busy loading her luggage in the jeep, she noticed two persons near a black car and was surprised when one of them was pointing his camera towards her and taking pictures. As her jeep went past them she leaned outside the jeep and took pictures with her mobile phone, of these men and the car's registration number.

The 121 Km journey to Zakhama took over five hours, which included a halt for half an hour for lunch midway at Senapati. The sun sets quickly in the hills and as they approached the guest room of the Div HQ Officers Mess, the short twilight period had commenced. A sewadar (helper) who was waiting for her, took her luggage to her room.

"I will be here tomorrow morning at 0830 hours. The Div HQ office is at a walking distance, the sewadar will guide you to it," Puran said.

"Thank you Puran, that will be just fine," she said and returned his salute.

She changed her clothes quickly and told her sewadar that she would only have hot milk for dinner as she was not hungry.

The guest room building was a single storey prefabricated steel framed structure which had its outer walls and roof cladded with CGI sheets. Laminated boards covered the walls internally and fiber tiles were used for false ceiling.

She looked around the room and found it aesthetically tasteful with all the modern amenities in the right place. While she was watching the television, her sewadar placed milk on the bedside table and left wishing her. Before sleeping, she uploaded and sent the pictures of the persons and the car taken at the airport to her people at SAG HQ at Gurgaon, and requested them to send their details to her as soon as possible.

She woke up early in the morning and went for her usual morning five kilometres run on the cemented track within the boundaries of the Div HQ. She encountered a few persons who kept looking at her while they continued to run.

After a quick wash, she dressed up in white tops, blue jeans and black moccasins. Her sewadar who had served her with morning tea early in the morning, escorted her to the Officers Mess. She entered the dining hall and occupied an empty chair. She asked the waiter to bring plain omelette with toast and tea; curious glances from men and women in the dining hall did not bother her as she ate leisurely.

Her sewadar was waiting for her outside the Mess and escorted her towards the office buildings. At the entrance door he asked the sentry to take her to GOCs office.

As they approached the imposing rooms, the Aide De Camp (ADC) who saw her through his office window came out to receive her at the entrance.

"Welcome Captain, I am General's ADC, Major Kashif Abidi. The General has asked me to escort you to his office," he said.

"Thank you Sir! I am Capt Hina Rathore," she stood to attention and nodded.

Kashif gave her a stern look, and after a while smiled when he found that she had not moved.

"OK relax! Now that the intro is over, let us cut out the formalities! Call me Kashif from now on," he said with a straight face.

"Please call me Hina," she said and smiled.

"This way Hina please," he said and she followed him towards a large door a few steps away.

He knocked and opened the door which immediately closed behind him. After a few seconds he opened it and kept the door ajar, allowing her to enter the room.

"Hello Hina welcome to Zakhama!" Maj Gen Ranbir Singh got up from his chair came over to her and shook her hand.

"Come sit down," he said pointing to the single sofa as he sat down in the bigger one.

"Thank you Sir for meeting me. I am very grateful to you," she said as she occupied the sofa.

"Rakesh, your boss spoke to me yesterday. He said you are Brijesh's daughter and that renders you to be my daughter too! I have known Brijesh since we were very young. Though we have not kept in touch, the pleasant childhood memories are fresh with me!" Ranbir said feeling sentimental. Hina looked down suppressing her emotions.

"Everything will be alright! We are going to find Brijesh! You have my word," he said.

"Sir, you have touched my heart by calling me your daughter! I really feel honored!" She replied with humility and softness in her voice. He smiled and patted her on her head.

"Sir, my father in a way encouraged me to join the army. Perhaps, he wanted to fulfill his own missed desire. He was selected by the SSB and would have been your junior, if his eyesight had met the prescribed standards. He is the one who has inspired me to join the SAG," she remarked.

"That is very like him! The kidnapping and killing has shocked us all. The local administration relied on their police to protect him and his team, which is wrong. In Nagaland it is only the Army that can protect the outsiders!" Ranbir said and sighed.

"Sir, he has been away for over a week now and there is no news about him. I know the Army and our intelligence agencies are doing their best to find and rescue him. Sir, I cannot rest until we find him! I have taken a month's leave and intend to devote myself day and night searching for him, and I am confident that I will!" She spoke with a firm and determined voice.

"I am with you! However, wait for a few more days before you start your search. My boys are in touch with the locals and we hope to get a breakthrough. Go and get an update from Bhaskar my Colonel Intelligence (Col Int) who is totally involved in the search mission and will keep you informed regularly," Ranbir said and pressed the buzzer. The ADC entered the room and stood near him.

"Escort Hina to Bhaskar and let him brief her on our efforts to find Brijesh. Ask him to meet me later for my further instructions on the matter," Ranbir told Kashif, who left the room with Hina following him.

They found Bhaskar talking with his subordinate who left the room when he saw them entering. Kashif introduced Hina and conveyed GOC's instructions to him.

"We have a few leads that we are working on. It is a tough task to get the locals to inform us voluntarily. We are offering lucrative incentives and hopefully someone will fall for it soon. Our agents are working overtime in this area and beyond. Hopefully we will get lucky soon," Col Int said as she sat across his table facing him.

"I am certain your Int staff will succeed Sir! However, I need to go over to Tuensang," she smiled and replied.

Bhaskar had been instructed by the GOC to assist Hina through all available means and meet all her requirements. Besides, he was also shaken up by the killings and kidnapping.

"We will make all arrangements for your journey to Tuensang and your stay. Go and rest in your room. Kashif will call you up soon with the details," he said, getting up and shaking her hand. She left the room with Kashif who escorted her to the building exit door.

It was late in the evening when she heard her doorbell ring. Upon opening the door, she found Kashif standing on the porch holding a bag in his hand and with a broad smile on his face.

"May I come in, I have some news for you," he said.

She looked at the tall and handsome figure with sharp features more closely now. He was in her age group and appeared a bit different from others, a bit more polished, sophisticated and appealing!

"Please come in. I was under the impression that I would get the information through a phone call from you," she said.

"Oh, I could have done that! It did not strike me! I hope I am not putting you to any inconvenience? Maybe I should leave and call you up on the phone!" He said and moved towards the door.

She felt embarrassed and hastened forward, held his hand and stopped him.

"Please sit down! I am sorry if I said that I have annoyed you!" She pleaded, not leaving his hand. Kashif with a bemused smile sat in the chair and told her to sit.

"Our Col Int and his team did some research from the information gathered by their agents and have come up with certain findings. Your father was friendly with a Chief from the Changs tribe. He made many trips to his village and as the team members close to him are dead the name and location of the Chief's village remains unknown. The traditional territory of the Changs lies in the central Tuensang district. Their principal village was Mozungjami Hakű from which the tribe expanded to other villages and dispersed all over," he paused and looked at her. She remained pensive going over the information in her mind." I now have some information to start the search. I need to go to Tuensang and get further details from the locals there. I will start early tomorrow morning, I am sure the bus service to Tuensang is regular. Please convey my sincere thanks to the GOC. I shall ever remain grateful to him," she said, showing excitement.

Kashif looked at her with a heavy heart. Her father meant so much to her, he realised.

"Hey! Hold onto your horses! A bus journey for you is too dangerous! Puran Bahadur will take you in the jeep to Tuensang. A vehicle with armed soldiers will escort you. On arrival please contact Matthew Thoma our liaison man, who will make arrangements for your stay and connect you with people who can assist you. I already have had a word with Matthew and he will speak to you any time you call him up," Kashif told her and she looked at him and smiled.

"Please stop treating me like a child! I put on the same uniform that you are wearing! However, I will abide with the instructions, which are probably from the GOC," she said. He felt amused and gave her a wry smile.

"The GOC has asked me to keep in touch with you. Please note down my mobile phone number," he said and spoke it out, which she stored in her mobile phone.

"Please store my mobile number too," she said and pressed his number on her mobile and heard his phone ring.

"You will not get any transmitting signals beyond Tuensang and in the jungles. For contacting us or passing any message go to the nearest Army post. The Brigade HQ knows that you are in their area. Keep in touch and good luck!" He told her and left the room.

In the morning they started their journey at 5 am as she wanted to reach the destination before sunset. The National Highway from Zakhama to Tuensang passes through Mokokchung, another district HQ. Although the distance was 257 Km the time taken to cover it was around nine and a half hours on the winding hilly road.

The front escort vehicle maintained a steady speed as the driver maneuvered the turns and twists on the road with deft and skill. She combed the countryside closely for any untoward movements or flashes from metallic objects. They were carrying pack breakfast and lunch packets and sufficient quantity of water. The convoy stopped after every two hours for ten minutes for the radiator water to cool down and she consumed her meals during these halts.

Beyond Mokokchung the road took greater turns and twists as the hills were more pronounced and higher. She was deep in her thoughts when she heard the sound of machine gun fire and saw bullets hitting the ground very close to the jeep. Puran stopped the jeep instantly on the berm. They jumped out and crawled to the nearest undergrowth. The men in the escort vehicle did likewise.

She crawled on her elbows without raising her head, distancing herself as much from the jeep as she could. Looking sideways, she noticed that the jawans were firing back at the assailants who were positioned on the ridge some 300 yards away. She instructed the marksman to engage the machine gun from which the bullets were coming towards them.

The firing continued for ten minutes unabated from both sides when suddenly the enemy stopped. However, the soldiers continued and when she was about to shout cease fire, she saw the glimpse of a rocket fired by the enemy rocket launcher.

The rocket hit the jeep and it burst into flames. Covering her ears, she pressed her body to the ground to minimize the effects of the deafening sound and the tremendous blast. She remained lying on the ground for some time, until she was satisfied that the danger had passed with no more rockets fired at them.

When she got up, she looked in the direction from where the enemy had fired with their machine gun and rocket. She noticed a car moving away towards Tuensang. It appeared to be the same car she had noticed at the airport car park. She met the soldiers and found them in good shape.

She rang Kashif on her mobile and briefly narrated the details of the incident emphasising that the perpetrators of the assault were on the road going to Tuensang.

Within twenty minutes a helicopter from Tuensang reached her site and landed on a level ground close to her. The pilot sat in the chopper, kept it running and sent the copilot to meet her.

"Capt Hina Rathore, I am Capt Passi. We have been instructed to evacuate you to Tuensang," he said. She nodded and asked Puran to call the convoy commander.

"The persons who had fired at us are in a black car and are driving ahead towards Tuensang. Talk to your Commander over the radio for further instructions," she told the convoy commander when he met her.

"Yes Madam! I have already spoken to him about the incident and he is sending reinforcements from our Post near Tuensang." he said. She nodded, he saluted and left.

"Give me your rifle and a spare filled magazine and go with the convoy," she told Puran, who looked at her and was about to speak when she stopped him.

"Do not worry Puran, Capt Passi will arrange to send your rifle to you and I will also inform Kashif," she said. Puran looked at Passi who nodded.

"I will personally bring them to your unit which I think is 3/4 Gorkha Rifle (GR)," he assured Puran who handed over the rifle and magazine to Hina.

She entered the chopper and spoke to the pilot giving him directions.

"Please follow the road leading to Tuensang and keep the chopper around 300 feet above the ground," she said.

The pilot followed her instructions and continued at a low height over the winding road. The black car was nowhere in sight, though through the binoculars Hina noticed the Army vehicles coming from Tuensang. Frustrated, she looked downwards and noticed a dirt track branching out from the main road.

She grabbed the copilot's headset and spoke to the pilot.

"I am looking for a black car and I do not see it on the road. We should have caught up with it by now. Let us follow the dirt track on the left, maybe we can get lucky there," she said.

The chopper followed the dirt track at the low altitude and after flying for another three minutes she saw the car.

"That is our target and I am going to take it head on! Please fly ahead and return facing the car. Keep low as you approach it," she said to the pilot.

As the chopper closed on to the car head on, she opened the door, slid down and sat on the landing skid while maintaining her balance. Lifting the rifle she fired a burst on the approaching vehicle. The bullets shattered the windshield and killed the occupants sitting in front.

The chopper flew over the car and returned following the same path. The car had hit a rock and had exploded. She saw a person who had escaped unhurt was running away from the burning vehicle. Taking aim, she shot the man who fell on the ground, never to rise again.

"Let's now go to Tuensang," she said over the headset!

☐

6

For the past half an hour the hare and hound chase was in motion at a fast pace through the thick bushes and over the rugged terrain. The hare were the hapless five young boys who had left the sanctuary of their confinement, where they were held hostages to be used as foot soldiers by the Patriotic People Party of Nagaland (PPPN), a terrorist organisation declared by the Government of India. The hounds were the security guards of the PPPN camp located near Hpakant village in Myanmar. Though the hare were agile, swift and accustomed to the hilly forest, they were not as seasoned to the area as their adversaries who were hunting them. They deftly dodged the bullets shot at them, and kept a brisk pace outrunning their pursuers until they reached the area where the line of trees and the undergrowth ended.

As they proceeded with caution and reached the center of the area, a barrage of bullets fired by gunmen, hidden in the trees, hit them. They fell to the ground, a few wounded and some dead. The group is led by Loheleniyu. The leader emerged from the trees closed on them, and kept firing at the hapless boys even when they were dead.

"Severe their heads from their bodies and put them in the bag. Make a bamboo matting platform and lay the bodies on it," Loheleniyu instructed his men.

The funeral pyre was completed in half an hour and the bodies with heads missing were laid on it and left there. They returned to their camp satisfied with the success of their mission.

The camp was spread over an area of twelve acres. The entire ground was covered with fairly dense trees, but the undergrowth had been cleared completely. Cotton camouflage nets with tree branches and leaves spread over them, covered the buildings and installations. As a routine, a team in a helicopter flew over the area every other day to inspect the effectiveness of the camouflage from the sky. Instructions to remedy the observed flaws were remedied promptly. So far the camp had remained invisible on the satellite and drone radar screens.

"We caught and killed the boys who had escaped from the camp," Loheleniyu told his boss Kiyanelie, the supreme leader of the PPPN, in his office.

Kiyanelie got up from his chair and came towards Loheleniyu and patted him on his shoulders.

"Please ensure that there is no repeat. No one should ever escape," Kiyanelie told him.

"It will not be repeated. We have their severed heads," he said, emptying the sack as the heads rolled out from it. Kiyanelie stared at the faces scattered on the ground.

"I suggest, for a few days we display them prominently in our camp and then send them to the Baan (communal house) in the village," Loheleniyu said.

"Yes, do it. We now have to get their replacements immediately. Plan a raid and bring in as many boys and girls as you can. Go across to India and choose a village with lax internal security and well away from Indian security forces camps," Kiyanelie said.

"Do you think the Myanmar authorities will allow the display of severed heads in the Baan? If I am not wrong the Britishers had banned headhunting in 1940," Choti Suh Sazo his friend and second in command reminded Kiyanelie.

"Yes they did, but we will continue. To us Konyaks, headhunting indicates the power of a warrior. It is driven by and founded on certain beliefs, code of honor, principles of loyalty and sacrifice. These heads are our trophies to be hung in the Baan of our villages. The number of hunted heads hung is a measure of our strength," Kiyanelie replied.

Sazo sighed audibly and looked at Kiyanelie with a wry smile.

"It is not the heads of Nagas that you should be hunting! Clear your ideas from your foggy head and prioritize them correctly. We hounded the Britishers long back, and they left us alone. They tried with all their might but we did not surrender. We moved into the hills and continued to live with our old traditions and culture. Sadly, some of us got influenced and ensnared by their priests and evangelists and lost everything we had. They changed our beliefs, language and our way of life. Now we have new rulers who want to further subdue and subjugate us and annex our territories! It is them we have to fight and throw out!" Sazo spoke with bitterness. Kiyanelie looked at him and nodded in agreement.

"I know exactly what you mean. You and me are victims of this new regime for the past several years. They call us rebels, destroy our houses, murder us and our dear ones. Our crime is that we ask them to let us live our lives according to the wishes of our people in our land!" Kinyalie replied. He sighed, looked with resignation at Loheleniyu and instructed him.

"Do as you have suggested, hang the heads wherever you want to, but if the local authorities object, listen to them and do as they instruct you," he said. Loheleniyu nodded and left the office.

"Let us go around in the camp to meet people and see what they are up to," Kiyanelie said and moved out of the room, with Sazo following him.

Their first stop was at the tattoo hut. A lady came forward requesting them to sit on a chair placed in the hut.

"We are fine, we do not require any more tattoos on our body! You can see there is no space left anywhere!" Kiyanelie told her, pointing to his face, hands, chest, arms and calves.

"Our ears too are pierced!" Sazo said, pulling them down. The lady giggled loud and pointed to his face.

"Your facial tattoo is fading! When was the last head you hunted and brought it home?" She asked.

"Oh! Long back, much before you were born! We both hung them in the Baan! Maybe they are still there! Here see this bronze skull, this was the last one," Sazo said pointing to the upper most of the five skulls in the chain around his neck. Kiyanelie did the same though he had only three skulls in his necklace.

They left her and proceeded towards the hut where Jangalu (machetes) were manufactured. They spoke to the iron smith and encouraged him to increase its production.

"I have been thinking about the conversation you had with your friend the DG of NSG. I presume that he is the same one, you mention quite often. Your closeness to him has given me an idea! Let us discuss it in the office," Sazo said on leaving the Jangalu hut. Kiyanelie looked at him with bemusement.

"Fine, let us hear it," Kiyanelie replied and turned to walk towards his office.

"Though I may not like him, yet I admire the late Gen Zia Ul Haq, President of Pakistan." Sazo spoke thoughtfully.

"I am a bit confused! How did Zia Ul Haq come in all of a sudden?" Kiyanelie remarked, looking at him with surprise.

"I know it is difficult for you to grasp my devious thoughts! I do not blame you! You, a graduate from an elite St Anthony College in Shillong cannot easily read the mind of someone from a rustic provincial College in Imphal! You face your problems squarely and headlong irrespective of the consequences! Whereas, I am shrewd, scheming and cut many corners to get what I want!" Sazo said with a smile.

"OK you have made your point! So what is it about Zia?" Kiyanelie asked.

"General Zia used money given by the US against India for starting a proxy war in Kashmir. The militancy and infiltration in Kashmir is the result of Zia's 'Bleed India Through A Thousand Cuts' doctrine. This has worked, but unfortunately partially. His soldiers are getting regularly killed in encounters as they face a very large and formidable Indian Army presence," Sazo explained.

"How do you connect it to our cause? The Indian Army troops here too retaliate ferociously through surgical strikes across the border. We have lost many more men than they have," Kiyanelie said.

"That is exactly the point! Both Zia and us are fighting the might of Indian Army and getting nowhere! Our men are killed for no purpose other than headlines in the media! We are trying to crush the Indian sledge hammer with our peanuts! We have to rise to the next level where we make the Indian sledge hammer ineffective. We create such a situation which raises our esteem in the eyes of our people and our enemy is left helpless and vulnerable!" Sazo spoke enthusiastically.

"How will that be?" He asked.

"We cannot do it alone. We have to get help from our Chinese and Pakistani friends. Call them up for a meeting," Sazo told them.

"OK, but I have to tell them the agenda. Give me some details," he said.

"Tell them it is top secret. We will disclose everything in the meeting," Sazo said.

"At least tell me what it is?" He insisted.

"Ring up your friend the Director General of NSG. Tell him that you and all your men are prepared to surrender their arms to the Prime Minister of India in Nagaland at a mutually agreed place. Give them a day to reply," Sazo said.

"What are you talking about? Are you out of your mind? Impossible! I cannot do it!" He burst out in a loud voice.

"Do as I tell you if you want success! It is a concrete step forward towards liberating Nagaland from India!" Sazo said emphatically.

"What is the catch? What are you hiding from me?" He inquired, showing deep concern.

"All in good time! Ring him first! I will spell out everything after you speak to him," Sazo replied.

He got up, drank water from the glass, refilled it and handed it to Kiyanelie, who placed it on the table.

Kiyanelie held his cell phone, paused for quite some time and dialed Shashi DG NSG.

□

7

The chopper landed on the helipad and took off as soon as she jumped out from it on the tarmac. She waved at the pilot raising his hand and gave her a thumbs up. With a smile on her face she headed towards the two member reception party waiting for her at the fringe of the helipad.

"Welcome Ma'am, I am Matthew Thoma," he said, extending her hand.

"Capt Hina Rathore, please call me Hina," she said and shook his hand.

"This way please," he said pointing towards the car which was parked not very far off. He drove her to his office which was part of the District Commissioners complex. She got out holding her mobile phone in her hand and moved away from the car.

"Please give me a few minutes. I have an important personal call to make," she said, moving further away. She heard a voice after the first ring, apparently the person was expecting the call.

"I have not received an answer to my last text." she said after greeting the SAG contact.

"Someone will contact you soon. I am texting the password. Remember it and then delete," he instructed.

"I will," she replied.

"OK, Take care," he said and hung up.

She was perplexed at the abrupt end to her call and the reason for sending the password to her. She wanted to narrate a few details of the recent ambush, but shrugged her shoulders and headed towards Matthew who was entering his office.

"Please sit down and make yourself comfortable. I am aware of the horrible attack on you and the convoy. This is the second incident in this area after kidnapping a few days back. I do not know when will this stop," he said.

She remained silent and sipped tea from the cup placed in front of her on the table by the office boy.

"I met Mr Brijesh, who has been kidnapped, quite often. He is a very humble and noble person, always smiling?" Matthew told her. Hina smiled and told him that Brijesh was her father.

"Oh! I am very sorry! The Army, the intelligence agencies and the local administration are combing the area for information, I am sure we will find him soon," he assured her.

"I am here to find him. I intend to stay here until we do," she replied. Matthew looked at her apprehensively and smiled.

"You are our guest, please stay as long as you want. We are concerned about your safety, especially after this incident we have to be very careful. Kashif has asked me to take you to the VIP inspection bungalow, where you will be protected by heavily armed soldiers and not the paramilitary guards who are sent for all the civilian dignitaries," Matthew stated.

Hina smiled with the thought that Kashif had not only become her mentor but also her protector!

"Mr John Letho is the head of Tuensang Health and Education Mission (THEM), a non-governmental organisation (NGO). They are mainly funded by the Christian church. He is a Naga, from Rongmei tribe and a devout Christian. He was very friendly with your father and they met regularly. He was the last person your father met before he was kidnapped. He will meet you at the inspection bungalow today at five in the evening. I will drop you there now and you can call me up any time if you require my services," he told her and gave her his mobile phone number which she stored in her cell phone.

The VIP inspection bungalow was nothing less than a five star hotel. The building was perched on a hilltop which provided a 360 degree visibility of Tuensang city. She stood on the porch and admired the pretty houses built on the terraces of the green hills. Though the sun shone brightly, the cool mountain breeze touched her pleasantly making her feel serene and peaceful. How could violence and hatred breed here in such a beautiful place? She shrugged, and looked at Matthew who was seeking her permission to leave.

"Oh! I am extremely sorry I was lost in my thoughts! I love this place! Thank you very much! I will be in touch with you," she said and shook his hand.

She was pleasantly surprised to see her luggage neatly stacked in a corner in her room. Opening her suitcase she took out shalwar and kameez which she was going to wear after her bath. Her uniform had stains and patches of mud stuck from crawling on the ground during the encounter and needed to be washed. Hearing a knock on the door she stepped forward and opened it. She was surprised to see Puran with a broad smile on his face.

"Come in Puran! Nice to see you. I hope you got back your rifle and magazines?" She asked him. He saluted her and entered the room closing the door behind.

"Yes my weapon and magazines are with me," he said lifting the rifle, "I am here with three more colleagues to provide protection. One of us will always be sitting in the hall just outside your door."

"Thank you Puran! There are a few things required to be done. Please tell the room attendant to meet me after half an hour," she told him. He saluted and left, shutting the door.

She let the warm water flow over her head onto her body and arms for a long period. When she washed herself after applying soap, she felt the tiredness and fatigue ooze out from the pores. Wiping herself with the towel, she looked at her hands and legs which had cuts and scratches and attended to them with antiseptic cream.

The doorbell rang after she had changed into shalwar kameez and was about to lie down to rest. She got up and opened the door to find the attendant, to whom she handed over her uniform and under garments and told him to have it washed and pressed by the next evening. An hour later, she was served lunch in her room which she found tasty. She set the alarm on her mobile phone to wake her up at 4.30 pm and hit the bed; slumber soon caught up with the fatigue and exhaustion leaving her gradually.

The loud alarm rings woke her. Reluctantly she got up to dress and was ready when the attendant informed her that a gentleman was waiting in the lounge to meet her.

"Good evening Ma'am I am John Letho. Mr Matthew has asked me to meet you," a fairly tall athletically built man got up and greeted her as she entered the room.

His facial features were sharp with piercing eyes, he was fair skin and thick tuft of black hair covered his head. She shook his hand and requested him to sit on the sofa.

"Thank you for sparing your time to come here. Mr Matthew must have mentioned the reason for our meeting. It is totally personal and very close to my heart. My father Brijesh Rathore has been missing for over ten days now. We have not heard from him or from anyone else about him," she told him.

"Your father was a regular visitor to my house. We sat in the evenings spend hours talking and discussing various issues. He is a well read intelligent person whose knowledge on various subjects is exhaustive and very authentic," John said.

"Yes, I have learnt a lot from him. Did he mention about the work he was involved in here? She asked

"No. He always avoided talking about the work he was doing here. I suppose it is very secretive," John replied.

"It is my father's nature to be secretive about any project he is associated with. You were the last person to see him. Was he disturbed or apprehensive of any looming danger?" She asked.

"No, he appeared as normal as ever with his famous smile. You being his daughter, you are my friend too. I will do my best to track him down. In the meantime, if you have the time and inclination it will be my pleasure to show you the modest effort and labor that THEM is involved in improving the conditions of our brothers and sisters and their children in this beautiful Tuensang district," he suggested to her.

"My first priority is to meet my father. However, I really look forward to see and meet people here. My knowledge about Nagaland is very fuzzy. I have only heard and read about Nagaland and mostly negative, all about killings and destruction. I came very close to it when my convoy was ambushed today," she said and sighed. John looked down and kept silent.

"I will accompany you tomorrow. Please take me wherever you want to," she said. John smiled and got up.

"Thank you, I will be here at 9 am," he said. They shook hands and he left. She felt better after the meeting and looked forward to meeting John.

The attendant served her dinner in her room which she barely touched as fatigue had not left her completely and she still felt weary and run down. Under normal circumstances she would have walked for about 5 Kms or so in the open air to refresh herself. Today she hit the bed early and within a few minutes fell asleep.

Her mobile phone alarm woke her up at 4 am forcing her to sit up with a start. Reluctantly she got up, changed into her sports attire and running shoes and came out of her room. She found the guard who stood up from his chair with a start and saluted her.

"I am going for a run and will be back soon," she told him.

Stepping out of the building, she decided to run on the cemented track which was inside and along the boundary wall. After her first round, she was surprised to find the guards positioned at vantage points along her route to protect her. She smiled and waved at them. When her cell phone indicated that she had completed 5 Km she returned to her room for yoga exercises.

After a quick bath, she wore her grey pants and white tops and had a quick breakfast in the room. She met John, as he arrived in his new Land Rover sharp at 9 am. They greeted each other and he opened the car door for her to sit in the front seat.

"We are going to Pangsha village located near Noklak, which is approximately 26 Km driving distance. Due to the winding roads, we will take around one hour or so to get there," he said, as he started the vehicle. She nodded and looked ahead towards the gate where the sentry was checking a vehicle.

"Why is the army vehicle with soldiers following our car?" John asked, looking in the rear view mirror. She turned and looked behind and saw Puran driving the truck.

"Oh! They are for my protection! After yesterday's incident

the army authorities are taking precautions," she replied. He shrugged his shoulders and drove on.

"The Army takes special care of its officers!" he said.

"The Army takes care of every soldier," she corrected him.

"How I wish the Army cared for the Nagas too!" He remarked. She looked at him astonished at the serious tone in which he had spoken.

"What do you mean? Please clarify," she asked looking at him.

"Oh! We have all these killings and destruction, which was a routine earlier and had ceased for sometime due to political dialogues. It is picking up again! The people are fed up and they want the army to leave," he said.

"I feel sad to hear from you that people want the Army to leave, when it is here to protect them," she replied.

"The people want freedom! The Britishers too kept away and never interfered with the Nagas, and refrained from even discussing hegemony over the tribal community. They respected the tribal's independence and liberty," he said.

She kept silent and looked out of the window towards the distant hills with terraced fields which painted a pretty picture.

"The only statement that I can unequivocally make is that Nagaland is legally a part of India! I am a soldier and not a politician. Let us end this discussion right now," she sighed and said.

For the rest of the journey they remained silent. Pangsha village spread along the highest hilly ridge in the area, was well camouflaged by the dense vegetation from all sides. The tarmac single lane road leading to it was in good condition. She noticed the Church tower rising above the trees as they came closer to the village gate. They stopped near a building from where she could hear children's voices from within it.

"I will first take you to St Andrew School which was established by THEM seven years back. We encountered galore problems especially from the young boys. Growing up for the Naga children is all play and fun. For them, hunting and helping their parents in the fields in cultivation is everything. As they live together in a dormitory, they lead a carefree undisciplined life with no direction or fruitful purpose. Regular schooling spoils their fun and is a jail to them. However, over the years through persuasion, motivation and recreation we created an environment wherein they not only read their books but also participate in games and sports. Another important aspect which we highlight is good and clean hygiene which is sadly missing in most of the villages," John kept talking, as he escorted her into the school building. They spent around twenty minutes in the school, meeting the teachers and a few students.

"What is coming up there?" Hina asked John, while standing in the room and pointing through the window towards a bulldozer leveling the ground at some distance.

"Oh! The ground is being leveled for additional basketball and volleyball fields," John replied.

"I see men in uniform working with the dozer," she said.

"Yes most of the ground leveling is carried out by dozer teams from the army," he stated.

"Even the ground on which this school buildings stand?" she looked at him and queried.

"Yes," he said.

"What else does the army do for the village?' She asked.

"Many other things. It's what they call fraternisation with the locals," he replied. They walked out of the school building and proceeded towards playing grounds.

"I see men in uniform playing volleyball with your school children," she pointed to the ground where the game was in progress.

"That again is part of fraternisation. There is an army post on a hilltop not very far from here and soldiers from there come here to play regularly," he replied.

She wanted to question him on the comments he had made earlier on the locals' unhappiness with the army, but refrained.

He took her to a clinic not very far from the school where she met a nurse and a male nursing assistant.

"This clinic provides basic medical needs to the villagers. We have a full time trained nurse and a nursing assistant. THEM is responsible for providing medicines and equipment," John clarified.

"What about the doctor? Who prescribes the medicines to the patients?" She asked.

John looked away from her, moved closer to the nursing assistant and whispered in his ears. The assistant left the room immediately.

"Madam, the army doctor visits us twice a week. Her Battalion location is fifteen minutes drive from us. In emergency cases we take the patient to the Government Hospital in Tuensang," the nurse responded.

She thanked the nurse and took the glass of water from the assistant, who had returned carrying it in a tray.

"Our main problems here a few years back were, rampant drug addiction among men and HIV aids mainly in women. The women were terribly scared when drug addicted men returned from work in the evening to their house. The men were violent, abusive and made the lives of their family members miserable. Now due to better understanding through education and counselling, drug addiction has lowered considerably leading to improved family life. HIV aids cases have also reduced largely on account of easy access to condoms and contraceptives," John explained to her as they rode back to the inspection bungalow.

"Any news regarding my father's whereabouts?" She asked John when he left the vehicle and came over to her at the bungalows doorstep.

"Not yet, I have not heard from my men who are at it. Hopefully, by this evening I will be able to give you some news," he replied.

"Thank you for the trip! It was quite educational! I will wait for your call. You have my cell phone number with you," she said, shook her hand and entered the building.

She remained in her room waiting anxiously for the call from John. It was around 9 pm that her cell phone started ringing. She grabbed it and pressed the button.

"Good evening! John here! I have some good news for you! Your father used to visit a lady who lives in Khejok village. Her name is Vamuzo, she is a widow and has two grown up children. Her husband died a few years back. She says she knows your father's whereabouts and will divulge it only to you! According to her she is following your fathers instructions, given to her when he left her before disappearing," he informed her. Hina felt very relieved as well as intrigued.

"Thank you very much! You have been extremely helpful! I'll find my way now," she told him.

"You are welcome, it is my pleasure to help you! Unfortunately, Khejok is not marked on any map. You require a guide to take you there," he said.

"Do you know anyone? I will recompense him handsomely," she stated.

"Yes, the person who gave me this information lives there. I will ask him to guide you to the village. There is no need for any compensation to be given to him," John replied.

"Fine, we'll leave early in the morning tomorrow. I will be ready by 6 am," she said.

"His name is Keshoho and he will be there with the land rover and two guards at 6 am," he told her.

"I have army guards who will insist on accompanying me," she pointed out to him.

"I am sorry that is not acceptable. Keshoho will be singled out and may suffer at the hands of the rebels, when they see him openly moving around with army soldiers. He will certainly refuse to go with you and the soldiers," he insisted.

She paused to assess the situation and after a while spoke to him.

"OK. I will ask the army men to stand down! Please send Keshoho with the vehicle by 6 am," she said and hung up.

She considered calling up Matthew to brief him on her travel plans and seek his advice on whether she should proceed without army security cover. However, considering the lateness of the hour, she decided to postpone it for the next morning before leaving. Opening the door, she spoke to the guard and asked him to fetch Puran.

She divulged her next day's arrangements to Puran as she could not reach Kashif on her mobile. Puran heard her, though he felt uneasy when he learnt that she was leaving without the army escort.

She got up early in the morning and freshened up quickly. On the ankle under the trouser she strapped the holster with a semi automatic Springfield pistol in it. In addition in her trouser pockets she also had a range of knives encased in leather casings and a compass. The guard knocked at the door and informed her that a vehicle with four persons were waiting for her.

"Good morning Madam, I am Keshoho your guide and these three are your guards who will be travelling with you," he greeted Hina, when she stepped out of the building.

Keshoho was middle aged with rugged features. He was taller, leaner and more energetic than his brethren. She greeted him and went over to shake hands with Puran and the army guards who had lined up near their vehicle. She thanked them and bid them goodbye. After checking that her luggage was in place, she occupied the front seat of the Land Rover. When the three men had settled down in the rear seat, Keshoho started the vehicle.

The road was winding downwards with sharp turns at every 200 yards or so. Though its surface condition was fairly good but at places it was so narrow that Keshoho found it demanding to keep the four wheels of the car on the road. Hina was perplexed that neither Keshoho nor others spoke during the journey. Her attempts at conversation with them were responded either through a smile or nodding. She kept to herself and enjoyed the morning breeze coming through the open windows. After driving for nearly an hour, the condition of the road worsened with the surface strewn with rocks and boulders.

"We have to stop here and do the rest of travelling on foot," Keshoho said, applying the brakes and switching off the engine.

The men got down from the vehicle, stretched their limbs and went into the bushes to ease themselves.

"How far is the village from here?" Hina asked Keshoho who came over to her after easing himself.

"The ocean turns blue when the sun rises!" Keshoho whispered.

She turned her head sharply towards him, startled and amazed. She could not believe that she would meet her contact here in the wilderness.

Recovering quickly, she looked down and whispered, "The river shines when the moon is full!"

Keshoho moved away from her as the men converged and surrounded her.

"OK please take my luggage and let us start walking," she spoke out loudly.

The men looked at each other and conversed among themselves in their language.

"We will leave the luggage here and bring a horse from the village to carry it," one of the men spoke out.

"What is your name?" She asked the speaker.

"Ranphan," he said.

"OK Ranphan, will my luggage be safe if it is left in the vehicle?" She asked.

"Yes. Now start walking!" He told her brusquely, and signaled one of the men to lead.

Keshoho joined them as they walked in a single file. As they marched forward, the undergrowth became more dense and thick with the trees too getting closer. The Nagas had to cut the branches and clear the area to move forward. They struggled along for half an hour and stopped when an open piece of ground appeared all of a sudden.

"We halt here!" Ranphan said, and gave out a loud bird call.

Within seconds five Nagas armed with pistols and dahs, emerged from the bushes and surrounded Hina.

"Kneel down and offer your prayers to your God before we kill you!" Ranphan told her as the Naga pointed his pistol at her.

She was stunned! Felt the earth slipping away from her feet. She had never expected this terrible reception! Vulnerable and helpless, she looked towards Keshoho, who nodded and hooked his finger.

Taking the hint, she bent down on her knees, in a split of a second snatched the pistol strapped to her ankle, and fired at the nearest Naga. Before others could react, she shot two more. From the corner of her eyes she saw a Naga aim at her but felt relieved when Keshoho stepped forward and chopped his arm with his dah.

She got up to kill the remaining Nagas, who were hiding

behind the trees. She looked around and found Ranphan and the two who had come with her, attacking Keshoho with their dah's. Taking two steps sideways she aimed and shot Ranphan who stumbled and fell on Keshoho bringing him down on the ground. The other Naga hesitated before striking Keshoho with his dah, giving her ample time to shoot and kill him.

A bullet fired from the pistol by a Naga hiding in the bushes hit her. Crying out loudly she fell to the ground feeling pain in her left hand. Her pistol flew away from her hand and landed at a distance. Finding that she no longer had the pistol in her hand, the Naga came out from the bushes and stood near her pointing his pistol at her.

She closed her eyes, heard the sound of a fired bullet, but felt no pain! Surprised to be alive, she raised her head and laughed out loud! Through her bleary eyes, she saw Kashif firing his pistol at her assailant who was lying on the ground, close to her!

□

8

Their prey, the spotted Lansing had eluded them for nearly half an hour. They had noticed it accidentally during their regular hunt in the forest for birds and animals. The dusky brown animal having long slender body, short limbs with elongated neck and head, and a long tail. It fed on rodents, frogs and snakes. It was a prized animal as it would fetch them a high price in the Tuensang market. They desperately wanted it! The three teenage Nagas pursuing the animal aimed their arrows at him and missed. Their target kept moving faster and further and remained out of range from the bullets fired from their rifles.

The chase continued relentlessly and as they closed in rapidly, the animal slowed down and was within their firing range. One of the Nagas paused to take aim, but to their surprise before he could fire they noticed the Lansing drop on the ground and heard the sound of gunfire from behind them. They swung around and noticed a girl holding a rifle drop down from a nearby tree. Before they realised the girl brushed past them towards the fallen animal. They ran after her and halted as she knelt to feel the animal's body.

"He is dead!" She said and got up.

"Sano! What are you doing here?" A boy asked her.

"I am hunting for my food, Luikham! You all are doing the same!" She rebuked him.

"But we are men! It is our duty to hunt for food! You are a girl, you have to help your mother!" Luikham said, showing his annoyance.

"I do help my mother when she requires it. We do not have a

male member to hunt for our food!" Sano said and bent down to pick up the dead animal.

"Leave it, we will carry it to the village. I am going to complain to the Chief," he said.

Sano shrugged her shoulders, turned and left them. Luikham cut a long and fairly stout branch from a tree and shaved it closely. He asked his two mates to tie the animals feet, hang it on the wooden staff and carry it by supporting its ends on their shoulders.

"Why don't you behave like other girls?" Luikham asked her when he caught up with her.

"I do behave like other girls! I do all the household chores, cleaning, cooking, washing and much more!" She replied emphatically. He remained silent trying to keep pace with her fast strides.

"I weave and make beautiful shawls. See the one I am wearing? It is woven by me. I make Zutho (wine from rice) and help my friends during the cultivation season. I am a normal Naga girl," She kept talking while walking.

"Sano, you are an extraordinary girl! You are beautiful, your face is pretty and your eyes are so large! Your slim and lean body sways my heart when you walk and dance! You are the most pretty and graceful girl that I have seen! The problem with you is that you are arrogant, domineering, impudent and bossy, especially with men!" Luikham told her, showing his frustration.

"I do not want to have any further discussion with you," she said and abruptly increased her pace.

They reached the village by noon. She left the rifle in her friend's house and headed towards her home. Luikham and his mates took the dead animal to the Chief's house and left it there. They told the Chief that it was Sano who had killed the animal and requested him to take action against her.

"Let me prepare food today," Sano told her mother Monalisa who was busy weaving a shawl.

"Go ahead, I have cleaned the fish for you to cook. We will have fish and rice for lunch today," she said.

Sano lit the firewood in the oven which was made from stone and mud. Soon the flames from it started heating the earthen pot containing fish and rice.

"Tomorrow is the Muong Lem festival. We have to make Zutho for ourselves and others. My weaving is nearly over, and now we both have lovely garments to wear," she said, holding up the shawls, tops and skirts for her to see.

"That's nice!" Sano said admiring the garments.

As they ate their meal she narrated the hunting incident pertaining to the Lansing she had killed.

"I only hope the Chief does not stop you from hunting. We need the meat of the animals and birds that you kill," her mother told her.

Sano nodded her head, and after finishing her meal got busy cleaning up the utensils and the floor. Taking out a book from the wooden box she sat down on the floor to read it. Monalisa sat next to her knitting a pattern on a skirt with colored threads.

Her mother was the only person who cared for her after her father's untimely death, due to malaria, when she was very young. Sano had grown up under her guidance and tutelage which had given her greater freedom to act and speak. She learnt the skill sets of her tribe from her friends and had mastered them through patience, diligence and hard work. It was her mother who had taught her to read and write.

Unknown to her mother, she had practiced shooting with a friend's rifle in the dense forest. Through her inbuilt talent and quick grasp she soon hit the targets regularly. Her mother learned of her feat when Sano confessed that the meat they were having for dinner was of a squirrel hunted and shot by her. Initially she was shocked, but later relented and encouraged her daughter to pursue hunting the animals. Sano continued to hunt as and when she had the opportunity.

"Is he coming today?" She asked her mother taking her eyes away from her book.

"No. Brijesh is not joining us in the festival!" Monalisa heaved a sigh and replied in a sad voice. Sano looked at her with surprise, closed her book and kept it on the shelf.

"I too feel sad I am going to miss him. Why is he missing this festival?" She asked.

"He was kidnapped a few days back. No one knows where he is," Monalisa murmured.

"What! How did you know?" Sano inquired in a shocked tone.

"I heard it on the radio a few days back. The police are investigating but so far they have not found him," she said.

"He is a nice man. I like him," Sano comforted her.

"He likes you too! He said he has a daughter just like you, nearly your age" she said.

"How did you meet him?" Sano asked her. Monalisa gave her a candid look and smiled.

"Oh! About two months back, Longayo, our village chief, asked me to assist Brijesh and his team in their work in the village. I was to arrange their meals, accommodation and other logistics requirements. Brijesh chose me as my English was good and he could understand me. I needed the money so I accepted," She said.

"You soon became thick friends, how did this happen?" Sano smiled and asked her.

"He is very inquisitive and in a hurry to learn about our social and cultural customs and traditions. I spent a lot of time with him alone, and we got to like each other's company," she replied and smiled

"Did he make a pass?" Sano asked with a mischievous smile.

"No never! He was always very polite, gentle and courteous," she replied.

"I hope they find him," Sano said.

Their conversation was disturbed by a knock on the door. Sano opened the door and spoke to a girl who had a message from the Chief.

"The Chief wants to meet us tomorrow early in the morning in front of Morung'"she told her mother, who nodded and continued knitting. The sun had set and Sano, feeling tired, wanted to retire and rest.

"I am going to the dormitory to sleep and will meet you tomorrow morning," Sano said, kissing her on her cheek and leaving.

There was only one oil lamp burning in the girls dormitory; she tiptoed to her bed, lay down and closed her eyes. The day-long hunt had taken its toll, her sinews and muscles were stiff and weary. Gradually as her body relaxed and sleep caught up with her.

She woke up suddenly when she felt pressure on her right leg calf. In the dim light she could see the tail of a snake twirling under her skirt and felt it slithering on her thighs. She jumped up, and in one motion held the snake's tail, pulled it out and banged its body on the floor. Placing her foot on its head, she pressed it until it stopped jerking in her hand. She noticed that the snake was over three feet long, healthy and poisonous.

Opening a box, she took out a jute bag in which she put the dead snake and felt happy that for the next two days she and her mother would enjoy the delicacy of cooked snake meat.

She took a piece of string tied one end to a small wooden stick and applied the tourniquet above the wound. With her pocket knife, she cut the area of the snake bite and squeezed her calf so that blood drained out from it. Taking out cotton from her box she cleaned the wound and put the herbal bamboo shoot paste on it. Pressing fresh cotton on the paste she covered it with a strip of cloth and tied it around her calf.

She was aware that she and her tribe did not consume salt therefore they had immunity from poisonous insect bites. However, as an extra precaution, from a pouch she took out the powder made from the bark of the Letoso plant and swallowed it as an antidote. She lay on the bed, the pain in her calf soon subsided and she slept peacefully.

In the morning she took the bag containing the snake to her house and showed it to her mother. Cutting the snake into small pieces, she washed them and put them in an earthen bowl containing hot water.

After finishing their morning chores and breakfast, she along with her mother left the house to meet the Chief.

"Good morning Monalisa! I see Sano is with you, good morning to you Sano!" Longayo Chief of Yuinsai village greeted them and took them inside the Morung to meet others.

The younger men stood up and greeted the Chief as he entered the room with the ladies. They all sat down, and Sano noticed the presence of all the village elders in the gathering.

"Monalisa, we will not detain you here for long as you and Sano have a lot of work to do for this evening's festivities. In your presence, we will only discuss whether we should allow our girls to hunt birds and animals for food. Prior to your arrival the council members have discussed among themselves and through our revered elder we will now like to have his views," the Chief said, and looked towards a wizened old man.

"Let me ask you a question Sano, why do you go to hunt? Is it that you fancy doing it, or is there any other reason?" The elder queried.

"With due respect and reverence, I have to submit that I started hunting not out of choice or fancy, but due to necessity," she replied.

"What do you mean? Can you be more specific?" He asked.

"Me and my mother were mostly starved of meat as we have no male members to hunt for us. Our produce of rice and soybeans are barely sufficient to meet our daily consumption. With great difficulty we can save some of these products and by selling or trading them we purchase our basic necessities. We eat meat on an average only twice a month, counting those days when our hosts serve us on our festivals," Sano replied.

There was silence all round, the elders looked at one another, some shaking their heads and others deep in thought.

"We take pride that we have no beggars in our tribe or in any other tribe in Nagaland! We help each other and look after each other without being condescending or hurting any egos. Let us now reexamine our tradition on the ban on our women to hunt animals, especially in light of the live problem posed by Sano. Give us sometime we will revert to you in due course," the elder spoke out. Monalisa nodded her head and felt relieved.

"Regarding the other issue, the animal killed by Sano can be sold. However, the proceeds obtained from the sale will be kept with the Chief until the larger issue is resolved," the elder continued. Monalisa thanked the Chief and the council members and left the room with Sano.

For the rest of the day both mother and daughter were busy collecting firewood and helping in the preparation of the feast. By dusk they returned to their home to dress up for the occasion.

Both wore sleeveless vatchi (top), Sano's was colored red and her mother's white. Their pfemhou (skirt) had different colorful patterns knitted on them. The multi colored shawls around their shoulders enhanced the elegance of their attire and gave a regal look. The jewelry on their body parts sparkled brightly, whenever the light fell on them.

The rituals for appeasing the deity had commenced when they reached the festival site. A huge fire was burning, with people sitting around it. While an aged man recited the invocations, pigs and goats were slaughtered on the wooden block in front of the carved stone pillar. This continued until they heard the loud sounds of drum beats from behind the pillar. Soon a large number of men and women wearing traditional clothing and jewelry emerged dancing. The offerings were quickly removed and kept aside.

The dancers winded their steps towards a raised platform, where earthen pitchers with wine and glasses were kept. After a while, the drums stopped beating, the dancers dipped their glasses in the pitchers and took out the wine from them. They sipped the wine and mixed with the crowded horde, who taking cue from them quickly converged towards the pitchers. Within a short period every man woman and grown up child had a glass of wine in their hands. Soon the wine started taking its effect as shouts, shrieks and verbal gibberish rent the air. The drums sounded again, the drummers arranged themselves in rows and circles and danced with the fast rhythmic beats. Many women joined the men, dancing and singing in the chorus.

Monalisa was with a group of middle aged ladies who sat and watched the dancers perform. She had consumed a glass of wine and enjoyed the music and the dancing by her friends. Sano stood near the group where her mother swayed to the drum beats. She was not fond of alcohol and avoided drinking it, especially on such occasions, where the taste and the quality were doubtful.

She, however, was very fond of music and dancing, the elegant and feisty dancers lured her to join them. She soon lost herself to the drumbeats and the lilting music and moved in rhythmic steps with the dancers. The elation in her heart expanded and tingling in her body increased as she swayed and glided in the milieu filled with magical resonance. She was lost in another world!

Her sweet trance was cut short when a hand encircled her waist and pulled her. She looked sideways to find Luikham lurching next to her. He leaned towards her and spoke in her ears.

"Let us leave the dancers," he said. The smell from his mouth forewarned her and she stepped away.

"I see you want to continue to dance! We have danced enough! Come with me, we will find a place and make love!" He said coming closer to her.

She felt flustered, looked around and continued dancing. He stepped towards her with the intention of embracing her. She stuck out her hand and grabbed him by the shoulder, pulled him away from the dancers and took him to a nearby house whose doors were open. He looked at her with amusement and anticipation!

"Oh! Where is the bed? Never mind we will lie on the floor," he said and attempted to pull her down. She shrugged him off and stepped away.

"Luikham the wine is affecting you! Either you go back to the festival crowd or go home and sleep! Do not come near me! I do not want to have anything to do with you!" She shouted at him.

"Sano! You think you are special? All the girls in the village sleep with the boys before they get married! I want to marry you!" he said, stepping towards her.

"Not all the girls sleep with different boys, only a few of them! Look what happens to these girls who keep sleeping with different boys! They get diseases and the boys get diseases and they all die horribly! I am not going to marry anyone!" She shouted at him.

Moving erratically Luikham plunged forward to hold her and bring her down. She sidestepped and he fell on the floor with his head hitting the hard ground. She bent down to check his breath as he lay heedless on the floor. He was alive, probably unconscious. Closing the door she stepped out and joined the festive crowd.

The dancers had swelled as more men and women had joined in large numbers. Young boys and girls who had joined were jumping laughing and yelling out loud with gay spontaneity and abandon.

Food arrived around midnight and was served on plantain

leaves laid out on the ground. Sano sat next to her mother and helped herself with rice and pork. She and her mother left immediately after finishing their meal and went home. Changing her clothes, Sano left for her dormitory and slept as soon as she hit the bed.

The dancing continued as most of the dancers, having consumed a large quantity of liquor preferred not to eat. It was nearing dawn when the festival site was ultimately empty of the participants, who staggered to their homes in severely inebriated condition. The fire's flame had lost its intensity, but the embers were still alive and red.

The Chief, who had consumed far less wine than the others, got up early in the morning and came out of his hut to take a round of the festival grounds. He was a satisfied man, the festivities had no untoward incident and his people had enjoyed the occasion.

The sharp rays beat his face as he looked up at the early morning sun. He blinked when he found a person with an awkward smile on his face standing in front of him. With his palm he covered the sun's rays from his eyes and moved forward for a closer look.

Observing that the man was from a different tribe, he stepped back and raised his voice and asked, "Who are you?"

"I am Loheleniyu from the Konyak tribe!" The man replied.

"A Konyak from Myanmar! Why are you here?" The Chief frowned and questioned him.

"I am here on a mission, Chief! Please listen carefully! I need young boys and girls from your village. The boys will become fine soldiers of our army and fight against our enemy India and the girls will help them," Loheleniyu the commander of Kyanelie's insurgent army smiled and said.

The Chief looked at him, shocked at his impertinence and arrogance. Losing his temper, with anger and contempt, he shouted at him rudely.

"Get out of my village immediately, before I call my men," he said.

"Your men are all fast asleep! After all night drinking and dancing they are now having sweet dreams! Look around, we cannot find even the sentry at the gate!" Loheleniyu said condescendingly and raising his arm high above his head circled it around. The Chief turned around, saw unfamiliar armed men wherever his eyes could reach.

"Your village is surrounded and I am certain you do not want a bloodbath," Loheleniyu told him.

Crestfallen and dejected, the Chief left his adversary and rushed towards the Morung and the girls dormitory. He stood at the doors of each building blocking entry to the rooms. Loheleniyu ordered his men to push him away and enter the buildings.

In a swift operation and with minor resistance, the boys and the girls were rounded up and taken away. Sano saw the helpless situation she was in and followed her companions. She trudged along silently with the rest of the prisoners.

□

9

Shashi stood facing Sikandar Lodi tomb in Lodhi Garden expecting Suresh Mathur the NSA to arrive any moment. Out of curiosity he approached a group where a tour guide was busy narrating the history of the monument to his audience in his resonating voice. He stood there and listened to him chronicle the details of the tomb.

"It was built by his son Ibrahim Lodi in 1517 the last Sultan of Delhi from the Lodi dynasty. He was defeated by Babur in the First Battle of Panipat in 1526, paving the way for the advent of the Mughal Empire."

A tug at his elbow from behind made him turn to find Suresh facing him with a frown on his forehead.

"Follow me after a few seconds," he whispered and left him.

He waited for a while allowing a few yards gap between them before proceeding at a moderate pace. Suresh walked ahead with confidence of being familiar with the surroundings and lead him to a bench under a shady tree well away from the track used by the early morning walkers and hidden by an tall and dense evergreen plant hedge.

"Come and sit down here Shashi," he called out to Shashi, who shook his hands and sat next to him on the bench.

"A nice and peaceful surrounding," Suresh said and looked at him.

"Yes, this is the first time I have come here. It is a good place for our discussion, thank you," Shashi said. Suresh sighed audibly and looked up towards the sky.

"You know Shashi, everyone desires peace and tranquility! It appears we are likely to contribute our bit to it! It is great news that Kiyanelie and his men are surrendering unconditionally! The PM is thrilled! His popularity will certainly go up!" He smiled and patted Shashi on his shoulder.

"Yes! It will be a landmark achievement. At last peace will return to the region," Shashi added.

"Tell me, you were close to Kiyanelie, why and how did he become a rebel and took to insurgency? I am sure he must have given you his reasons even if you had not asked him?" Suresh asked.

Shashi knew the answers. He remembered Kiyanelie's distress and anger when he had raged like a wounded animal over the phone for full fifteen minutes.

"His entire family which included his parents, a grown up sister, two younger brothers were killed and his entire village destroyed in an action by an Assam Rifle Battalion," Shashi replied.

Suresh looked shocked, this was the first instant he had learnt about the gory happening.

"How did this happen? How can an entire village be destroyed?" He asked.

"A cordon and search turned into a search and disaster operation. Naga rebels had entered his village and were demanding money and rice. They killed two villagers who refused their demands. An SOS message was sent by the village Chief through an informant to the Brigade HQ. An Assam Rifle Battalion was tasked to go to the village to capture the insurgents. The Battalion sent a platoon consisting of around 25 armed men under an officer. They discovered that there were far many more rebels than the informant had intimated to the Battalion. In the skirmish the insurgents surrounded and massacred the entire platoon, however, two wounded soldiers managed to escape and informed the Battalion. Suspecting that the villagers had on purpose sent a false alarm and that they had held back the presence of the actual numbers of insurgents, the entire Battalion went into action. Two of its rifle Companies surrounded the village while the third entered it.

On reaching the Morung they found the dead bodies of their colleagues spread all over on the ground. Their heads were missing, they searched everywhere but could not find!" Shashi said and paused. Suresh sighed and looked away shaking his head.

"Rest you may well visualise, Sir! The men of the Battalion were shocked beyond belief! They were bloodthirsty for revenge and retribution! The Battalion retreated to a safe distance and the CO asked for and got artillery fire, which completely razed the village! They shot and killed all those who tried to leave the village! As soon as the arty fire stopped the companies charged into the village and killed those who had survived! There was a major hue and cry from all over Nagaland. Overnight, the Battalion was shifted to Dimapur and the CO posted out," Shashi said.

"Where was Kiyanelie when his village was razed?" Suresh asked.

"He was in a College in Imphal. He had just finished the Civil Services exams and was leaving for home the next day. After a year, I learnt through a newspaper report that he had taken over the insurgent group on the death of its leader," Shashi replied.

"Sad very sad! However, we have to continue to do our job as professionals. I come to this place quite often, it gives me peace and privacy. Kiyanelie wants his message presently to remain secretive, this is the place which is ideally suited for discussion," he said.

"Yes, Kiyanelie was very emphatic on ensuring that the surrender news is kept absolutely secret for the time being. I told him that only you and the PM will have this information," Shashi said.

"Tell him that the PM is keen that he and his men should surrender as early as possible. A month from now would be ideal," Suresh said.

"Any particular reason for the hurry?" Shashi asked.

"The PM is keen that he must include this as a successful achievement in his 15th August speech from the Red Fort. Moreover, the longer it is delayed the more are the chances of it getting leaked and encountering roadblocks from vested interests," Suresh replied.

"Has he agreed to the venue?" Shashi queried.

"Yes, the ceremony can be held in the Sitni which is the village Kiyanelie has chosen," Suresh said.

"It is very close to the Myanmar border," Shashi remarked.

"We have our presence there. Our intelligence agencies both RAW and IB have agents in the village and the army presence can be increased very quickly from the adjoining posts. Moreover, your men will be guarding the PM during the meeting. The locals too are friendly and are fed up with the rebels," Suresh elaborated.

"Can we propose 10th August as a suitable date?" It is four weeks from now," Shashi said.

Suresh retrieved a small diary from his pocket and went through its pages.

"I notice that the PM has no major engagement on 10th August. We can plan on this date unless you hear anything to the contrary from me," he replied and got up.

"I leave the nitty-gritty of the ceremony to you and the army. You will be in charge of coordinating it. As a caution, send your men to Nagaland only a day before the event. We do not want to alarm the locals for some of them may not be in favor of the peaceful surrender," he said and got up. Shashi followed him as they started walking towards the gate.

"Can I inform the Home Secretary so that the Home Minister is aware?" Shashi asked.

"No, do not tell anything to the Home Secretary as yet. Leave it to the PM to inform the Home Minister," Suresh replied.

They walked together a few yards and separated as they approached the monument. Shashi stayed back to join a group and ambled with them perambulating the monument for a short while.

Filled with anxiety and trepidation, Shashi reached his office. He felt very uneasy from withholding information from his immediate bosses. The Home Minister (HM) and his Secretary may not directly question him for not informing them, however, they will at the back of their minds have a reason to question his loyalty and integrity once they become aware that he was fully involved in it and did not keep them in the loop. He might as well get prepared for his next transfer, which certainly would be in an area where he will either spend the rest of his remaining three years twiddling his thumbs, or amidst the naxals in a remote jungle.

He rang up his wife on his cellphone and learnt that his only daughter was on her way from Pune and would land at the airport by 10 pm.

"I am not going to receive her! I will send the driver to bring her!" Usha, his wife told him.

"Why is she coming back so soon?" He asked her.

"She doesn't like her in-laws and Pune! She wants to stay with us in Delhi!" Usha replied.

"What about Akash, her husband? What does he have to say? Did you speak to him?" He queried.

"Yes, I spoke to him, he wants a divorce as early as possible." she replied.

Shashi was shocked and stupefied and remained silent; he had anticipated the brewing trouble between his daughter and her husband, but did not expect that it could lead to a divorce so soon.

"Do not worry, I will speak to them. We will find a solution," Usha told him and wiped her eyes.

"Thank God they did not have any child after the first one was stillborn! Please speak to them and find a way out," he said and hung up.

He rang the bell and told the office orderly to open the Communication Room which was adjacent to his office room. The array of phones, monitors and other telecommunication gadgets greeted him when he entered the room. He told the orderly to leave and picked up the receiver from the phone, whose line was secure with the latest scrambler. He had spoken to Kiyanelie through it earlier and had learnt from him that he too had similar gadget attached to his phone. This allowed them to speak freely without fear of eavesdropping or interference.

"I have spoken to the NSA. The PM has agreed to all your conditions," he said.

"That is good news!" Kiyanelie said with enthusiasm.

"He wants the surrender to take place at Sitni on 10th August" Shashi told him.

Kiyanelie looked towards Sazo who nodded and raised his thumb.

"Let us have it on 10th August," Kiyanelie said.

"That is all for the time being. I will let you know if there are any changes," Shashi told him.

"I have a small requirement. A man will meet you at your home at 8 pm today. He will deliver a letter, please read it carefully and act on it. Please do treat my man properly," Kiyanelie said and hung up.

Shashi left his office early for home as he was keen to receive the letter in person and also to prevent Kiyanelie's man from conversing with any member of his household.

Exactly at 8 pm he heard the doorbell. His servant ushered the man into the living room.

"Good evening Sir I am Soni and I have been asked to deliver this letter to you," a fairly tall man with dark features said, handing over the letter.

"Good evening. Thank you, please wait in the verandah where Ramu will bring a cup of tea," Shashi said after taking the letter from him.

The man went out reluctantly dragging his feet and looking back. Shashi opened the envelope with the letter opener and read it. His head spun and he felt dizzy as he went through the contents. He could not believe that this letter was written by Kyanelie with whom he had spent a wonderful period of his life. He read it again more deliberately concentrating on each word. It read:

Dear Shashi

Cutting short formalities and trivialities, I request you to read this letter carefully and follow its contents.

Please ensure that the NSG personnel sent with the PM for the meeting on 10th August are NOT from SAG.

The NSG Guard Commander must ensure that during the meeting with the PM there are no armed men from the army on the dais and within a hundred yards from it.

Only one unarmed civilian will remain on the dais with the PM.

All other Guards should withdraw to the helipad and wait for him there.

As we are to be accorded complete amnesty and freedom on completion of the meeting, no one should follow the convoy of vehicles in which me and my men will leave the venue.

The safety and security of the PM is our joint responsibility therefore the instructions mentioned in Serials 1 to 4 should be strictly adhered to by your security Guards. Failure to do so may end the meeting abruptly and could endanger the lives of persons attending it.

Please read the instructions carefully and pass them on to your men, guarding the PM, for strict compliance. My team will be closely watching their adherence.

For the services rendered you will be given $10,000 by us, half in advance and half after the meeting is over. Please text your acceptance to me by sending N through a message to my cell phone.

The moment I see N, from you on my mobile, I will transfer 5,000 dollars to your Cayman Island account No 786555443421666, which we have obtained without much difficulty. I too have a fairly large deposit in our organisation's name in the same bank!

Please note that in case you do not accept these simple instructions, the surrender ceremony will not take place. I visualise that this will cause many problems for you!

Please do not reveal the contents of this letter to your superiors or anyone else. We are constantly watching you and any false move will endanger your and your family's lives. After you have read it please memorise the contents and hand over the envelope with the letter to Soni.

Give my fond regards to Usha.

Yours,

Signed Kiyanelie

Shashi got up, went to the Puja room and stood facing the idol of his favorite deity. He closed his eyes, raised his folded hands reciting the Sanskrit shlokas, and remained standing for the next five minutes with his head bowed. When his heart beat slowed down and the turmoil in his mind had subsided, he came out of the room and called out for his servant to bring Soni to the living room.

"Here, take it and go," he told Soni, who, having checked the contents of the envelope, greeted him with folded hands and left.

Picking up his mobile phone he held it for a long time wrestling with his conscience! He felt lonely and isolated, there was no one he could turn to seek advice, not even from his wife!

He typed N and sent the message on his cellphone. Quickly, logged on to his online Cayman bank account on his laptop and waited. A few minutes later, $5,000 appeared credited in his account!

□

10

The men with Kashif collected the rifles and ammunition from the dead assailants and laid the dead bodies in a row at the center of the opening. Hina lay on the ground and pressed her injured hand tightly with the other hand to reduce the flow of the blood from the wound. She winced when Kashif lifted her, held her shoulders and made her sit up. From his pack he removed the first aid box and took out its contents. Holding her injured hand firmly, he cleaned the wound with cotton swab moistened with Dettol. As she felt the burning sensation she let out a cry while shaking her wounded hand. Kashif noticed that the wound was not deep as the bullet had only grazed her palm and left a fairly deep cut in the flesh.

"You are lucky, the wound is a superficial gash! The bullet has cut the flesh without damaging the bones," Kashif spoke after applying the antiseptic and bandaging the wound.

"Yes, I am indeed lucky that the wound is on the palm of my left hand," she replied, getting up.

"Let us move out from here quickly before enemy reinforcements arrive," Kashif said and signaled his men to follow him.

She followed him placing her wounded hand in a cloth sling, which he had placed across her shoulder. They walked at a fast pace often changing into a trot and within half an hour came out of the dense forest. A truck stood next to the Land Rover, which was at the same place they had left it. The men boarded the truck and followed the Land Rover driven by Keshoho.

"How did you find us here?" Hina asked him.

"Oh, luckily Keshoho had spoken to me when John asked him to take you to the village and told me the route you were taking. Puran gave me your message which made me suspicious. I checked with our intelligence guys and they reported that the area where you were going is active with hostiles. Recently an army patrol was ambushed very close to the spot you were about to be shot! I then decided to come here to save you, which I certainly did!" Kashif said and smiled.

"That is indeed very kind of you! I owe you one! But it beats me! You the ADC to the GOC located in Zakhama, flew to Tuensang at night to lead a patrol to save me?" She looked at him mockingly and queried.

"Yes, you do have very valid issues that should be needling you! Firstly, I was ADC to the GOC for only a week as the permanent incumbent was out of station. Secondly, I returned to my Battalion which is near Tuensang two days back by road," he smiled and retorted.

"Why did you not meet me in Tuensang?" She asked.

"Well I am here, when you really need me!" He smiled and said.

"Thank you!" She said and pressed his hand.

Keshoho stopped the car before reaching Tuensagn. Hina and Kashif got down and traveled to the Battalion in a jeep which was waiting for them on the predesignated spot. Puran drove his jeep to the Battalion Medical Inspection (MI) room.

"Find the RMO immediately," Kashif said to the nursing assistant on entering the room. He asked Hina to make herself comfortable while they waited for Capt Mahesh Gupta, the Regimental Medical Officer (RMO).

The pain in her hand had reduced considerably, though she felt feverish with slight shivering. Mahesh arrived soon and immediately examined her wound. He checked all her vital signs, her blood pressure and heart beats were normal.

"The wound is superficial. No bones are damaged, she can move her fingers and arm without any pain. I will just stitch up the cut in her palm," Mahesh told Kashif, who nodded.

"You do have a slight temperature, possibly due to the wound. With an antibiotics course and some rest you will be fine, Ma'am," Mahesh said with a smile.

"Please call me Hina and thank you," she replied.

Mahesh took her to the treatment room where he cleaned the wound and stitched the cut in her palm. She remained calm and quiet all along and felt relieved when he bandaged the cotton swab placed on her wound. She swallowed the tablet given by the nursing assistant and kept the rest in her pocket. They left the MI room for the Officers Mess which was in one corner of the Battalion premises.

"You will be staying in our guest room until we get fresh orders. Your meals will be served in your room." Kashif told her and asked Puran to drop her luggage in her room.

Tired and weary she quickly removed her shoes and without changing her clothes sank into the bed, stretched her legs and soon fell asleep.

Repeated knocks on the door woke her up from her deep slumber. For a moment she felt lost and could not place herself, feeling baffled and anxious. She heard a familiar voice calling her name and gradually perceived her condition and remembered the location.

"Good evening Hina, hope you slept well" Kashif said when she opened the door. She looked outside and noticed that the sun had set and the brief twilight period was ending.

"Oh my God! It is now nearly seven in the evening! I have slept for over three hours!" she gasped and closed the door.

"Yes you have, and that is good for you. How are you feeling now?" Kashif asked her.

"Better," she said, touching her forehead. The fever had left, and the pain from the wound had reduced considerably.

"Good! Now here is what we are going to do. Freshen up quickly, put on civies, have some snacks with tea, and send for me as soon as you are ready. The sewadar is here to help you," Kashif said, pointing to the soldier standing near the door.

"And do not forget your medicines," he said, closing the door.

It took her over half an hour before she asked the sewadar to inform Kashif that she was ready and waiting for him.

"That is really fast! I hope you have not missed out anything?" Kashif asked sarcastically, upon entering her room.

"I have not missed out on anything! I am all dressed up to go! Someone here needs a lesson on patience!" She smiled and replied.

"Great, now I am a pupil of a very learned guru! You look great in jeans and a jacket!" He said admiring her.

"Thank you! You are really a fast learner! Now where are we going?" She asked.

"I do not know. I have been asked to escort you up to the bridge, which is nearly a mile or so from here. I will hand you over to Keshoho, who will meet us there," Kashif told her.

"OK! Let us go," She said, tying the pistol holster to her ankle.

They met Keshoho as he came out from a mini van parked on the berm close to the RCC bridge. After exchanging greetings he escorted her and made her sit in the front seat of the van. They waved at Kashif and sped away along the highway towards Tuensang. After a mile Keshoho stopped the van and parked it on the side of the road.

"Please change into this Naga dress." he said, handed a bundle to her and got down from the van.

Hina quickly undressed, wore the skirt and the top he had given her and wrapped the shawl around her shoulders. She folded her clothes neatly and kept them on the corner of the seat.

"Where are we going?" She asked him when he returned and started the vehicle.

"To a safe house. Your boss has been trying to contact you ever since I spoke to him after arriving here. I rang Kashif who told me that you were sleeping and would not disturb you. It was only when your boss spoke to the Battalion commander that he knocked at your door," Keshoho told her.

She speculated at the urgent need by her boss to contact her and figured that the mornings encounter could probably be the reason.

"Has my boss mentioned the reason he wanted me to speak to him?" She asked.

"No, he only asked me about your safety," he said.

They drove along the well lighted main street with shops lined up on either side of the road. Keshoho turned the car into a side street and after driving 500 yards he halted in front of a house with brick walls. They got down from the van and she followed him to the house. He opened the building door, they entered the room and encountered an old lady who shut the door behind them. Hina followed him as he walked through the passage between the rooms.

At the end of the passage he stopped and opened a door to his right and entered another room. She smelt the strong stench coming from the carcass of dead animals hung from the roof. She also noticed the smoked meat kept in the shelves lined along the walls. Soon the sour stench filled her nostrils, churning her stomach. Taking out a kerchief she pressed it on her nose and mouth.

She saw Keshoho using his forefinger to push a large cupboard with cement shelves which were filled with bones and skins. The cupboard revolved towards him creating an open space in the wall. She hurried her steps and followed Keshoho through the opening. He restored the cupboard to its original position once they had entered the connecting narrow room filled with wooden carvings scattered on the carpet. When Keshoho bent down and lifted a carving and turned it over, she noticed a concealed steel panel, which when lifted, revealed steps going down.

He allowed her to go down the stairs and followed her after shutting down the opening. They were now in the basement which was fairly spacious and divided into two rooms. There was the bedroom with attached toilet and the office where telephones, transmitters, receivers, television sets and assorted equipment were neatly and appropriately positioned.

She sat in a chair in the office while Keshoho dialed a number and waited for the response from the other end.

"Wahid speaking from Al Kabir," he heard a voice speak.

"Kiran from Shah Sons. Your order is ready. Please give dispatch instructions," Keshoho said.

"You will receive it tomorrow," he heard the reply and replaced the receiver.

"Contact has been made and soon you will get the call from your boss. I am leaving as I am not supposed to listen to your conversation. Once you finish please press this button and I will be here," he said and left after indicating the switch on the table.

The bell rang after a few minutes, she noticed a red light flickering from a phone. She lifted its receiver and held it to her ear.

"Hello Hina, we are using the latest scrambler, you can talk freely. How are you? I have learnt that you suffered a bullet injury?" Shashi, DG, NSG asked her.

"Yes Sir, a slight wound on my left hand palm. The doctor has attended to the injury and I am OK," she replied.

"Big relief! I was really worried especially after the attack on you by the militants," Shashi said.

"Why did they attack me when I was coming to Tuensang?" She queried. She had to wait before he replied after a fairly long pause.

"A case of mistaken identity! They thought that you were a RAW agent," he said.

"How can they be so foolish, Sir! RAW agents do not wear Army uniforms." she replied

"OK Hina, let me tell you the truth. The RAW agent, from Myanmar was onto something vitally important to our National security. He had transmitted to his boss that he would speak to him once he reached Tuensang. He was ambushed and killed close to Tuensang," he said.

"It seems to add up, Sir! Someone in our organisation arranged to leak the information that I am the replacement of the dead RAW agent! I am still alive with God's blessings! Keshoho said you wanted to talk to me about something urgent?" She queried.

"Yes, it is about John from THEM! IB has told us that he is an anti-national agent! It was he who sent you on a wild goose chase and have you killed by the militants! We think that in the recent murder of the RAW agent, John has a hand and he is involved with the insurgents," Shashi said.

"Why don't you take action to throw out THEM from Nagaland and debar them forever?" She asked

"THEM is a large organisation and is doing wonderful work in Sikkim and Arunachal Pradesh. It is not THEM but it is only John who is supporting the Naga insurgents," he replied.

"THEM should be told to remove him," she countered.

"We need proof! John is well known in Tuensang and to remove him without any valid reason will antagonise the Nagas," he said. She paused, waiting for him to continue.

"The attack on you by the militants in the forest, has now confirmed our earlier suspicion about John," he said.

"Just a minute Sir! It implies that you were aware of John's activities and in spite of that I was sent to him to help me find my father?" She spoke in a serious tone.

Shashi kept quiet and sighed.

"Is Matthew with the militants too?" She asked.

"Yes, our intelligence people are onto him," he replied.

"Were the GOC and Maj Kashif following your directions? Were they aware of John's involvement?" She asked.

"No, they are not aware of John's involvement with the militants and they were following directions given by their higher Headquarters and not by us," he said.

"But originally initiated by you," she prompted. She heard Shashi give a loud sigh and possibly drink water.

"Listen Hina, you want us to help you to find your father. The RAW now wants us to find the killers of their agent that would lead them to unravel the likely threat to our country which our agent had hinted before he was killed," he told her in an authoritative tone.

"So you use me as bait, Sir! I am a goat tied to the peg while you all wait on the machan to kill the tiger when he approaches to eat me! Indeed, you are playing a very clever ancient sport," she exclaimed heatedly.

"It is the end result that matters! The attack on you proves that John and Matthew are guilty of conniving with the Naga insurgents! We now have to find from them if they know or have details of the likely operations by the insurgents," he said. She kept silent as she anticipated that he would continue further.

"Instructions are with the GOC to arrest Matthew and carry out a raid on THEM office and capture John. I want you to join the army raid party primarily to ensure that you get information for me about the rebel leader, Kiyaneli's plans from John," he instructed her.

"I am in Nagaland on leave only to find my father! Who is searching for him now?," she called out passionately.

"I am sorry Hina, it is the national interest which is always first and foremost with us. Once we tide over this problem, I give my firm promise that we will together organise a search for your father," he replied, trying to soothe her.

"I have no other option but to follow your instructions Sir!" She retorted exhibiting her helplessness.

"Thank you! Please keep in touch, you can call me up at any hour with your reports, goodbye," he said and hung up.

She pressed the call button on the table and waited for Keshoho to join her.

Feeling sad at the deceit played out by Shashi she was certain that there were better methods of finding evidence against John without her involvement. Her confidence and trust in Shashi diminished considerably; she had heard from others and now noticed it herself, most officers from his organisation placed their self interest foremost even at the cost of others, and cleverly disguised their actions as national interests.

"We are to join a raid party from the army, let us return to the Battalion immediately," she told Keshoho.

"I will drop you at the bridge," Kashif has all the information that is required for the raid," he told her.

"OK! Let us go," she said and followed him climbing up the stairs. They did not meet the old lady while leaving the house.

"Why did you not warn me that John was mixed with the insurgents?" She queried Keshoho.

"I was told not to! I could reveal my identity to you only when your life was in danger! When we stopped to ease ourselves before walking through the forest I heard the escorts say that they were going to kill you once they meet their friends at the forest opening. I revealed myself to you then, as your life was under threat," he replied and started the van. She sighed and looked away with a heavy feeling in her heart.

"John is the insurgent's conduit between China and Pakistan. He also collects money from the local sympathizers to spend on weapons and ammunition which are routed through Bangladesh into insurgents camps at Myanmar," he said.

He stopped the vehicle well short of the bridge and got out. Hina changed her dress got into civvies came out of the van and stood with him looking towards the bridge. Soon they saw a number of vehicle lights approaching and stop on the road. Keshoho nodded and she commenced her walk towards the bridge in long strides. Keshoho turned the van around and left towards Tuensang.

"How are you feeling?" Kashif asked her when she had occupied the front seat of the Jeep.

"Just fine. No complaints," she replied with a sigh.

Kashif looked at her closely but chose to remain silent. He started the vehicle and blinked the jeeps light signalling the vehicle in the front to proceed. Two more trucks filled with armed soldiers followed his Jeep.

"Welcome to the party I hope you enjoy the raid," he said with a smirk.

They crossed downtown which now was hushed and tranquil with insignificant numbers of persons and vehicles on the road. The convoy stopped a mile after crossing the main built up areas. The men got down from the vehicles and grouped into five parties each with five soldiers. They left the road and silently entered the line of trees.

Kashif with Hina joined the last group and soon came out of the line of trees. They knelt down on the ground in front of a large house which had an imposing courtyard.

"That is THEM office and John lives there," Kashif told her.

They positioned themselves on the ground and she soon heard the group commanders confirming on Kashif's phone.

"Jaya Mahakali Ayo Gorkhali," Kashif repeated twice on his phone and got up.

She saw the group in front of her moving towards the gate, open it, and proceed towards the building. As she followed them to reach the gate she observed that the front group had reached the doorstep of the house. Suddenly, the courtyard lit up with bright lights and guns started firing from the building towards the party ahead of her. As a reflex action she dropped quickly and lay on the ground facing the building. The firing increased and chunks of grass shot up as the bullets hit the ground in front of her.

She withdrew further back and removing the pistol from her ankle holster fired at the nearest light destroying it. Soon bullets from all directions were hitting the lights positioned in the yard and on the building.

'I think it is safe enough now, let us move forward," Kashif said when all the lights had been extinguished.

The front party had entered the building and were searching each room. Finding no one on the ground floor they climbed the stairs and entered the rooms on the upper floor. They found one person lying in a pool of blood in each room. As two of the injured occupants were still alive the group leader asked for help to evacuate them.

Men from Kashif's group rushed up the stairs with stretchers and carried the wounded men to the vehicle where a nursing assistant with a first aid box treated them.

Kashif and Hina entered the house, proceeded towards the CEOs office room and searched every nook and corner. The computer system and other electronic devices had been removed and taken away earlier by the soldiers.

"Look what we have here?" Hina spoke on opening a door in a wall.

"A bedroom meant for Maharaja!" Kashif exclaimed entering the room.

They looked around the room searching table drawers, cupboards, boxes and suitcases. A bullet from Kashif's revolver opened the lock of the built in locker which had cash and documents stacked in it.

From the corner of her eyes, Hina saw a portion of the carpet close to the table on the other side of the bed lift up from the floor. Soon a man emerged from the opening with a pistol in his hand, pointing at them.

"Duck Kashif !" She shouted, pulling him down.

The bullets from the assailant missed them as they fell and lay on their stomach on the floor. As the man bent down to shoot at them from under the bed, she took aim and shot him on his forehead. He fell dead and rolled over the stairs into the room below.

"We are quits now!" She told Kashif, as they climbed down the stairs and entered the basement.

"Agreed and thanks," Kashif smiled and replied.

Aligned along the wall were the latest high frequency broadband communication equipment rendering access to satellites for voice, video, and digital facilities. They searched for papers and files but found CDs and pen drives only.

"Let us leave these to our IT personnel to sort them out," Kashif said.

Coming out of the house Kashif rang up the group leaders for the situation report. There were no casualties or injuries to his men. Barring two the rest of the militants were killed.

Hina took the opportunity and dialed her boss who responded promptly.

"Sir, John is not here and we have not gathered any new information," she said.

"No problem. Matthew has given us some information which we need to verify," he said.

"Any further instructions for me Sir?' She asked

"Yes. You will accompany an army patrol to the Myanmar border for gaining further confirmatory information," Shashi said and hung up.

□

11

Pressure was mounting on her from her grandparents. With each passing day Hina found herself as distant in her effort to find her father as she was on the first day when she had met the GOC in his office in Zakhama. Her telephonic conversations with her Dadi were frustrating and painful.

She picked up her mobile after hearing it ring for sometime and noticed that the caller was her Dadi. With consternation and pang she pressed the button.

"Gudiya, where is my son? Did you find him?" Dadi asked, without greeting her.

"No Dadi Ma! Everyone here is doing their best to locate him! I have some leads which I am working on, we will find him soon," she reassured her soothingly.

"Beti, I am having lots of premonitions, all frightening and with bad forebodings! I get very little sleep! I do not want anything to happen to him, please do something urgently!" Dadi cried out, wiping her tears.

"Nothing will happen to him as long as I am alive!" Hina assured her with firmness in her voice.

"I know darling, I know you love him very much and he also loves you more than anyone! You know he refuses to remarry because he cares for you and wants you to always be happy!" Dadi told her.

"I know Dadi Ma, he has sacrificed everything for me!" Hina exclaimed painfully. Dadi could not bear her agony any longer and abruptly hung up, leaving Hina dismayed and restless.

Next day on meeting Kashif she narrated her conversation with her boss Shashi. He was equally astonished that Shashi was taking advantage of her presence in Nagaland to further his interests and put her in a dangerous situation without recalling her from her leave. He told her that an Army boss would never even think of exploiting his junior in this manner; he would certainly lose the respect of the men under him and that of his colleagues. On learning about such an act the boss's superiors would frown on him and remove him from his position at the earliest opportunity.

"From my limited exposure so far my observation regarding the difference between Army Officers and those from the police and civil cadres is that we in the army, breathe live and die with and for our men. Whereas, the police officers do care for their men but from a distance and for most remain detached and self centered. For us in the army the comfort and the safety of our men comes before our own, for them it is not so.

Moreover, our life is totally different from theirs. We have our own ethos and culture, defined and refined through centuries of experience in and out of the battlefield. Whereas, their experience is primarily in dealing with law and order through bureaucratic handling and often by erratic means. Their ethics permit them to flatter and suck up to anyone who is useful to them, especially to the wily politicians, to whom human values, right, wrong and morality ends once these are in conflict with their personal intentions and interests," Kashif spoke at length in an agitated voice.

Hina listened silently wondering why she ended up in this predicament and fervently wished that she soon would come out of the quagmire.

During the course of the day the Battalion received orders from the Brigade HQ to send a reconnaissance patrol near the Myanmar border. Specific terms of reference stated that the patrol's task was to obtain intelligence on the intention of the insurgents, the details of their camps, hideouts, weapons and equipment. Col Atul Dutta the CO briefed Hina and Kashif on the sand model highlighting the fact that though it was not mentioned in the instructions issued by the Brigade, the patrol will have to cross the International Border to obtain the information.

Kashif, Hina and ten soldiers from the Battalion constituted the patrol party and were to proceed to Nokalak in vehicles from there to Shirang in case the road was motorable, if not then they had to cover the distance on foot. The Assam Rifle Battalion post at Shirang was their staging area for crossing the border.

Satellite pictures taken recently indicated increased activity of men and vehicles in Hpakan village in Myanmar. As the insurgents took refuge under forest cover the extent size and other details of the happenings in the rebel camp were not obtainable through the cameras. It was for the patrol to physically reconnoiter to get as much information as possible.

After his briefing, when Atul informed Ravi Sharma the Brigade Comdr that he was ready to send the patrol, he was told by him to wait for further orders. Instructions from the Brigade Comdr soon arrived through a courier informing them that there was no requirement to send the patrol by the Battalion. Only Hina and a sewadar were to leave for Shirang by helicopter at 7 am the next day.

"It appears that crossing the border has been ruled out. All the best to you Hina! Keep safe, looking forward to meeting you soon!" Atul told her after he had read out the instructions.

Hina was perplexed with the major change in the plan. She sought Kashif's advice who was of the opinion that many more changes are likely to occur in the future, and therefore it would be prudent to wait and watch before she confronts her boss.

Next morning the chopper landed on time, and the rotor blades kept whirring as Hina boarded it along with Puran. Kashif was there at the helipad, waving to her as the helicopter took off. She waved back with a sad and forlorn feeling, moving her hand in slow motion.

The life threatening encounters they both had faced together during the past few days had aroused poignant feelings in Hina. Kashif, to her was much more than a brother officer now. He had unfolded into a trusted and a very dear friend with whom she felt very safe and comfortable! As she saw him waving, a soft pleasant emotion percolated for him in her heart! She winced, and shook her head to stop such delusions, and looked out from the chopper towards the forest above which they were flying. The weather was clear with no clouds visible as far as her eyes could scan. In her line of duty, she was aware that she would be flying in helicopters on many such occasions in more arduous terrain and difficult conditions.

On arrival, she was received at the helipad by Subedar Roy Burman the post commander, who guided her to a jeep parked 100 yards away. As she was about to sit in the jeep she heard a voice call out to her. She turned and noticed the helicopter pilot coming towards her carrying a bag. She glanced back and felt relieved to find Puran sitting in the rear seat with her backpack.

"Ma'am, there are few items I have to hand over and also to brief you about them. We need some privacy, therefore please step over and follow me," he said. Hina followed him to a rocky outcrop hidden in the tall undergrowth from where they remained invisible to others.

"These are certain surveillance devices which you are required to carry with you as part of your mission," he said. He removed the items from the bag and laid them on a flat surface of the rock.

Hina was surprised, she had no clue about her mission. No one had mentioned her role to her so far. Nevertheless, having come this far, she listened to the pilot as he described the gadgets to her.

"This is Iridium GO portable satellite hotspot, designed to upload and download data via Iridiums world spanning satellite network. When you place it in the room the activities within its walls are visible to the controller on their receiver screen via the satellite." he pointed to a medium size black cylindrical object. She picked it, felt its weight and put it in the bag.

"Ranger R Radar is a lightweight handheld radar system designed to detect people through walls. With an effective range of up to 50 feet the system can see through walls, floors and ceilings made of reinforced concrete, cement block, wood, brick, glass and other common non metallic construction materials," he said, picking up the object and handing it to her. She took it and placed it in the bag.

"Finally, the Button Mini Camera as the name signifies it can be hidden in a convenient place of the body and it will record clearly all that is visible to it," he said.

"Thank you sir, you have been very helpful. Let us hope that these devices perform," she said, shaking his hand.

He wished her well and proceeded towards the chopper. She returned to the jeep and handed over the bag to Puran.

Roy, who was waiting near her jeep, handed a sealed envelope to her. She noticed it was marked Top Secret with the NSG seal stamped on it. She tore it open and read the contents. The instructions were brief, she was to lead a patrol to perform the tasks she had been briefed earlier. Her team members were from Assam Rifle Battalion and further instructions would be given to her on arrival at Sitni village. She looked at Roy and nodded. He saluted her and sat in his vehicle and proceeded towards the Post, her vehicle followed his jeep. When she alighted from her jeep, a fairly tall middle aged man in uniform saluted her smartly.

"He is my second in command, Naib Subedar Bhuban Das. He is in touch with the locals, especially the drug smugglers who are very scared of him. He has led patrols across the border on a number of occasions," Roy said as they walked towards a hut which appeared to be an office.

"Will he lead our patrol?" She asked him.

"No Madam, I am not feeling well. Havildar Manoj Sharma will go with you," Bhuban butted in.

"Manoj is a very capable soldier and he too has crossed the border several times. Two other equally good and experienced soldiers Kanak Kumar and Kirti Goswami will be in the team," Roy said.

"Only three members in the patrol?" She asked

"Yes Madam, we received orders to send three soldiers from our post. There will also be a fourth person, Hoki Sema the naga guide who is very familiar with the area. Although I have met him only today but he has been highly recommended by Bhuban Das," Roy told her.

"OK, when do we leave?" She asked.

"You all can leave at any time, but it is better to travel in the bus going to Sitni village which is very close to the border. Manoj knows the village head, who has always cooperated with us," Roy told her.

"What time does this bus leave?" She asked him.

"At 1400 hours and normally reaches Sitni in two hours," Manoj interjected.

"Fine, we have another five hours to spare. I would prefer to rest," she said.

"We have prepared a room for you. Puran is already there with your belongings," Roy informed her. She got up and followed Roy who escorted her to her room where she met Puran. Roy saluted her and left.

"What's this for?" She asked Puran when she saw the Naga dress spread over her bed.

"The dress is for you to wear when you leave with the patrol. One more dress is in that bag with other articles that you will require during your journey. All the members of the patrol will be in Naga dress," he said.

"OK Puran, go and rest. I will meet you before I leave," she said.

"I will bring your lunch as soon as it is ready," he said.

"Fine, thank you," she said and shut the door after Puran had left.

She changed into the Naga dress and took out the devices from the bag to examine them. Sitting on the bed, she inserted the battery cells in each of the devices to test them. She could see the images on her mobile phone screen when she connected it to Iridium GO. She pointed the Ranger R Radar towards the wall facing her and noticed on its screen a blurred image of an armed person standing outside her door, which she assumed was the guard for her protection. On switching on the Button Mini Camera she observed that it was capturing the pictures in the room. She removed the battery cells and put the devices into the bag in which her dress and other items were kept.

Puran served her hot lunch consisting of rice, dal, fish and yogurt, she ate them with relish. At Tuensang for the journey, she had packed in her backpack, parathas (flat bread with dried oil), boiled eggs and pickles; she left them in the bag for later consumption.

After taking a rest she left the room, covered her head and walked with the rest of the party to the bus stop which was a mile away from the Post. En route several Nagas crossed them and she was glad that they passed by with casual glances towards her. They boarded the bus and occupied the vacant seats. Manoj came over to her with a dark lean scrubbed faced Naga, who had a permanent smile on his face.

"This is Hoki Sema, the guide who is going to assist us," he said introducing him. She shook Hoki's hand and nodded.

"Come sit next to me," she said, pointing towards the vacant seat. Manoj left and sat three rows behind them.

"So, when did you come here?" She asked Hoki.

"By early morning bus," he replied.

"How long will it take us to reach our destination from Sitni?' She asked.

"Around three hours by foot. There is only a track and in the hilly region there is some climbing," he replied.

She nodded and preferred to look outside through the window and observe the countryside.

"Madam you look very pretty in the Naga dress," He said leaning towards her. She gave him a sharp look and looked sideways towards the passengers.

"Sorry Madam! I really like our women to wear traditional dresses. They look free, buoyant, cheerful and appeal to me very much. Girls in modern dresses look so stiff and formal they give people like me a complex. They pretend to be superior and distant," he kept speaking.

She did not reply but looked out of the window, admiring the green and dense foliage along the road.

Taking the hint Hoki kept quiet and closed his eyes and rested his head on the backrest. After an hour the bus stopped for the engine to cool down and also to allow the passengers to stretch their limbs. The next hours' journey proved further taxing and uncomfortable due to the poor condition of the road.

They reached Sitni village, which was well populated

considering its isolated location and proximity to the international border. The huts too were larger and looked more sturdy and were enclosed by a stone wall built all along the village perimeter.

Manoj lead them to the village Chief's house. He greeted them and escorted them to the Marung. Hina was pleasantly surprised to notice Keshoho sitting alone in a corner. On seeing her he stood up and approached her in quick steps.

"Very happy to see you, Keshoho. Are you joining the patrol?" She asked.

"Yes, Madam. I will be going with you," he said. Hina was delighted, she now had at least one member in the team, whom she knew and could trust.

"Let me introduce you to other members." she said, naming each as Keshoho shook hands with them.

"This is Hoki Sema, who will guide us to the location," she said.

Keshoho's demeanor changed immediately, and she noticed that he looked at Hoki with surprise, anger and disgust!

"Where has he come from?" He asked furiously. Hina was totally taken aback and replied in a low voice.

"From across the border to lead us to HPakan village, our mission objective. Why do you ask this question?" She queried.

"Because he works for John at their THEM office! I have seen him there a number of times!" Keshoho spoke in throttled voice.

"Oh my God! You mean that John is in HPakan with the insurgents and has sent him here to escort us?" She cried out in despair.

"Yes! I am going to find out further details from him," Keshoho said, stepping towards Hoki with closed fists.

"You will stand where you are, and then slowly step back" Hoki said as he quickly went behind Hina, encircled her chest firmly with his left hand, took out a sharp knife with the other hand from his pocket and placed it on her throat. Hina froze and kept still, breathing slowly and silently.

"Stop it! They are my guests! Leave her and go! We will give you protection to reach the border," the Chief told Hoki, who looked at him and shook his head.

"My boss wants her dead or alive! He has given a commitment to someone! Now all of you step back and let us pass through the door," he said.

They all started moving away from the door giving enough room to Hoki to go through it. As he took a longer step forward to get outside in the open, his grip on her shoulders weakened. Hina pushed him hard with her back, he stumbled allowing her to turn, bent down and hit him hard on his groin with her right foot. He cried out loudly, the knife dropped from his hand and he fell down writhing in pain. Keshoho stepped forward and kept kicking him on the stomach until he passed out and lay still breathing in weak bursts. On Chief's directions, a Naga fetched a bucket of water and splashed it on his face. He opened his eyes with a startled look.

Keshoho lifted him, dragged him to an inner room where he dumped him on the chair and tied him up with a rope. Hina, Manoj and the Chief followed and surrounded him.

"If you answer my questions truthfully we will do you no further harm and leave you with the Chief, who will decide your fate," Keshoho told him with a firm voice.

"I do not know anything other than what John told me. He instructed me to get Hina alive or kill her if that was not possible," Hoki murmured through his cut lips. Keshoho looked at him angrily and taking out the silencer from his pocket fixed it to his gun.

"This may revive your memory," he said and shot the first two fingers of his right hand. Hoki screamed and copious tears flowed down from his eyes.

"Please stop it! I will answer all your questions truthfully," he said.

"Who sent you?" Keshoho asked.

"Our leader Kiyanelie and John asked me to go to the Army post in Shirang and meet Nb Sub Bhuban Das for detailed instructions. They had received information from Bhuban Das that RAW spy Hina was preparing to cross the border with some men. John was very specific that she should be captured alive or killed," he said.

"What operation is Kiyanelie planning and when?" Hina asked him.

"They are planning something big! I do not know the details! They are waiting for the advisors from China and Pakistan, who may arrive any day now. Artillery guns and machine guns are supposed to arrive from China through Bangladesh," he replied sobbing like a child.

"How many men are there in the camp?" She asked.

"Nearly two thousand, which includes young boys and girls, who were recently kidnapped from Nagaland villages," he replied.

"We want you to mark the camp on the map and the safest route to it. Remember if you fool us and we do not return, our man who will be here, will kill you," Hina told him.

They untied him and gave him a red marker. He looked at the map for some moment and marked the camp area and the route to it. After he had completed the markings, Keshoho tied him again to the chair.

"I have marked the easiest, the shortest and safest route for you," Hoki said.

"Why is this route safe?" Hina asked him.

"It is the route on which you will not meet any armed men. This safe route will take you to the boys and girls dormitory area where the sentries are not very alert as they indulge with them," he replied.

"Where exactly are they planning to attack?" Hina repeated her question.

"I really do not know. I was never asked to attend any meeting. I have told you all that I have heard and observed," he pleaded.

"I think he is telling us the truth, let us now decide what we should do," Hina said and returned to the Morung hall. The rest followed her leaving Hoki behind. Manoj sent Kanak Kumar to guard him.

"The first action that we should take is to have Nb Sub Bhuban Das placed under arrest. As we are maintaining radio silence and there is no landline from here to Shirang, Manoj please send Kirti Goswami to Shirang with a letter from me to Sub Roy. The second and more important act is to decide whether the information which we have now is sufficient to terminate the patrol and return to our units," Hina stated. Both Keshoho and Manoj remained silent.

"If you have more information about the enemy you lose lesser men in the battle! My suggestion is that you continue with your patrol. I will give you a man who will guide you and assist you." the Chief said.

"Then it is decided that we continue with our mission," Hina said sitting down on the bench.

She took out her letter pad from the bag and wrote the letter to Roy informing him of Bhuban Dass's treachery. She put the letter in an envelope and handed it to Kirti, who left immediately to catch the last bus leaving for Shirang village. The Chief left them to look for the guide.

"I will be back soon" Keshoho told her and entered the inner room.

He asked Kanak to leave as he wanted to speak to Hoki in private. After Kanak left, he approached Hoki, shot him in the chest several times with his silencer gun and returned to join the rest.

"I am ready to leave," he announced. Observing his abrupt to and fro movements, Hina looked at him curiously.

"What happened to Hoki?" She asked.

"You do not have to worry about him anymore," Keshoho said looking away. She sighed and kept quiet.

They left in the early hours of the night after their meals. In the dense forest, the light from the stars entered the rare openings created by random barren trees whose leaves had withered down. For most of the journey darkness engulfed them. But it did not prevent their guide Sukhose to reduce the pace of their march; the Chief had sent his best scout to assist the patrol. The border crossing posed no problem as the guards on both sides were temporarily absent from their posts. The Chief had ensured safe passage through his influence with the guard commanders.

They continued to walk with very brief halts for resting their strained muscles. It was after nearly three hours since they had marched that Sukhose finally halted, raised his hand and asked them to go to the ground. They lay flat on their bellies breathing softly; they heard the faint whine of a motor engine coming from in front of them.

"We are close to the camp, the sound is from the generator," Sukhose said, and started crawling on his elbows. They followed him, taking care not to disturb the stillness of the silent night, by evading the fallen twigs and dry leaves.

"Oh my God! It is a huge well organised camp, very well camouflaged!" Hina gasped.

They had reached the fringe of the vast opening and from their elevated location they had a birds eye view of the camp. All the huts were covered with camouflage nets with leaves and branches entwined on them. No wonder the satellites could not distinguish them from the normal trees. Covered lights lit up the pathways and the area around the huts.

"Let us familiarise ourselves with the layout and identify the huts of our interest. From the markings made by Hoki, the boys and girls dormitory should be near the generator hut located at the rear end of the camp," she said looking into the map held by her.

"Yes. The office building is in the center where the light is still on. Most probably the weapons are stored in these buildings which are likely to be heavily guarded," Keshoho added, pointing out on the map with a twig.

"OK, we go towards the dormitories as Hoki had recommended, but first let us destroy the generator by filling up sand and mud in its fuel tank, and damage the mains cable box from where the electric power is distributed through the cables to the buildings. Before that, I need to note down the grid references and take pictures from my high resolution camera," she said while taking pictures of different locations of the camp.

"Let us go now. Manoj you lead. Kirti you cover him as he moves. The rest of us will follow at some distance," she said and got up.

Keeping in the shadows of trees and with stealth they approached the dormitory huts which were close to one another. On Hina's signal Keshoho and Kirti approached the sentries guarding the hut entrances and decimated them after a minor scuffle. From one of the huts they heard a man's voice, giggles and light shrieks from the girls.

Upon entering this hut Keshoho looked towards the direction of the noise, and in the hazy light he noticed a man half naked with his knees resting on the bed, and jumping over a naked woman lying under him.

Taking quick steps, he reached the bed and shot the man on his temple with his silencer gun. The man slumped and fell on the girls breasts with blood spurting out from the wound. The girl let out a loud shriek when she saw Keshoho lurking over her and the blood running down her bare chest. She pushed the body to one side and attempted to get up. Keshoho forced her down with one hand and with the other pressed her mouth with his palm. When the girl stopped shrieking he removed his hand.

"Please keep absolute silence. You do not have to be afraid. We know you have been kidnapped. We are here to gain information so that we can come and rescue you later," he whispered to the girls around him who had gathered on hearing the shrieks. The girls stood still in shock and kept quiet.

The door opened and Hina entered the hut, the girls let out a gasp in surprise on seeing her. She raised her hand to stop them from any further sound.

"We do not have much time and we have to finish our mission quickly. I want one of you to take me to the locations of the offices, the radio and wireless set up, the computer rooms, and their conference hall. Is there a volunteer?" She asked and waited for a few seconds before leaving the room. No one replied to her.

"Carry all the dead men into the forest and bury them immediately, you will face problems if you do not," Keshoho told the girls and left the hut.

"Madam, I will take you to all the places that you have mentioned. I work in the office as an assistant," Hina heard a fairly tall pretty girl as she came out through the door behind her.

"Thank you! Please lead me, we are very short of time," Hina requested.

She asked Keshoho to gather the rest of the team at the designated RV point, where she would join up after finishing her work.

The girl led Hina to the office complex, and to their advantage, suddenly the entire camp came under darkness. Manoj and Kirti had finally rendered the generator useless beyond any repair. Keeping under the shadows from the moonlight, the girl forged ahead. Hina increased her pace and soon caught up with her. She stopped when the girl halted in front of a fairly large building.

Hina asked her to crawl on her knees to get closer to the building. She followed her after retrieving the Ranger R Radar and its battery cells from her bag. Putting the battery cells in the Radar, she switched it on and faced it towards the hut. On its screen, she could clearly see inside the room with its furniture and other assorted equipment. She noticed a sudden movement on a chair. Looking closely, she noticed a person sitting on it. She kept observing the radar screen for a few more seconds and then switched it off.

"There is a person sitting on a chair in the room, do you know who it could be?" Hina asked her.

"Most probably he is the one who has come here recently," she said. Hina got up to go towards the room but was stopped by the girl.

"Let me meet him. The man likes me and I will seduce him! You follow and take care of him!" She whispered in her ear. Hina nodded and the girl approached the building, knocked at the door and entered on hearing a voice asking her to come in.

"Who is it?" Asked, the man sitting in the chair.

The girl walked up to him and sat down in his lap. Surprised and startled, he soon relaxed as he felt her soft body.

"Oh! It is you! Feeling lonely?" He asked her.

"Yes and scared too!" She replied, rubbing his bare chest with her palm after she had undone the shirt buttons.

"Do not worry, we will soon have the lights," he said, pulling her down by the shoulder and bent to kiss her.

Suddenly the girl felt the body go limp and fall over her. She immediately got up, pushing the body to drop on the floor.

She turned around and found Hina standing next to her. By pressing her thumbs on his temple pressure points Hina had killed the adversary.

"Madam that was real quick and painless! Burn in hell dear friend!" The girl said, looking down at him.

Hina pointed a beam from her pencil flashlight on the man's face. She was startled and dumbfounded to observe the least expected person staring at her with wide open eyes!

"John! You filthy swine! Good riddance of dirty rubbish!" She hissed furiously and kicked the body violently many times.

She searched the table drawers, cupboard shelves and wooden boxes for papers and documents for useful information. She read some of them using the mini torch and photographed them with the Button Mini camera. With her work completed in this room, she followed the girl who lead her to other huts.

On observing the Ranger R Radar screen she noticed that the huts containing the radio and wireless equipment and the computers were occupied by men who were asleep on their cots. She decided to leave these alone.

They entered the large Conference room which was empty. With the girl's help, she installed the Iridium GO on the inner wall facing the entrance door. This would show the pictures of all persons entering the hut during the meetings.

On completion of the tasks, they retraced their steps towards the dormitory hut.

"Thank you very much! You were great! Do not worry, in a day or two you all will be rescued," Hina told the girl extending her hand.

"I want to come with you," she said, ignoring Hina's hand.

Before Hina could answer, the girl strode towards the dead sentry's body, picked up his rifle and pointed it upwards.

"Don't do that! You will alert the entire camp!" Hina pleaded.

"Please take me with you! I can help you to return safely! I am very good with all the weapons! I can kill with rifle, knives, bows and arrows, spears and also with my hands! I know the jungle well because I have spent my entire life here!" The girl reasoned it out to her and lowered the rifle.

Time was running out for her. In the short experience they had together, the girl had impressed her.

"Fine! Keep the rifle, collect the magazines and follow me," she said.

The girl jumped with joy, collected the magazines from the bag of the dead sentry and caught up with Hina.

They found the rest of the party lying in firing position on their belly to provide covering fire in case required by her.

"Sorry, I forgot to ask your name," she asked the girl, as other men joined her.

"I am Sano," she said.

"I am Hina," she said and introduced the other members of the patrol to her.

Sukhose took over the lead as they filed in to return to their village.

"We have to reach Sitni dawn. The entire insurgency force will be on our tail when they discover the damage we have done to them," Hina told them as they strode rapidly towards their destination.

The fast pace of the march was wearing her down, after an hour she asked them to halt and rest. They had yet to cover more than half the distance and she felt her leg muscles stiffen. She bent down lifted the skirt a bit and commenced massaging her calf.

"Let me do it!" Sano said and sat on her knees in front of Hina.

She lifted her leg and allowed Sano to massage. Soon she felt her muscles relax, the delicate and deft massage of her calf had relieved the stiffness.

"You are better than an expert! Do you massage often?" She asked her.

"I massage my mother's legs when she is tired," Sano replied.

"Where is your mother now?" She asked.

"In my Yunasai village," Sano replied.

"You will soon be with your mother and I would love to meet her," she said, and got up after Sano had massaged both her legs.

"Thank you Sano! It is time to resume our march," she said and waved at Sukhose to proceed.

The early morning sun rays were playing up on the tree leaves above them, lighting up the forest now and then, thereby increasing the visibility thus making their task easier.

They were in the vicinity of the border when they heard the noise of choppers flying overhead. They stopped in their tracks and looked for suitable hiding places.

"The forest ends about 100 yards from here. The choppers will wait for us to come out into the open or may be, they drop armed men to flush us out," Sukhose told them.

"Let us wait and watch," Hina instructed.

They hid behind the trees listening to the choppers hovering not very far off! Soon they heard the choppers overhead flying away.

"It appears that the choppers have downloaded men, who will now enter the forest," Hina said.

No sooner had she finished speaking, they heard the sound of mortar shells fall at some distance behind them. The blast from the mortars touched them mildly, the shrapnel from shells hitting the tree trunks and branches.

"We have to move up closer to them to avoid the mortar shells," she said.

They ran forward 25 yards or so keeping themselves behind the trees, when Kushoho noticed the line of men advancing with their rifles pointing toward them. Using hand signals, he pointed them to Hina.

"Start firing only when you hear the bullet fired by me," she told everyone.

Soon she saw a man advancing towards her, she signaled everyone to halt and opened fire when the man was about 15 yards from her. The rest of the group fired their weapons immediately killing their targets. Taken by surprise the insurgents ran back in panic, leaving behind their dead and injured.

"Follow them and keep firing until we reach the last line of trees! It is easier for us to take them on when we are hidden and they are in the open," she cried out.

The men heard her loud and clear and kept firing at their assailants. Halting at the edge of the forest they took position behind the trees.

From here they observed that the fleeing insurgents had taken refuge behind the rocky boulders at some distance from them. On Hina's instructions they ceased firing and so did the enemy.

"They are waiting for reinforcement, which I am afraid will arrive soon," Hina said.

"What are we going to do?" Keshoho asked her. She looked towards him and smiled.

"We have two options. Keep them at bay by holding on to our position until dark or by fighting our way through and make a beeline for the border which is not far off," she said.

"It is better to fight and reach the border before their reinforcements arrive," Manoj suggested. Hina looked at others who gave their thumbs up.

"OK then, let's do it! As Kashif cries out, 'Joya Gorkhali'!" She said and got up.

She signaled Manoj, who started firing his rifle towards the boulders. Sukhose and Keshoho also stood up firing in that direction while sprinting towards the border.

Hina waved at Sano and Kanak to follow them. The enemy had now started firing at Manoj and were using light machine gun whose bullets were flying close to them.

Keshoho and Sukhose had reached a safe distance on the other side of the enemy location. Keshoho shouted out to Sukhose to open fire on the enemy, which he did and distracted the enemy. The enemy were under fire from opposite directions and stopped firing momentarily, which enabled Sano and Kanak to rush towards the border.

Observing that enemy fire had momentarily ceased, Hina asked Manoj to get up and follow her. Both kept firing with their weapons at the machine gun location as they ran past it.

The enemy machine gun shooters had changed their position by now and had a better view of the fleeing opponents. As Hina ran across them, a bullet hit her backpack. She stumbled and fell close to the boulders. Her rifle flew away from her hands and landed at a distance. Manoj who was ahead of her kept running towards the border and reached his colleagues.

Hina crawled and hid behind the highest boulder and did not raise herself for fear of being hit. She attempted to retrieve her weapon, but a bullet hit her rifle and damaged it. She lay helpless and noticed a rebel crawling towards her. As he closed in, he raised his rifle and aimed at her. She closed her eyes, rolled over sideways and waited for the inevitable to happen.

She heard the sound of bullets hitting a body close to her, and a man scream. Surprised, she opened her eyes and saw her assailant lying a few feet away flat on his face with blood flowing from his body. She looked sideways and found Sano smiling at her.

"What are you doing here?" She asked her.

"You wanted to meet my mother!" Sano smiled and replied.

"Oh yes! I certainly do!" She shouted with a loud laugh.

The intensity of bullets on the enemy had reduced however, the bullets flying over them kept increasing.

"Looks like we are short of ammunition. The end is near now. Let us give a last try!" She told Sano and started crawling towards her colleagues.

"You go ahead, I have some rounds left in my magazine, I am going for the guy with the machine gun," Sano said and started crawling towards the boulders. Hina's shouts to her to return and follow her fell on deaf ears, she continued undeterred.

Sano halted when she was barely ten yards from the machine gun which was hidden behind a boulder. She raised her head to look behind to see whether Hina had safely reached the border. She was shocked to see a projectile rushing towards her! In panic she rolled over and closed her eyes. The loud bang from the blast and the heat wave shook her up. She raised her head, looked in front and found the machine gun destroyed and scattered, with the men lying dead in the crater. Shrieking with delight she got up and ran towards Hina, who hugged her fiercely and kissed her cheeks.

"I too deserve the hugs!" She heard Kashif, with a broad smile on his face. Hina ran as fast as her legs could carry and embraced him.

"Yes you certainly do!" She said, hugging him furiously!

□

12

It was on the fifth day after the raid on her village that Monalisa left Yunsai and reached Sitni around midday. She found a large number of elders assembled in Morung engaged in a serious discussion. Without causing any disturbance she sat on the unoccupied bench in the last row. She looked ahead and recognised Longayo, her village chief who was listening to the conversation with great attention that Akai the Sitni village chief was having with the village elders. She was aware that Longayo had come to Sitni to confer with Akai and the elders of the village.

"Let us forget our differences with them and approach the State Government to ask the Indian Government to help us. I am sure the Indian Government will come forward. About six months back they had carried out a surgical strike to teach a lesson to the rebels. If we ask them I am confident that they will rescue our boys and girls," Akai told the gathering.

"Our emissary met the State Government Minister in Kohima and returned yesterday. The Indian Government has as yet not taken decision on any action on the rebels. They said that they will let us know soon, which to me is very vague," Longayo informed them.

She heard murmurs in the gathering depreciating the governments for not displaying urgency. A wizened old man, a regular speaker, cleared his throat and spoke out loudly. Everyone always heard him and paid attention to him on account of his vast historical and traditional knowledge which he dispensed without any inhibitions or fear.

"This is not the first instance that we have had to suffer from a foreign Government's duplicity, their mindless and heedless conduct. My great grandfather drafted in Naga Labour Corps was deployed in France in WWI and my father was a soldier in Assam Rifles in WWII; both served the British and fought with honor and bravery like so many others of our brethren did. The British in return annexed some of our territory by massacring our men and women in various battles. Ultimately we found refuge in the hills where they were scared to come," the old man said.

Majority of those assembled had heard him earlier and his repeated enunciation remained entrenched in their minds. On his insistent exhortations they read the books, old magazines and papers he purchased during his trips to Kohima and Dimapur. He distributed these to them free of cost. They read about the courageous fight put up by the Nagas against the Japanese in the ferocious Kohima battle and the generous compensation the British handed over to them that brought them a little closer to the white man. They read about the early Baptist and other missionaries in their midst who helped them though in contrast they were badly treated by the Indian National Army (INA) which left a bitter aftertaste and this persisted for decades.

"After the Indian independence from the British we too wanted an independent country for the Nagas, but they refused, and gave us truncated freedom. We were elated when Gandhi told our leaders that 'The Nagas have every right to be independent. I want you to feel that India is yours. I feel that the Naga Hills are mine just as much as they are yours. Why wait for August 15 to declare independence? I will come to Kohima and ask the Army to shoot me before they shoot one Naga!" Brave words, but he never turned up!

"When everything we tried failed, we took to violence to get our freedom which they have coined as insurgency! Much later they did give us a token gift, when Nagaland became a separate state. Some of our people have remained dissatisfied and continue with the struggle through violence, though most have reconciled even though the elected State Government is not what we expected. Their tall promises for our development and betterment are all hollow and false. We need total independence, where we can live and die as our forefathers did!" The old man said, concluding his diatribe.

Both Longayo and Akai shook their heads conveying their disagreement with him but remained silent to avoid further discussion on the issue.

"The Konyaks have kidnapped our boys and girls and they are going to use them to fight the Indians. My sources have informed me that they are mounting a special operation very soon. They are waiting for their Chinese and Pakistani friends to deliver some more arms and equipment. They may get these in a day or two, then in their skirmishes against the Indian forces our boys will be used as fodder by them," Longayo said.

"What do you suggest?" Another old man asked.

"We go and rescue them!" Longayo replied.

"I have heard that they have over two thousand fully armed men in their camp, in addition they have light artillery, mortars and rocket launchers. Can you face this well equipped force?" The elder asked.

Longoya remained silent as he was aware that about 800 armed men was the maximum they could muster. He was also not confident whether they could launch a surprise attack although they had detailed information of the locations and the defenses in the insurgents camp.

"What should be done then?" He asked.

There was a murmur in the crowd as many attempted to speak out simultaneously.

"We do nothing now and wait for the Indian Army to help us or the rebels to finish whatever they are planning," the elder who spoke earlier said out loud. A pin drop silence followed after his utterance.

"Is there anyone who does not agree or has a better suggestion?" He asked.

No one spoke, each waiting for an intervention by someone else. The elder got up and left the room and the rest followed him.

Only Akai, Longayo and Monalisa were the ones who remained behind.

"I have come to say goodbye," Monalisa said, looking towards Akai and Longayo.

"Where are you going?" Akai asked him.

"To the rebel camp at HPakang," she said and smiled wryly. The two chiefs looked at one another perplexed.

"Why?" Akai queried.

"To bring back my daughter Sano!" She said with a heavy heart.

"You are out of your mind! Are you going alone?" Akai, stunned and astonished, asked her.

"Yes! The Lord is my guardian!" She said in a simple tone.

"I have known you for all these years and watched you closely. You are a true Naga fighter in all respects! Go and God be with you," Longayo told her, giving his blessings.

"Take as many rifles and pistols as you want! You do not have to pay for these but return them after you have used them," Akai told her and blessed her.

She knew a person in the village who would help her to get across the border. Early next morning she met him and he gave her his cycle for the journey.

"Please show this paper, in case you meet any guard whether Indian or from Myanmar. Pay them each 500 rupees and they will let you cross the border without asking any questions," he said handing the paper to her.

"Use this cycle for the journey. For most of the distance the track is fairly good though it gets rough in the hilly portion. You will reach HPakang before midday, if you halt for small breaks only. On reaching the village please handover the cycle to Thila, she is a widow and known to everyone in the village. For your return journey you can collect the cycle from her," he said.

"I will work it out! Thank you," she said, handing a thousand rupees to him.

"Thank you and wish you a pleasant journey," he said, shaking her hand.

She tied the rifles on the crossbar of the cycle and fastened the backpack to her body. She kept riding for the next hour without any halt. There were no Indian guards in sight on the border, however, on traversing the no man's land she had met a Myanmar soldier who stopped her. He permitted her to proceed without questioning after she had shown him the paper and handed over the money.

She reached HPakang village well before midday and found a person who took her to Thila, who greeted her warmly. Removing the rifle from the crossbar she handed the cycle to Thila.

"I have come here to find some work. Can you help me?" She asked.

Thila looked at her closely, measuring up her suitability for the jobs she knew.

"There are a few jobs in the nearby camp," she said.

"What kind of Job?" Monalisa asked.

"Can you make wine?" Thila queried.

"Yes, I do it all the time in my village," she replied.

"Come with me, I am going to the camp," Thila told her.

Monalisa looked at her with astonishment and silently thanked God.

They reached the camp on foot as it was only a mile away. Monalisa was overtaken with surprise and filled with frustration on observing the hectic activities in various parts of the camp. Men and women were busy firing rifles and pistols at the range. Some practiced unarmed combat, while a few were busy with demolition and booby traps.

They halted in front of a hut from which she could smell the odor of the fermented rice fumes permeating the surroundings.

"Remove the wine after it is fully fermented in these huge cemented pits and pour it in the steel cans placed outside the hut. Get busy! I will inform the supervisor about you," Thila told her and left.

Monalisa picked up a bucket and as she was about to enter the hut she stopped and stood still. Right in front of her, she recognised Luikham drop a sack of rice which he was carrying on his head.

She ran towards him and hugged him and looked at him with moist eyes.

"Luikham, where is Sano?" She asked him.

"She has left the camp! She is not here anymore," Luikham replied, flustered and taken aback on meeting her.

□

13

Her decision to share the room with Sano was turning out to be very congenial. She found in her lovable and practical person, who kept to herself, spoke respectfully when addressed and remained very cordial. She had won Hina over with the courage and skill she had displayed during the encounter. She had saved Hina from serious injury and probably saved her life.

In Hina, Sano too had discovered a unique personality, she appealed to her sensitive and emotional feelings.

After the arduous journey Sano lay on the bed relaxing peacefully with her eyes closed. She heard a noise, got up from the bed, picked up the pistol from the side table, cocked it, moved towards the door and opened it with a jerk.

"Oh ho! Relax Sano! It is me Kashif!" He said, stepping into the room. Sano lowered the pistol and allowed him to enter the room.

"Where is Hina?" He asked, looking around.

"She is in the washroom," she replied.

"Ask her to meet me in the Mess anteroom. You too come along with her," he said and left.

After finishing her chores Hina waited for Sano to freshen up. She loaned her jeans and top which though a size bigger did not show up much. Weary from yesterday's adventure and the early morning lengthy journey from the border, they took their time to get ready.

On entering the Mess anteroom they found Kashif sitting alone reading a newspaper.

"Ah nice to see young ladies all fresh and dressed up," he got up and said. He called the waiter and ordered fresh lime and soda for both.

"Your drink before you have breakfast! Now let us get down to business. You must be curious to hear about my amazing appearance to rescue you," he said with a smile.

"Certainly we want to hear! It is really amazing that you turn up every time at the last moment to save my life! I would much prefer that you show up earlier!" Hina remarked and smiled.

"OK, listen to the story. On learning about Bhuban Dass treachery the Brigade HQ ordered Assam Rifles Battalion to abandon the recce patrol and recall you and the men with you. By the time the instructions were received by the Battalion, your patrol had possibly crossed the border. I was then asked to rush to the border and join the backup team organised by the Assam Rifle Battalion. I traveled the entire night partially in the jeep and for most of the distance on foot to reach you! Now please thank the Almighty first and next me that I reached at the nick of time!" Kashif told them with a smirk.

"Thank you God for keeping me alive!" Hina said with folded hands.

"You see Hina, I am your archangel! Your guardian!' Kashif said pleasantly.

She leaned forward, held his hand and patted it.

"You have your breakfast and do whatever you want to. But meet me at 4 pm here. I will take you to our Mandir," he told them and got up.

"Thank you! You have read my mind! It will give me an opportunity to face and thank my God," she replied.

After finishing their breakfast they returned to their room and as fatigue had not left them, both hit their beds after changing their clothes. It was when her cell phone alarm vibrated at 3.45 pm that she realised that she had missed lunch. She dressed up quickly and left the room leaving Sano deep in slumber.

She found Kashif waiting for her at the Mess entrance from where they proceeded to the Mandir.

She entered the hall and stood in front of the idol silently thanking the deity. She prayed to Him for His blessings, to show her the path, to give her the strength to find and rescue her father. Taking out a few hundred rupees notes she placed it in the offering plate. She came out of the hall and met Kashif at the entrance. Looking around she noticed devotees sitting on the lawn and on benches.

"Can we sit on the bench under the shade of that tree?" She asked, pointing to a bench at some distance. Kashif nodded and followed her.

"Thank you for shepherding me to pay my obeisance to Bhagwan. It has been quite some time since I prayed in the Mandir," she said and sat next to him on the bench.

"You did good! We soldiers believe in God, whatever and wherever He may be. Our faith drives us! Irrespective of our different beliefs, we lay down our lives together with honor and dignity, believing in one another and devoted to our cause!" Kashif spoke feelingly.

"Wow! I really liked what you said and it is so true!" She responded.

"But tell me why are we sitting here? There is not much to look around," He asked her.

"Are you in a hurry? Can't you relax for sometime?" She inquired testily.

"No, I am not in a hurry! I am relaxed! Go ahead, shoot whatever is on your mind," he said with a smile.

She sighed out loud and looked directly into his eyes.

"Kashif are you married?" She asked. Totally taken aback, he sat up and looked at her, unbelievingly!

"No! Not yet!" he replied curtly.

"Do you have a girlfriend waiting for you?" She asked.

"No, never had time to even think about a girlfriend," he said, shaking his head.

She looked at him mischievously and smiled.

"Are you gay?" She asked. He looked at her and laughed out loud.

"No! I am not gay! I have no time to go out with girls! One day when I am ready, I will tell my mom to get me a girl," he said and continued to laugh.

"And when will that be?" She asked promptly.

"I think she already has someone in her mind," he replied.

"Oh! Now I see! You are Momma's boy! How cute!" She said laughing loudly and clapping her hands.

"Please stop it! Let us change the topic!" He said feigning annoyance.

"OK! But it beats me! You have so much faith in your mother! She is very lucky!" She responded, enjoying the banter.

He kept quiet, got up and proceeded in the direction of her room and she followed him.

"I would love to meet your mother someday," she said walking with him.

"Sure you will! But let us find your father first!" Kashif said.

She looked at him and realised the earnestness in his voice. Her heart went out to him.

"Come what may, I am going to find him even if I have to do it alone with no outside help!" She said with a determined look.

They reached her room and Sano opened the door.

"How are you Sano? Hope you are not getting bored?" Kashif asked her.

"No," she said looking towards Hina," but I want to go to my village. I want to meet my mother. I know she is in pain and grief and wants me!"

"We both will go in a day or two! The Battalion is making arrangements," Hina pacified her. Kashif nodded his head and patted Sano on her back.

"Cheer up Sano, you will soon be with your mother. I will leave now and if there is anything that you need you can send for me. Bye," he said and left the room.

"He is a nice guy," Sano remarked.

"Yes. Momma's boy!" Hina said and laughed.

"I think you like him! You both will make a nice couple!" Sano teased her.

"No way! His mother has selected a girl for him and I have to find my father first before I can think of anything else," Hina said with a frown on her forehead.

"What happened to your father?" Sano asked her.

"He was working in Tuensang and was kidnapped. He has been missing for the past fortnight," she told her.

"What? Is his name Brijesh?" Sano asked her, showing her excitement.

"Yes he is Brijesh Singh Rathore. How do you know his name?" Hina asked her.

"I met him during his regular visits to our village. My mother worked with him," Sano replied.

"What is her name?' Hina queried.

'Monalisa," Sano replied.

"Is your mother an engineer?" Hina asked her.

"No. She helped him in all the administrative requirements. She is fluent in English and good at office work," Sano replied.

"I am very glad. Now together we will find him," Hina said, embracing her.

She moved towards the toilet to change her clothes when she heard her cell phone ring. She picked it up and heard the caller; it was Keshoho informing her that a jeep would pick her up in another 15 minutes and bring her to the road bridge from where he would take her in his van to the safe house. She thought for a moment and rang up Kashif who informed her that he was aware of the instructions given to her by Keshoho.

Hina assumed that she was summoned by her boss probably for a debriefing and sat down to recollect the events and encounters she had faced throughout last night across the border.

She arrived at the bridge and walked the distance to meet Keshoho waiting in his van. He got down from the vehicle and she changed into her Naga dress sitting inside the van. The evening traffic was building up as they crossed downtown avoiding the rickshaws and the unruly pedestrians. She found the house empty, though the stench from the skins of animals persisted heavily. She got down into the basement by the staircase and sat in the chair positioned in front of the array of the electronic communication equipment.

"Give me a minute," Keshosho said and moved across to press the audio buttons to adjust the volume. Speaking out the code words he connected her to her boss, Shashi, DG, NSG.

"Hello Hina, how are you?" He asked her.

"Alive so far Sir, no thanks to you!" She replied in a sarcastic tone.

"It seems you have not lost your sense of humour! Anyway, we have been briefed by Keshoho and wish to congratulate you on your successful mission. The pictures you took are very useful especially to our RAW friends. One of whom is with you in the room presently," he remarked.

She looked at Keshoho who pointed his finger behind her. She swirled around and noticed a man who was seated in a chair hidden behind a temporary screen. He got up and advanced towards her.

"I am Ramamurthy Iyengar, you can call me Ram," he said and thrust his hand forward to shake her hand.

Middle aged with specks of white hair, thick eyeglasses, slightly drooping shoulders and a small paunch, Ram to her looked more of an upper grade clerk in a government office rather than a spy agent of a premier intelligence agency.

"Glad to meet you," she said, stood up and grasped his hand.

"Please finish your discussions with Shashi, after that we two have enough time to talk," Ram said.

"Sir, Ram and I have met, what are further instructions for me?" She asked her boss over the phone.

"Nothing from me, but do whatever Ram and the Army tells you to do." Shashi replied.

"Sir, please allow me to find my father! My aged grandparents' anxiety is growing everyday," she pleaded.

"I did mention it earlier that as soon as this mission is over, we will jointly launch the search for your father. Listen to what Ram has to say and consider these as instructions coming from me! Good bye," Shashi said and disconnected the communication network.

Hina slumped in her chair feeling frustrated and helpless. She got up when Keshoho placed a chair next to her for Ram.

"My sympathies are with you. I can imagine your plight. Our suggestion is that as you are so deeply involved in this ongoing affair, it is better for all of us that you continue until its completion," Ram said.

"OK Sir, I am ready. Please go ahead with your briefing," Hina said.

Ram looked at Keshoho and requested him to leave the room.

"It is not that we do not trust Keshoho, he has been with us for a very long time and is an extremely reliable agent! There are certain things which need to be known by only those who are closely concerned with them," Ram explained.

Hina silently accepted the frustrating fact that she was getting embroiled deeper in affairs which were well beyond her apprehension and her liking.

"Placing the Iridium GO portable satellite hotspot in rebel camp conference room has given us a window through which we can gain a lot. In another five minutes the rebel leader Kiyanelie is having a meeting with his Chinese and Pakistani friends. Thanks to you we will be able to view it on our computer screen," he said.

"How is that possible?" She asked, excited.

"Many miles away high above in the sky our satellite and drone are homed on to our Iridium GO in Kiyanelie's Conference room. They are patched onto our system, and will stream live the activities taking place in the conference room to us here, on our computer screen,' he said and switched on the computer.

After a short gap images appeared on the monitor screen. She noticed the room with vacant chairs and tables covered with white sheets. She was amazed at the clarity and sharpness of the pictures. She looked at Ram when he opened his bag to remove a notebook and place it on his lap. He then took out a ball point pen from his pocket and held it between his fingers.

Soon on the screen, she saw a man carrying glasses of water on a tray, opened the door, placed the glasses on the table in front of each chair and left. After some time a number of men entered the room of whom two were distinctly recognizable as they were wearing dark suits without ties.

"The man in front is Chinese and behind him with the bushy beard is Pakistani," Ram told her.

The last to enter were a tall handsome person and a middle aged man with a receding hairline. Both were dressed in their traditional dress and they occupied the chairs at the head of the table.

"The tall man in front is Kiyanelie, the rebel leader and with him is the ugly one, Sazo his advisor and henchman," Ram said.

"There is no audio," Hina observed.

"Yes, this device only has video projection facility," Ram said and pulled his chair closer to the computer screen.

For the next half hour she continued watching the screen aimlessly, however from the corner of her eyes she observed that Ram was busy. He kept looking at the screen and simultaneously kept writing in the notebook without removing his eyes from the computer. She leaned forward and noticed number of dots and dashes filled on the page,

Her curiosity aroused, she concentrated on the screen and after scanning it several times she concentrated on the man in the dark suit with his back towards them. He was holding out his right hand behind his back prominently for them to notice and moved the middle and forefinger regularly. Amused, she smiled at the ludicrousness of the situation where a person is playing with his fingers probably to a musical tune in a serious conference.

After a while the finger tapping stopped, Ram got up, carried his chair away from her, placed it at a distance and sitting on it immersed himself in writing in the notebook. She watched him as he continued for a while without raising his head.

"We are having a serious problem, we have to act quickly," Ram looked at her and said, "give me a few minutes, I have to send this message to my HQ.

He tore the written page from the notebook, scanned it and sent it through email as an attachment.

"Now we wait here until we receive further orders," he said.

"I am totally confused, please enlighten me," Hina smiled and requested.

"I know you are a bright girl and you would have noticed a man in a dark suit tapping his fingers during the meeting. He is our agent in Pakistan who is attending the meeting on behalf of the Pakistan Government. We had communicated to him the location of Iridium GO in the room before the meeting. He positioned himself such that he could send Morse code signals with his fingers as the meeting progressed," Ram explained.

"How did you decipher the movement of the fingers into letters?" She asked.

"Very simple! Imagine using the Morse code. Tap by the middle finger are dashes and by the forefinger dots. In this paper I noted down the number of dots and dashes while he was tapping and deciphered them to get the text," Ram smiled and replied.

"Can I see the paper?" She asked.

"I am sorry we are required to destroy the paper once its contents have been sent to our HQ," he said. He tore up the paper into bits, put them in the ashtray and burnt them with his cigarette lighter.

Hina left him and returned to sit in her chair in front of the monitor. She observed the participants sipping tea and probably engaged in small talk.

"The meeting is over, they are leaving the room!" She said.

Ram pressed the call bell button on the table and soon Keshoho came down the stairs with a tray containing water glasses and tea mugs. Both drank the water quickly but held onto their mugs. Keshoho left them carrying the empty glasses.

Ram felt his cell phone vibrate, he switched it on, opened the email inbox and read the message. The instructions were short and crisp and required no reply.

"These are the instructions for you," he said and read it out.

"Go to Nagpur with Ganguli as a poet and stay with Kartar to meet Gulshan in Nishat Garden." She was completely baffled and looked at Ram.

"Give me a few minutes to decipher the message," he smiled and said.

From his pocket he retrieved a different note book. Opening its pages he obtained the hidden meanings of the words mentioned in the message.

"Go to HPakang village as a Naga. Stay with Rangmutil to meet Afzal Beg in rebel camp." Ram read it out.

"Do I go alone?" She asked.

"No, not at all! You are the mission leader and you have to select your core team of a section strength. You are free to choose persons known to you. Your team will stay in Sitni village and move only on your orders," he said.

"Nothing is known about my father! What are you going to do to find him?" She asked.

"I will let you know as soon as I receive any instructions," Ram replied reassuring her.

"Are you coming with me?" She asked.

"No. I will move separately and will remain in Sitni village. We will give you a satellite mobile phone with which you can safely communicate without any danger of interceptions by the enemy," he said.

"When do I leave?" She asked.

"As soon as you can assemble your team," he replied. She nodded and shook her shoulders helplessly.

"Any more questions?" He asked. Getting no reply from her he pressed the call bell button. She got up to leave and waited for him to climb the steps.

"You go ahead, I will leave later," he said.

Keshoho waited for her to climb the stairs and followed her. He dropped her off at the bridge from there she rode to the camp on the jeep which was waiting for her.

She had called up Kashif on her mobile phone for an urgent meeting and found him sitting in her room with Sano.

"Before you speak, let me inform you that our Battalion has received a message to offer you all assistance," Kashif told her. She heaved a sigh of relief and sat down on her bed.

"Come here Kashif! Sit near me I have a lot to tell you," she said.

Kashif got up from the chair and sat on her bed facing her. She narrated the details of the evening's happening which he heard in silence and did not interrupt her, all the while admiring her ability to withstand the ongoing tension and pressure she was subjected with.

'I took a month's leave and came here to find my father, and look what I have got into! Oh my God this is insane!" Hina cried out.

"Calm down Hina! Your father is alive and we will find him! Now choose your team quickly for your mission," Kashif told her.

"My core team main members are you, Keshoho, Manoj, Kana, Kirti and Sukhose, the rest you can select," she told Kashif.

"When do we move?" He asked her.

"By first light tomorrow morning," she replied.

"I will send an immediate message to the Assam Rifles Battalion to send their men to Sitni to meet us at midday tomorrow. Puran and two others will travel with us. Keshoho too will be told to be at Sitni at the earliest," he said, with a smile. She got up to go towards the toilet.

"Let us go to the Mess and grab some food so that we can sleep early." Kashif told her.

"Give me three minutes. Oh Sano! I cannot go anywhere without you! You are coming!" Hina said, looking towards her. Sano smiled and nodded her head.

Next morning as they drove towards Sitni she leaned out from the jonga to feel the pleasant and soothing morning breeze. She was enjoying the ride with Kashif at the wheels. So far no one had spoken including Sano, who sat in the rear seat with the driver. The bumpy ride shook them continuously leaving little room for them to have any conversation. After an hour's drive they stopped for breakfast. Puran who was travelling in the truck handed them a packet containing puri and bhaji (spicy mashed potato) which they relished. A cup of hot tea followed and they were ready to commence their journey.

"Will you come with me to meet Afzal Beg?" She asked Kashif.

"No! You will have to meet him alone," he replied.

"Can I take Sano with me?" She asked.

"Yes. There should be no problem," he replied. She looked back and found Sano leaning forward listening to their conversation.

"I want to go with you to the camp. I could help in rescuing some of my people," she said.

"We will do it together!" Hina told her.

As they approached the village Kashif drove the jeep along the winding narrow track and passed through the gate unhindered. He stopped the vehicle in front of the Marung. The truck following him was not far behind and the men got down from it as soon as it stopped. Akai the Chief with few Nagas came out to receive them. He shook hands with Kashif and asked his men to guide the soldiers to their hut.

"We meet again," the Chief smiled as he spoke to Hina.

"Yes I am happy to meet you! I would have liked to stay longer, I am afraid I have to leave within a few hours," she informed him.

The Chief nodded and led them into the room where plates filled with rice and fish were kept for them for their lunch. Kashif was touched by the gesture and thanked him.

"There are bags filled with rice and spices and six crates of rum in the truck. Please accept these as humble token of our friendship," he told the Chief, who held his hand and thanked him.

They ate their lunch with the Chief and his followers joining them.

"Sukhose will guide you on a shorter direct route which will cut down the time by half," the Chief told Hina.

After lunch the Chief with his followers left them with Sukhose remaining behind. They waited in the Marung for Keshoho who arrived shortly. He refused to eat, when offered, as he had taken his lunch in a restaurant. He requested Hina to move to another room where he could speak to her in privacy.

"You are to travel dressed as a Naga girl and meet Rangmutil. I know where he lives in HPakang village. I will give the details of his location to Sukhose. Rangmutil will provide you with all the facilities for your stay there. No one else will go with you. For the rest of the world you are dumb and deaf, so do not attempt to speak to anyone in the village," he told her.

"Can I take Sano with me?" she asked.

'You are to go with Sukhose and no other person," Keshoho emphasised.

"When do I leave?" She inquired.

"Right now! It is better if you reach before dark," he replied.

Hina came out of the Morung, lifted her backpack from the jeep and tied it to her body. She took Sano aside and spoke to her at length. Sano was furious for being left out and insisted on accompanying her. With an affectionate hug to Kashif, Hina left with Sukhose without bidding goodbye to Sano, who was nowhere in sight.

The afternoon sun beat on them as they covered the rocky and steep track. For the past few days she had walked much more than her routine 5 Km that she ran every morning and this was telling on her. She kept up the pace and refused to rest when Sukhose halted after covering half the distance. They reached HPakang village before sunset and Sukhose greeted the men and women as he passed them on the way to Rangmutil's residence.

"You have made it in a good time! I was waiting for you," he said and ushered them into the house. She removed her backpack and put it in a corner, sat on the bench and drank the water offered by Rangmutil, who left them to prepare tea.

The knock on the door was soft and lasted for a few seconds. Hina waited for sometime and as the knocks increased and became louder she got up to open it.

"Oh my God! What are you doing here?" She cried out when Sano entered the room.

"I could not leave you alone so I am here!" Sano replied, grinning with her mouth wide open. Hina held her tightly, laughed and planted many kisses on her cheeks!

□

14

The request for the meeting with Suresh Mathur NSA, was made by Bhupinder Singh, director RAW, and was held in the underground conference room. In attendance were the IB director Unnikrishnan and the DG NSG, Shashi Damodar Kulkarni.

"Before I question the reasons for your request for this meeting, I want an update on Brijesh. The PM is extremely worried!" Suresh said and looked at Bhupinder.

"I and Unnikrishnan have a combined task force to get information on Brijesh. We have learnt that Brijesh is not in Nagaland or anywhere else in India. The rebel leader in Myanmar may be aware of his location but Brijesh is not with them. Our team is on the job and soon we will find him out," Bhupinder replied.

"Please give it the utmost urgent priority," Suresh told him.

"Yes, we are fully engaged and will leave no stone unturned," Bhupinder pledged.

"Only a few days remain for Kiyanali and his men to surrender to the PM. I hope the preparations for his safety and security are in full swing at the ceremony location?" Suresh enquired.

"My boys are engaged in identifying and flushing out those who could pose a threat to him. So far the police have rounded up 15 suspects in Nagaland," Unnikrishnan stated. Suresh looked at Shashi, who was busy reading from a paper held in his hand.

"My team is ready to guard the PM when he arrives at Sitni. The Army has to provide overall protection for which I have contacted the Director General Military Operations (DGMO) and he has confirmed that orders to all concerned have been issued," Shashi told him.

"Good! Bhupinder you have requested this meeting, let us know the reason?" Suresh asked him.

"Yes, I wanted to share the information on the latest development. I received some details from my agent stationed at Tuensang," Bhupinder replied.

"OK! Let us have them," Suresh said.

"A meeting between the Chinese and Pakistani agents with Kiyanelie took place last night. Our agent attending that meeting has sent a coded message for our actions. As I do not have a suitable agent located in Nagaland to provide immediate assistance, I have requested Shashi to loan me the person who had planted our electronic devices in the camp a few days back," Bhupinder said.

"Shashi, can you do that?" Suresh asked.

"On receiving Bhupinders request, I have told my contact to take further instructions from the RAW agent located at Tuensang," Shashi replied.

"We need to send someone to meet our Pakistani agent in the rebel camp. He at grave personal risk to himself, has sent the coded message during the meeting with the participants sitting close to him. The message intimates that possibly Kiyaneli is involved with Brijesh's kidnapping. To confirm it the agent is investigating further. He wants to meet someone from us as he possibly will get the answer by then, and pass on the details personally," Bhupinder replied.

Suresh's eyes lit up upon hearing the information, it gave him some hope.

"I am of the opinion that there is no requirement to send anyone to the rebel camp. I cannot visualise Kiyanelie holding Brijesh as captive when he has offered unconditional surrender! If the agent is caught it will jeopardize the surrender meeting," Shashi intervened quickly and emphatically.

"Shashi, you do have a point. Unni how do you feel about it?" Suresh asked.

"I will go with Bhupinder, someone should go and meet our Pakistani agent in the rebel camp," Unnikrishnan replied.

"I also feel the same. The agent should be extremely cautious. Under no circumstances should he get caught. Bhupinder, please send someone immediately, and let us know the moment you have the information," Suresh said.

Shashi was tempted to argue further but realised that the NSA had made up his mind and he remained silent.

"Anticipating that we all would want our agent to cross the border and meet our agent in the rebel camp, I have already passed the instructions to my contact at Sitni to direct Shashi's person to proceed to the rebel camp. The meeting will take place tonight," Bhupinder said.

Shashi, completely astounded, looked towards Suresh with dismay and frustration.

"Considering the urgency of the situation you took the correct decision, Bhupinder! I hope that this person who is from Shashi's setup and who has helped us so far, will have a successful meeting and get us useful information. So that's it! Please ensure that the surrender ceremony kicks off peacefully and that all our safety and security concerns are dealt with seriously and effectively," Suresh said and got up. Rest of them followed him to the elevator and dispersed after leaving him.

Throughout the journey to his office Shashi's thoughts were in turmoil. Kiyanelie would never take it kindly if he discovered about the meeting Hina is scheduled to have with the Pakistani agent in his camp. The letter from Kiyanelie had specifically warned him not to use the SAG. He has failed to comply with it and was certain it would lead to very dire consequences. What if they catch Hina? What if she told them that she was from SAG and that he had sent her? Kiyanelie was no longer the genial and friendly person, with whom he had spent good time as a student and later while commanding the Battalion. He was an animal, a monster, who would go to any extent to take revenge.

For him, his and the family's safety mattered foremost above all other considerations! He would go to any extent to ensure that they remain protected!

Upon reaching his office he headed to the Communications Room, entered it, picked up the receiver and dialed the number.

"Shashi, how are you?" Kiyanelie asked him from the other end.

□

15

For the past week Monalisa had spent the night sleeping in the camp in the hut next to the one where they worked fermenting wine from rice. The demand for the liquor had increased manifolds due to the arrival of a large contingent of Nagas from adjoining villages. To maintain her good relationship with the camp authorities, Thila had consented to their suggestion that she and her setup should work round the clock.

She used Luikham and the boys to clean and deposit the rice into the open earthen vessels which were half buried in the ground. From there the fermented wine was poured into earthen pitchers and carried by the girls and disposed of in huge copper containers which were similarly buried in the Marung. Further distribution from these containers to the men was made under the arrangements of the supervisor.

"Can I go to the village now?" Monalisa asked Thila as they came out from the brewery.

"What is the hurry? We will go tomorrow morning," Thila suggested.

"I have to meet Rangmutil, he is a friend of my late husband," Monalisa replied.

"You go, we have sufficient wine for the next day. But come back tomorrow morning," Thila instructed her. Monalisa thanked her, collected her belongings and left the camp.

It was Akai the Sitni village chief who had suggested her to meet Rangmutil, who could help her to meet Sano. The evening sun was touching the horizon when she stood in front of his door and knocked. After a number of knocks the door opened and she walked into the room feeling tired. As she raised her head she stood still and stared with total surprise when she saw the face a few inches away from her.

"Mother!" Sano shrieked.

She plunged and hugged Monalisa tightly, almost cracking her ribs. Hearing her shriek, others came out from their rooms and joined them.

"My darling, my sweetheart!" Monalisa pressed her to her bosom planting kisses on her cheeks and forehead.

They kept holding each other with tears of joy in their eyes until Rangmutil stepped forward and rested his hand on Monalisa's shoulder and gently separated them.

"Mother, this is Hina, Brijesh's daughter!" Sano told her pointing towards Hina who was watching the poignant moment with gratification.

Monalisa, completely astonished, stepped towards Hina, held her by the shoulders and hugged her.

"You are my daughter from now on!" She said, planting a kiss on her cheek.

"You said it mother! Ever Since we met, Hina has been more than a sister to me! I love her, will always be her sister and best friend," Sano said, with tears rolling down her eyes and holding Hina tightly.

Monalisa smiled and put her arms around them holding them firmly. For her reunion with her daughter was God sent, she silently thanked Jesus Christ and prayed for their safety and long life.

"We can now return to Yunsai tomorrow morning," Monalisa said.

"We will have to wait until Hina completes her mission," Sano said.

"What mission?" Monalisa asked.

Hina asked her to sit down on the bench and briefly narrated the details of her mission.

"I have been instructed by my boss to meet Afzal Beg tomorrow in the evening at seven at Black Rock Spring. He will give me certain vital information which I have to pass on to my boss," Hina concluded.

"Why did you not refuse him, it is too risky," Monalisa said!

"I did refuse but they did not accept. I have no other option but to follow their orders!" Hina said.

"I know where Black Rock Spring is. We go there in the morning to wash ourselves. I will come with you," Monalisa told her.

"No, please not that again! My mission may get compromised! I will go alone dressed as a Naga girl and no one will recognise me especially in the dark. Rangmutil will guide me to the place," Hina replied. She insisted that both of them should return to Yunsai where she would meet them on completion of her task.

"As you wish my dear! Tomorrow morning I will go to the camp to say goodbye to Thila, who has been very helpful and kind to me," Monalisa said.

"Thila? I had been to her house today and did not find her. Is she the same person who makes wine for the camp?" Sano asked her mother.

"Yes, she is the same one, how do you know her?" Monalisa asked her.

"I used to carry her wine in pitchers to the large containers from the brewery. I am coming with you tomorrow. I have to meet my friends there," Sano replied.

Rangmutil who had left the house while the family reunion was in session returned with eggs and chicken meat. He handed these to Monalisa and asked her to prepare them for their breakfast and lunch.

"We are attending the Thingyan (Myanmar New Year) festival with the Buddhists and will have dinner with them," Rangmutil said.

They dispersed to their respective rooms and after washing up the ladies got busy with the cooking.

In the evening they watched the Thingyan festivities from a distance, not participating in it as it was different from their tribal customs. There was music and dancing and merrymaking but all divergent and dissimilar. They were not quite impressed with the use of garden hoses, huge syringes made of bamboo brass or plastic water pistols, water balloons and fire hoses, all of them used for squirting water on girls by the boys. They left the place after tasting the insipid vegetarian food served to them.

Monalisa got up early in the morning to prepare the day's meal. She was soon joined by Sano and Hina, while Rangmutil gathered firewood and carried water from the spring to store in the pitchers. After their breakfast, Monalisa and Sano left for the camp and on reaching it found Thila giving instructions to the girls, who held a small earthen pitchers filled with wine, on their shoulders. Thila looked at them curiously and smiled.

"So Sano is your daughter?" She asked Monalisa, who smiled and nodded.

"Where have you been all these days Sano? I knew you worked in the office after leaving us, but have not seen you for sometime," Thila stated.

"I was sick, now I am alright," Sano replied and looked around.

She saw a few girls standing at a distance chattering loudly, she excused herself and joined them. This was her first meeting with them after the night raid. They spoke in whispers exchanging notes.

"I will not be here for long. I may leave in a few days," Monalisa told Thila.

"That is fine with me! You can leave whenever you want," Thila replied.

She accompanied Thila to the brewery hut leaving Sano, who picked up a pitcher and carried it along with other girls. Throughout the day both mother and daughter worked separately and left together at dusk to join Hina at Rangmutil's hut.

"You look so sweet and good in our dress. I will knit and weave a better one as soon as I return to Yunsai," Monalisa told Hina, on observing her dressed in Naga clothes.

"Thank you very much! I would love to wear it! I am leaving now to meet Afzal Beg. Wish me a safe journey," Hina said. Rangmutil followed her as she moved towards the door.

"I am coming with you. I know the route. I went to Black Rock

Spring this afternoon with my friends," Sano said loudly. Hina turned and faced her with resignation and despair.

"My instructions are to go with Rangmutil." I cannot allow you to come with me," she pleaded, coming close to her.

"Take her with you! I will inform Ram. From what I have heard about her, she can protect you better than me!" Rangmutil said.

Hina looked at Monalisa who nodded her approval. She sighed loudly, smiled and held Sano's hand.

"Come my sister go bring your weapon," she said.

Before stepping out of the house Hina touched the elders feet in the Indian tradition; taken aback, they quickly recovered and offered her their blessings. The girls left the house for the rebel camp in the darkness of the night unaware of what lay ahead for them.

"We have to walk about half an hour or so," Sano said as they stepped out from the village gate.

"This afternoon my friends spoke to me privately near the Spring. One of them heard Kiyanelie the leader saying that very soon they will have a free and independent Nagaland. He said it in a meeting with some of his men close to him," Sano told Hina.

"Oh that is common! As a leader he has to keep the morale of his men high" Hina replied.

"My friend also met a doctor who told her that she should get all the girls who are sick treated immediately as the camp will wind up soon. He looked worried and kept on muttering and complaining about the leader's advisor," Sano continued.

"What did the leader's advisor say that upset the doctor?" Hina asked her.

"He told him that they all have to obey not only the leader but him too! Whenever he asks them to perform certain tasks, they should do it," Sano replied.

"The advisor considers himself close to the leader and therefore he is taking liberties. Keep your eyes and ears open, hear and watch closely especially the leader and his close associates," Hina told her.

"Yes I have already sounded a very close friend who takes the wine to the leaders office," Sano said.

Realising that they were approaching the camp, they slowed down and traversed in silence. Sano, raised her arm, stopped behind a thick tree and held Hina's hand.

"The Spring is another twenty yards ahead. I am going to hide behind this tree from where I can see you. I have checked this location during the day for clear visibility; the entire area around the spring is under my surveillance and I also picked up the night vision glasses from the camp. I can observe your movements clearly with it," Sano whispered while putting on the glasses.

"Perfect! I could not have asked for a better back up!" Hina smiled and whispered.

She waited for Sano to settle down before she moved ahead. The moonlight had lit up the water from the spring which flowed into a fairly large pond. She moved towards it and looked at her watch, another four more minutes remained.

"I never could imagine that I will meet a Naga girl!" She heard a man's voice from behind her.

She turned quickly and noticed a tall man in dark pants and shirt wearing glasses. He had a fairly long black beard which hid most of his face.

"Afzal Beg," he said and held out his hand.

"Zamthingla, how do you do! You can call me Zam," Hina said, shaking his hand. On the spur of the moment she had decided on her Naga name.

"I have come here..," before Afzal could complete the sentence, she saw him wince in pain and heard the sound of rifle fire from behind her.

Instinctively she dropped and hit the ground and a bullet whizzed past over her head, Afzal kept standing totally baffled and frozen with fear.

Hina looked up and saw two men advancing and firing at them. She shouted out to Afzal to drop to the ground which he did after a bullet pierced his heart. The men kept firing from their rifles as they advanced, their bullets grazing the earth close to her.

She lay still and slowly slid her arm towards her leg to retrieve the pistol tied to her ankle. The movement attracted an assailant who fired and the bullet furrowed through the flesh near her elbow. The pistol flew out from her hand and rested out of her reach. She winced in pain and felt that her life was about to end when she heard the sound of sudden spurt of bullets very close to her.

"Get up!" she heard a faint voice and opened her eyes.

"Oh my God I am alive?" She mumbled and sat up.

"Yes you are very much alive, and so am I though bleeding profusely, she heard the faint voice of Afzal who was sitting with his back resting against a rock very close to her.

She bent down, and removing a kerchief from her skirt pocket pressed it to the bullet wound to stop the bleeding.

"It's no use Zam! My time has come! I can feel the angels coming to take me!" Afzal spoke softly with a smile on his lips.

"No you are going to be fine! We will take care! Please tell me everything now, please hurry before they take us away!" Hina pleaded.

"Zam tell your people that Shinto is a traitor, he is with Kiyanelie...," Afzal said and stopped without completing the sentence. Hina shook him vigorously and urged him to speak, but to no avail. She kept shouting, asking him to speak up.

"He is dead! Leave him and get up. Let us go!" She heard a man say in a menacing voice.

Looking around she saw herself surrounded by a number of armed men. Getting up, she raised her hand above her head, waved it several times and let out a whistle from her mouth. The Nagas surrounding her thought that she had gone crazy.

It was a signal from her for Sano to withdraw and run away immediately. Sano who was closely watching her, took the cue and left, running with soft steps she headed towards the village.

"Stop acting crazy and move," Loheleniyu, the leader of the group, told her.

"Where am I going? What will you do with his body?' She asked, pointing to Afzal Beg's corpse.

"Just keep moving and shut up! We will bury the traitor here and inform his boss about his treachery," he shouted at her.

She followed the group leader trying to figure out who had betrayed them. In her present condition her mind hit a roadblock.

Though Afzal's last words kept ringing in her ears. She felt sorry for him, she had read that the lifespan of a spy was short and that of a double agent shorter, the odds forever remained unfavorably loaded against him!

"Who is Shinto?" She asked suddenly.

"Just shut up and walk!" Loheleniyu scolded her.

She looked down and kept walking showing her resentment by kicking the pebbles lying on the ground. Soon they stopped in front of a hut which looked familiar to her. It was the same office room in which she had sent John to his maker, few nights back.

"Get in!" Loheleniyu ordered, stepping behind her.

Holding her bleeding arm upwards, she entered the well lit up room and found the furniture exactly in the same place. Sitting at the head of the table were two middle aged persons, one fairly handsome looking the other an ugly duckling.

"Welcome Capt Hina Rathore from SAG! You are not only brave but you look very pretty too, especially in our dress!" The handsome man called out.

"So Shinto is the one who told you about my meeting with Afzal Beg?" Hina sneered at him.

"Shinto? Who is Shinto? Do you know him?" The handsome man said looking towards the ugly one who smiled and shook his head.

"Never mind! At least have the decency to tell me your names now that you know mine!" Hina said, showing her revulsion.

"I am Kiyanelie and he is Sazo," the handsome man said with a smile.

"Kiyanelie! The leader of around 1500 Nagas who is hiding in Myanmar like a rat! Who loots his own people, kidnaps their children, rapes their girls and women and ambushes and kills Indian Army men. You even tried to get me killed!" Hina said loudly, walked up and sat in a chair close to his.

Kiyanelie stood up stared furiously at her in anger but soon calmed down, patted the table with his hands and burst out laughing loudly. He beckoned a Naga and whispered in his ears. The Naga ran, fetched a first aid box from the cupboard and bandaged Hina's bleeding elbow.

"Ah! You will feel much better now! I do not want to get into a dialogue with you and waste my time. The whole world knows about me and I do not intend to change the popular perspective! I have a mission which I intend to finish. It will succeed soon, with your help Capt Hina! Please help me towards my goal by cooperating with me!" Kiyanelie said, standing close to her and looking into her eyes.

"Me? Never even if you torture me or kill me!" She said looking up to him.

Kiyanelie looked back at her with a wicked smile on his face.

"Even if we torture or kill your father?" He said and filled the room with his guffaws.

Perplexed and frustrated, Hina abruptly got up from the chair and hit him on his chin with a clenched fist. Kiyanelie staggered and fell on the table. Pushing himself with his hands he stood and looked at Hina. Loheleniyu moved forward to hold Hina and pin her down. Loheleniyu raised his hand, waved to him to leave her alone.

"My father? Where is my father? What have you done to him?" She shouted loudly. He came close to her menacingly but stopped a few feet in front of her. Wiped the blood trickle from his lips and spoke to her with a wry smile on his face.

"Calm down Capt Hina! Your father is safe and sound! We are keeping him alive and in one piece so that you can meet him, which you will very shortly!" he told her and looked at Sazo who smiled and nodded!

□

16

"He is a tough nut! Any other person would have given up by now! Look at him, he cannot stand, the soles of his feet have swollen up, he can neither sit because his bums too are like balloons! You must have broken a dozen bamboo canes by now!" Yang Lin the Chinese interrogator spoke pointing at Brijesh lying semi naked on the floor.

"I wish I was allowed to use iron rods and wooden staff to break his bones!" Khoula the Naga interrogator, a vicious tormentor, replied.

They stood and watched from the door as Brijesh crawled towards the pitcher, picked up the glass and dipped it in. With difficulty he filled the glass and drank the water in sips lying down on his sides. Khoula entered the room and snatched the glass from him, spilling the water on his chest. Yang joined him, both of them placed their hands under his armpit, lifted him and forced him to stand on his feet. Brijesh cried out with pain as his feet touched the ground. He wrestled with them in vain as they tied his hands with rope and fastened it to the overhead pegs fixed in the wall. He stood still so that the pain from his swollen feet would reduce.

"Brijesh you leave us with no choice! We have to raise the bar now! For the past one week we have used the cane and it has done its job. You can neither squat nor stand! From now on we intend to go further unless you tell us exactly the reasons for your presence in Tuensang with your team. We know that the mapping of underground water locations is a cover for something your Government is planning against us. You tell us what it is and we will let you go," Yang said, lifting Brijeshs head by pushing his chin up with his hand.

"I have nothing more to say other than what I have repeatedly told you for the past so many days. Our Government has not sent me here for any secret project that would harm your country," Brijesh spoke in a soft, tired voice.

Yang looked at Khoula, who went out and returned with a diode capacitor voltage multiplier which provided an alternating high voltage discharge and was powered by a battery. Yang held the two metal probes connected via wires to the electroshock device on Brijesh's upper shoulder, and above the upper hip.

"Oh my God! Help me!" Brijesh shouted as his body felt the intense shock and pain from the current when Khoula pressed the switch.

He repeated it several times until the shrieks stopped and he fainted. They loosened the ropes and he fell and lay on the ground unconscious.

"Enough for now. We will question him when he regains his consciousness." Yang said and closed the door as they left the room. They entered the adjoining room where two other persons sat chatting and drinking tea.

"My time spent here in Bhamo is total waste! The prisoner has given us no information! So far our torture has not worked though he has suffered sufficiently from it. Any sane person would have broken down by now. I think he has said everything he knows and there is nothing more we can get out from him." Yang told them. The men looked at him with concern and the person wearing dark glasses shook his head.

"Come sit down Yang. I will show you something which I have received today from Beijing," Chou Min said.

As Yang occupied his chair Chou his compatriot got up and shut the doors and closed the window curtains making the room dark. He switched on the projector and images appeared on the screen.

'These are pictures and videos which our agents have collected from their sources in India. You will notice that Brijesh is prominently present in the entire video. He is in a conference on satellites and drones, which are used for espionage and reconnaissance and is in discussions with a team of scientists on the development of effective weapons to destroy them. He works for the Indian Defense and Research Development Organisation and is actively involved in Operation Indradhanush!" Chou said and looked at Yang.

"What is Operation Indradhanush?' Yang asked

"That is exactly what we want to know from Brijesh. It has to do with missile interception from close to our border. It is so secretive that so far in spite of our best efforts we have remained clueless about it. Brijesh can provide us a breakthrough if he is made to spill out its details," Chou said.

"We have failed so far. We will try harder from now on," Yang assured him.

They dispersed and decided to meet again after Yang and Khoula finished interrogating Brijesh once he regained his consciousness. Within the next hour they paid several visits to his room and found him lying on the floor unconscious.

It was late in the afternoon, the loud sound above the roof woke up Brijesh. He opened his eyes and recognised the whirring noise of the helicopter blades which pierced his ear drums as it hovered overhead. He covered his ears with his palms and closed his eyes fearing that the chopper would fall any moment. Gradually, the noise subsided and he heaved a sigh of relief.

Persistent pain in his body from the electric shock had considerably numbed his sinews. He could barely move parts of his body. Any further torture would probably make him indifferent to pain. He had reached a state where he had become indifferent to pain and his mind had accepted it as fait accompli! He sighed, closed his eyes and prayed silently for a quick end to his life!

After a while the door opened with a loud noise that disturbed Brijesh's reverie. He looked up and observed Yang and Khoula standing next to him blocking the closed door.

"Wake up Brijesh!" Yang shouted.

He opened his eyes with a start. Yang quickly tied his hands and feet with ropes, Khoula fixed the two metal probes on his body and stood ready holding the switch. He looked towards the glass panel fixed on the wall, smiled and pressed the button.

The visitors who had arrived in the chopper were witnessing the torture from the adjoining room through the one way look through glass panel that was part of the wall. The loud full throate, heart rendering, pain filled roars from the adjoining room hurt the ears of the visitors, as they noticed the person toss and turn on the ground.

Hina who stood alongside was dazed and bewildered as she watched the horror filled spectacle. When Brijesh, struggling in pain, turned and faced her, she let out a gasp and wailed out loud! She had recognised her father's disheveled bearded face filled with agony and pain!

"Stop it! For heaven's sake stop it! I cannot stand it anymore!" She cried out loudly.

"Tell them to stop it immediately!" Sazo ordered the man standing next to him.

A man tapped the glass pane with his knuckles and waved his hand. Khoula heard the knock disconnected the metal probes from the body and kept them on the table.

"Oh my God! You bastards! What have you done to my father?" She cried and advanced towards Sazo with clenched fists. Two men grabbed and held her by her arms.

"You are no worse than animals! God will never forgive you and I swear that I will never forget you!" She continued shouting.

"Enough of this rubbish talk! Your father has the option to go free if he tells us everything he knows about Operation Indradhanush! So far he has refused and therefore he is suffering," Sazo told her in a stern voice.

"For his country he is prepared to offer any sacrifice. You go ahead and do whatever you want to do, but you will hear nothing from him!" Hina said.

"Even if he watches his loving daughter being raped and dishonored by these men? I doubt it!" He said and knocked on the door.

Yang and Khoula stepped out into the corridor, closing the door behind them.

"He has fainted again and this time it is serious. We have to send the doctor to revive him, which may take up to an hour or so," Yang said.

"Why an hour?" Sazo asked him.

"The doctor is in his clinic, which is around thirty miles from here," Yang replied.

"Ring him up. In the meantime lock her up in the store room and guard her closely. Deploy guards all around the perimeter, under no circumstances she should be allowed to escape. I want her father to see her when she is raped and tortured by our men," Sazo said and turned to head for his room.

The men held Hina, she struggled but soon her mind cleared and she controlled herself.

"Can I have a word with you privately?" She called out to Sazo.

"Yes, why not?" He said and signaled his men to step away.

She followed him to the living room and asked his men to leave them alone.

"OK, tell me what you want to know?" She asked.

"The Chinese have been mentioning Op Indhradhanush. What is it?" Sazo asked her.

"I know everything about Operation Indradhanush! Right from day one my father has confided in me," she said as they settled down on the sofa.

"Fine, let me hear it?" Sazo asked her.

"Only if you let my father go!" She replied.

"I will do that only after the information that you have given to me has been verified, found accurate and the Chinese are satisfied," he said.

"I will remain here with you as your hostage until all your formalities are completed. Please let my father go," she pleaded.

Sazo looked at her and felt the sincerity and seriousness in her voice as she begged him.

"I am sorry, I am not in a position to decide on the fate of your father. However, if you can give sufficient information, I can persuade my colleagues to release him," he said.

"Is that a firm undertaking by you? Will they listen to you?" She asked.

"Yes it is my promise and my colleagues invariably accept my requests," he told her.

Hina got up and paced the room in small steps, her head bowed in deep thought. Sazo kept looking at her, anxiously waiting for her to speak.

"OK! I need a notebook in which I can write down every detail that I know. I need to be alone for the next half an hour, so that my concentration is not disturbed," she said ultimately.

Sazo got up, opened the door and called out loudly giving instructions in the native language. Soon a man brought a notebook and a ballpoint pen which he handed to Sazo who gave them to Hina.

"You have half an hour to write. Lock the door from inside and open it only when you hear my voice," Sazo instructed her, looking at his wristwatch. He left the room, shutting it firmly and met Khoula waiting in the corridor.

"Put two men to guard the door and position the rest all around the house. In case she tries to escape, tell your men to shoot to kill her," Sazo said. Khoula nodded and left to organise the security, while Sazo entered a bedroom and lay down to rest.

Hina waited for five minutes before opening her room door and came out into the corridor where she was shocked to find two guards pointing their rifles at her.

"Please relax! I am not going anywhere! I am thirsty and I need a glass of water. Can someone please get it for me?" She requested.

The guards looked at one another and finally one of them left towards the kitchen which was at the end of the corridor.

"Can you come inside the room and help me push the sofa so that I can find my pen which has rolled under it?" She requested the guard standing in front of her.

"No. I am not supposed to move from here," he said.

"It will take you only two minutes. I am not going anywhere. I will be in the room with you, so please come in. I have only fifteen minutes remaining to write and submit the note to Sazo. He will be very angry with me if I do not give it to him in time," she pleaded earnestly.

The guard hesitated before stepping towards the door. She opened it completely, stepped aside, allowed him to enter and then closed it. They moved towards the large and heavy sofa. She bent down looking under it, covered it with her body and threw the ball point which rolled over near the wall.

"It is there next to the wall and I cannot reach it. Please push the sofa a little away from the wall," she said, getting up after looking under the sofa.

The guard placed his rifle on the carpet and with both hands started to push the sofa away from the wall. Hina bent down, in a flash grabbed the rifle from the carpet and hit the guard with its butt at the back of his head. The guard slumped noiselessly and lay on the carpet with blood flowing from his wound. She tore open the notebook and made a roll from its paper and shoved it into his mouth. Tearing the table cloth into long strips, she tied two strips over his mouth. She heard a knock on the door, stood up and picked up the weapon and moved cautiously to open it.

"Stand still without making noise!" She told the guard as he entered the room holding a glass filled with water in one hand and the rifle hanging from his shoulders.

Shocked to see the rifle pointing at him, the guard remained motionless when Hina removed his rifle from his shoulder.

"I am sorry but I have no other choice," she said as she landed a blow with the rifle butt on his temple. The guard fell down on the carpet spilling the water from the glass, however he did not lose his consciousness. He completely blacked when she hit him behind his head. She stuffed the cloth torn out from the tablecloth in his mouth, covered it with the strips and tied them.

Plucking the cable out from the table lamp she cut it into pieces with the pocket knife retrieved from the guard's pocket. She tied their hands and legs with the cable, all the while worried that time was running out for her. Before leaving the room she scribbled on a paper and left it on the center table.

The corridor was empty which enabled her to run across without any hindrance towards the room where her father was held captive. As she approached his room she heard the sound of steps and voices ahead of her and guessed that the doctor had arrived to meet her father. For her to save her father was now risky and an attempt to extricate him now was to endanger both their lives. Retracing her steps, she reached the end of the corridor and came out of the house where she noticed a guard loitering near the fence. She lay down on the ground and crawled towards the Land Rover parked ten yards away.

She was caught unawares, when all of a sudden, hell broke loose as men ran helter skelter inside and outside the building yelling and shouting. The guard close to her ran towards the house giving her an opportunity to rush to the Land Rover, break the glass window with the rifle and enter it. Swiftly she snatched out the starter wires, joined them and started the vehicle.

Sazo, filled with anger and in desperation, stood in the living room twisting the piece of paper in his palm. The note read, 'You bastards stop torturing my father! I will personally kill each one of you if he is hurt anymore!' Every word was written in capital letters!

□

17

Hina left the house which was in Bhamo, a small town close to the Chinese border and drove along the dirt track until she hit the main artery leading to Myitkyina, a major Myanmar city. The fairly wide road with an even asphalt surface allowed her to press the accelerator. As the car crossed over 100 mph, she held onto the steering wheel with firm hands and overtook the vehicles. She looked at the dashboard and noticed that the fuel tank was nearly three fourths full which was sufficient to carry her to her destination. For about an hour she maintained the speed until she noticed vehicles lined up ahead along the road. Slowing down, she stopped her car behind a Toyota Camry which was crawling slowly.

Looking ahead, she observed that the cars were stopped and checked by the Myanmar policemen who were identifying persons with a picture held in their hands and scrutinising the registration plates of the vehicles. Perturbed, she brought her car back to the center of the road, pressed the accelerator and at full throttle sped through the cordon leaving behind shocked policemen, who jumped aside in panic.

Recovering quickly they jumped into their vehicle, turned them around and followed her car. Hina was worried as her lead over the police cars kept reducing, the distance narrowing between them rapidly. She heard the rear glass window shatter followed by the sound of gunfire. In the rear view mirror she saw a large hole in the glass in the windscreen and a gaping hole in the seat backrest. Obviously her pursuers meant business as they were using high caliber weapons with large size bullets. The next bullet came through from behind and hit the front windscreen which tore and flew away.

She realised her precarious condition which now required her urgent immediate attention. Keeping her head low, she slowed down allowing the police cars to close in on her. From the rear view mirror when she observed that the front police car was about fifteen yards from her, she held the steering wheel with firm hands, using her strength turned her car 180 degrees, and headlong raced it towards the oncoming car. In panic, the policeman took evasive action, turned his car to the left. His car skidded along the steep slope and landed in a ditch nearly thirty yards away from the road.

The second police car which had a marginal time to react, halted, the policemen came out and kept firing at her onrushing Land Rover; the roof of her car riddled with bullets soon disappeared. She increased the speed and when only a few feet remained from the police car, she jerked her car door open and jumped out. Her Land Rover rammed into the standing police vehicle which overturned twice and fell into the deep ditch. The car burst into flames injuring the policemen seriously.

It was her spontaneous recollection of the 'safe fall drill' learnt during her training that saved her to some extent. In the hurry to get out, she could not get enough elevation to permit her to adjust her body position, this caused her to land on her back and bruise her left arm. When she rolled over, her head smashed into a protruding stone, knocking her out.

After passage of time the sound of wailing siren, and the loud chatting from men at some distance, woke her. She attempted to get up, felt dizzy, dropped down and fainted. Her eyes opened again when the sun had set. She found herself in the wilderness with stars shining above in the clear sky. The blood from her wounds had dried. Her arm pained and her temple pulsated painfully. Slowly, she lifted her wounded arm and moved the fingers and saw them respond. Her bones appeared to be intact giving her hope that her body was spared any immediate major attention.

Spreading her legs she sat up slowly, pushed herself up with her right hand and stood on her wobbling feet. The road was not very far from her, however, she had to wade through the thick undergrowth to reach it. She realised that it was this dense foliage that hid her, and eluded the policemen from finding her.

Her car was nowhere in sight, probably towed away. She stood swaying on the berm of the road and raised her hand to stop any vehicle going towards Myitkyina. From the headlights she recognised an oncoming vehicle to be a car. She stepped forward waving her hand. The loud screech from its tires was the last noise she heard as she slumped and blacked out inches in front of the car when it stopped.

The smell of medicines and the bad taste in her mouth from the anesthetic made her feel uncomfortable when she regained consciousness. On opening her eyes she found herself in a well lit room, lying on a soft mattress with her head resting on a cotton pillow. Her eyes looked sideways towards the drip stand from where the IV tube was connected to a vein at the back of her hand. She heaved a sigh of relief and closed her eyes and silently thanked the Almighty.

"Good morning I am glad you are awake! I am Chesa your nurse," she said upon entering the room to find Hina sitting upright on the bed.

"Good morning Chesa! I am feeling better but where am I?" Hina asked her.

"You are in Myitkyina General Hospital. You were brought here by a gentleman, in an unconscious condition. An emergency surgery was performed on the wound on your temple and stitches were given to the cuts on your left arm," Chesa replied.

"How serious are the injuries?" She asked Chesa.

"I do not know. I came in this morning, the night nurse will know. You can ask her or the doctor when you meet him," Chesa told her.

"I have to leave immediately! It is a question of life and death for me!" Hina said, showing anxiety and rising from her bed.

"Please sit down! You cannot leave now, your condition is not stable. I have read your report signed by the doctor. You have lost blood and your hemoglobin is less than nine, your blood pressure is abnormally low and your wounds are fresh requiring constant attention," Chesa said.

"Chesa, please! How can I convince you that my leaving now is much more important than my staying here! I have to prevent my father from being killed by people who are torturing him!" Hina cried out desperately.

"Oh my! You really require help! Let me speak to the authorities," Chesa said and turned to leave the room.

"No! Chesa please stop! The police are in league with the Naga rebel leader who has my father as his captive! On his instructions the police are on the lookout for me! Please do not go to the authorities or tell anyone," Hina pleaded.

Chesa paused to look at her, pulled a chair close to the bed and sat down. She held Hina's hand and smiled.

"I will not go to the authorities, but you have to tell me everything from the beginning. Please do not hide anything, just tell me the truth. You can rely on me, whatever you say will remain with me no one will know," Chesa comforted her, speaking softly and deliberately.

Realising her vulnerable situation, Hina decided to open out to her and narrated the events from her capture by the rebels, her witnessing her father's torture, to her escape from her captors and her encounter with the policemen. All along she emphasised that her aim was to rescue her father who was undergoing life threatening and unspeakable torture.

"If I do not go back to Tuensang immediately and organise a rescue mission, my father will be killed. I love him more than my life. I have to rescue him!" Hina concluded by showing her desperation.

Chesa listened silently without interrupting her, sharing her grief with visible pain showing on her face. She got up and commenced to check Hina's temperature and blood pressure.

"Do not worry! Let me see how best I can help you! Rest and take your medicine regularly," she said and left Hina, who felt helpless, kept quiet and lay down on her bed.

She rested throughout the day having long naps between meals. The painkiller tablets helped to reduce the discomfort she felt whenever she moved her arm or her head. As the IV transfusion continued her head cleared, her body relaxed and the dizziness gradually disappeared. However, her anxiety and restlessness aggravated and the doubt lingered in the correctness of her action of disclosing her identity to Chesa. She now had no other option left, but to pray to the Almighty for guidance and help!

In the evening, Chesa entered her room with a flurry holding a white coat and a cloth face mask, which doctors put on while performing operations.

"Please get up and put on these quickly!" She said handing over the coat and the mask to Hina.

Without questioning her, Hina got into the uniform and followed Chesa out of the room. They did not have to walk much when they entered a room with Cardiologist written on its door.

"Please sit down in the Cardiologist chair, cover your face with the mask, keep your head down and keep looking at the ECG reports lying on the table. You have to show that you are busy," Chesa told Hina, who looked at her with confusion showing on her face,

"The receptionist rang me and said that some very interesting visitors were inquiring about a girl matching your description," Chesa told her.

For a moment Hina felt the ground shifting below her feet and her heart sink, missing a beat.

"What did she tell them?" She asked.

"Nothing!" Chesa said and smiled.

Hina looked at her with pain showing in her eyes and sweat drops appearing on her forehead.

"Relax! It is the Hospital's policy not to reveal information about its patients to anyone, unless they come with a court order. So she told them nothing," she said. Hina heaved a sigh of relief and smiled.

"The visitors are from the Burmese Special Intelligence Department, as they could not produce any legal papers the receptionist refused to entertain them," Chesa stated.

"Then why are we here?" Hina asked.

"They met the Hospital Administrator who has agreed to take them to each ward to see the patients," Chesa replied.

"Have they started the search?" Hina asked her.

"Yes they will be in the surgical ward at any moment. I will leave you here and return with them," Chesa said and left the room.

Hina kept looking at the ECG charts hoping and praying that the detractors would not come to her room. But soon she heard voices outside the office, she looked up momentarily and noticed a tall elderly person enter the room with Chesa and two other men, one of whom she recognised. He was Khoula who had given electric shocks to her father. She lowered her head and kept looking at the reports on the table.

"Good evening doctor! Sorry to disturb you! These men here are looking for a patient whom they say is a fugitive from law. We are therefore checking every room. I see you have no patients and are all set to go to the OT. We will leave without disturbing you any further," the admin, the tall man, said, turned and left followed by Chesa.

Khoula, however, advanced towards the table and stood looking at Hina.

"The doctor is preparing for a heart surgery, which she has to perform within the next five minutes. Please leave her alone," Chesa called out standing at the open door.

Khoula dropped his keys on the floor and as he bent down to pick it up, he looked at Hina, who lowered her head further and started writing on the paper.

"Please let us go! Leave the doctor alone," the admin spoke out loudly.

Khoula picked up his keys and headed for the door. Before shutting the door he looked back and found Hina busy writing. He joined others to look into the rooms occupied by surgical ward patients, which included the one which Hina had vacated not very long back.

"Why is this room vacant?" The admin asked Chesa.

"I do not know Sir! I was with you!" Chesa replied with a smile.

He asked her to call the ward boy and the security man on duty who when questioned exhibited their ignorance.

"Who was the patient?" Khoula asked impatiently.

"A girl who had met with an accident was brought to the hospital last night," Chesa said.

"Does she look like the girl in the picture?" Khoula took out a picture and showed it to Chesa who examined it closely.

"I am not sure, but there is a resemblance. Yes, I think it is her picture," Chesa said, holding the picture in her hand.

"Is she the one, the fugitive? She must have left the hospital by now and headed for her home," the admin said.

Khoula looked at him, without speaking he left them and rushed towards the cardiologist's room. Upon entering he found it empty; he checked the toilet and the cupboards and found no sign of the doctor.

"Where is the doctor?" He asked.

"She must be in the operating room performing surgery," Chesa said.

"Can you call her up?" Khoula asked.

"What? That is impossible," the Admin said.

"OK, give me her number," instructed the security man from the Government, the other man with them.

"I cannot! It is against hospital regulations," Admin said with a smile.

"Thank you! I will be in touch," Khoula said and left with the security man.

"What does he want with the doctor?" Admin queried.

"I don't know!" Chesa told Admin, and informing him that she had to attend to her patients excused herself.

Relieved that Hina had left the Cardiologists room in time, Chesa headed towards her office to meet the night nurse to brief her. Through the window she saw her sitting on her chair busy writing with a pen in a register. When she entered the room she was shocked when the 'nurse' looked up and smiled at her!

"Oh my God! Is it you Hina? I just can't believe my eyes!" She cried out.

"Shh... please lower your voice! Even walls have ears!" Hina said, smiled, got up and hugged her.

"Where is the night nurse?" Chesa asked her.

"She has not come so far," Hina replied.

"I was really worried when the Naga rushed towards the Cardiologists room! A big relief to find you are here!" She exclaimed.

"I had an intuition that he would return on finding my bed empty! I have met him earlier, he was the one giving electric shocks to my father. I had a hunch that he had recognised me but was uncertain. As soon as he left, I came out of the cardiologist room, asked a patient and he directed me to your room," Hina said.

"Thank God your intuition worked! You cannot stay here anymore! We have to get you out of this hospital at the earliest," Chesa said.

"I have been thinking about it. I have to leave under a disguise to fool the rebels who will be keeping a close watch at every exit," Hina said and came close to Chesa and stood next to her.

"You and I are nearly the same height and girth. I can wear your uniform and leave the hospital in an ambulance as a nurse," Hina suggested, holding her hand.

Chesa smiled and nodded her head, the idea appealed to her. She took out her normal clothes from her locker and entered the toilet. A few minutes later she came out dressed in her casual wear and handed her nurses attire to Hina who took it and left to wear them.

"You make a pretty picture in these clothes. Go and sit in the nurse/s relaxation room. I will meet you after I have handed over the charge to the night nurse, who should be here any moment," Chesa said.

Hina left her and as she was stepping out of the room she nearly collided with a nurse entering the room.

"Who is that nurse?" The night nurse asked Chesa as she settled down in her chair.

"Oh! A new girl who had lost directions" Chesa replied casually.

It did not take long for Chesa to brief the night nurse. Casually she mentioned that Hina's condition had improved and she was discharged at her request.

Hina was reading the newspaper, looked up and smiled when Chesa entered the room.

"An ambulance is carrying a patient and its driver has agreed to drop you at my aunt's house. I will be there to meet you when you arrive. I am going ahead on my scooter," Chesa told her.

They found the driver relaxing on his seat with his eyes closed. Chesa knocked on the glass window to wake him up.

"Kyle, this is nurse Mary, who is going with you. She is new here, let her sit with the patient so that she can look after her during the journey," Chesa told the driver, who nodded and got down to open the rear door of the ambulance. She left after instructing him to drop Hina at the location written in the paper which she gave him.

Hina entered the vehicle and sat down on the seat near the door. Soon a patient, an aged lady arrived in a wheelchair and was helped in the vehicle by the ward boy. The driver started the vehicle and stopped at the exit gate.

"I am carrying a patient to her home. You can note it down in the book" Kyle told the sentry.

"Is there anyone else with the patient inside the vehicle?" A man standing next to the sentry asked him.

"Nurse Mary is with her," the driver replied.

"Can you open the door? I want to see," the man asked.

The driver looked at the sentry who shrugged his shoulders indicating that they had to comply with the request. Kyle got down from his cabin and opened the rear door.

They saw an old lady resting on the bed on the stretcher being fed by a nurse whose back was towards them.

"Hurry up and drive! I am about to finish my meal! I need to sleep in my bed in my house!" The lady shouted at the driver in a stern voice.

The man wanted to have a closer look, but Kyle closed the door immediately and drove away the ambulance.

Hina looked out through the glass window and was shocked to see Khoula standing next to the sentry and arguing with him. She heaved a sigh of relief and smiled at the patient who returned the smile with curiosity written all over her face.

"You are running away from the hospital! I can make out that you are not a nurse!" She told Hina, who smiled at her and nodded.

"Do not worry! It is our secret! I will not tell anyone!" The lady said and closed her eyes.

The driver dropped Hina before dropping the patient at her residence. Chesa, who was waiting for her after thanking Kyle, took Hina inside the house and introduced her to her aunt, a middle aged lady on the heavier side.

"You are in no fit condition to travel, however you have to leave this country immediately! You are a hot potato now with the police and the Naga rebels, and they are good at hunting down people. Relax here for a day and then leave, which will give me time to make arrangements for your travel," Chesa told her, showing her the room.

"I do need to rest, I am feeling very tired. I want to sleep straight away," Hina said, removing her nurse's dress and putting on a dress given by Chesa's aunt.

"I will leave you with your medicine which you should take before you go to sleep. Have no worries, my aunt will take care of you. She is good at it," Chesa said and left her.

Hina fell asleep on the soft bed the moment she closed her eyes. The strain from the anxious moments she had faced during the day had drained her energy, in addition the injuries were taking a toll on her body. It was her unyielding professional training and attitude that had sustained her physically and mentally so far. The horrible torture her father was subjected to by Sazo and his men and her close escape from the authorities and the insurgents had further strengthened her resolve to rescue her father at any cost.

Her peaceful slumber that lasted over twelve hours ended when she felt a piercing pain in her arm as she turned over in her bed. She got up and decided to finish the morning chores before meeting Chesa's aunt. To ease the pain she swallowed a painkiller tablet.

Her activities in her room and the toilet had alerted Chesa's aunt who was sitting in her room as she came out.

"Good morning you seem to have slept well," she said.

"Good morning aunt! I had a wonderful sleep! I am sorry I got up so late," Hina told her.

"You were so tired! The lunch is laid out on the table, you can have it whenever you want. I have finished mine and will leave you for sometime. I have to do some shopping," she said and left the room.

After having her meal and medicine Hina lay on the bed and slept. She woke up when she heard voices from the other room and looking through the window found it dark outside. She quickly got up and left the bedroom.

"How are you feeling today?" Chesa asked her, holding her hand.

"Much better! The pain has left me though I still feel slightly weak," Hina told her.

"I am sure you will regain your strength soon. I am coming from the hospital and the search for you has not stopped," Chesa said.

"Is there any new development?" Hina asked.

The same two people had come again asking about you! They insisted that the girl missing from her room had not left the hospital. I told them that I will personally search all the wards and asked them to come tomorrow." Chesa said. Observing the anxiety on Hina's face she smiled.

"Do not worry! I will take care of them," Chesa comforted her.

"What is the program you have for me?" Hina asked her.

"I have discussed and tied up with my brother, and this is what we have thought best for you. Do not go North to Nagaland by following the Ledo Road as it runs close to HPakang where your enemies live. Go further South to Tamu which is close to Moreh near Imphal. The train from Myitkyina will take you to Shwebo. From there go by road to Tamu which passes through the major towns Kalemyo and Kalewa. From Tamu the distance to Moreh is not much and you will find many Indians there," Chesa said.

Her aunt pointed out the risks Hina will face due to her physical condition and the exposure in a hostile country. She advised her to delay her departure.

"Have no worries," Chesa looked at her aunt and held Hina's hands affectionately.

"The medicines will take care of your wounds during the

journey, but the moment you cross the border you should get a thorough check up. You will be travelling in a coupe compartment in the train for around 16 hours. At Shwebo my brother Hita will meet you with a car and will drive you right up to Tamu. The road upto Kalemyo is good but thereafter it is in bad shape to Kalewa and right upto Tamu. I have been on this road and if the going is good you will cover the journey in eight hours," Chesa explained to her.

Hina reached out and held Chesa's hands, her eyes moist with gratitude and gratefulness.

"Chesa my sweet, sweet dear, you have rekindled my faith in humanity! After all that has happened so far, I had almost given up hope in humans! Now a total stranger in a foreign land has proved me wrong! As much as I can thank you, it will never be adequate!" she said.

"Hold on dear! Do not get too emotional! Hear me out fully before thanking me! You will have to leave by tonight's train which leaves at 10.30 pm. I have arranged for a taxi to take you to the railway station," she said, handing the ticket, to Hina, who looked surprised on reading the name printed on it.

"You have a new name, you are Bennu. You are Burmese, your clothes are in this bag. Your berth is in a deluxe class coupe compartment, your companion is an old lady, besides her and the ticket collector no other person is likely to meet you. You can order your meals to be served in your compartment," Chesa told her.

Hina interlocked her eye with her! Her heart shot out to her and her mind spun in a whirl! Is Chesa for real or she was daydreaming! She bent down, lowering her head onto her lap!

"Oh my, wake up Hina! Here is some money for expenses during the journey. Keep it, you may have to grease the palms of the officials especially when you cross the border," she said handing over Burmese currency to her. Hina shook her head, took it quietly and put it in her pocket.

"Now let us sit down and have some tea! Oh yes, please take my visiting card, my mobile number is on it. I have also added my brother Hita's mobile number. Call me up after reaching India," she said and gave Hina her card.

They drank tea making small talk with Chesa doing most of the talking.

"Tell me Chesa, why are you going out of your way, knowing the grave risk to yourself, to help an unknown fugitive?" Hina asked her with moist eyes.

Chesa looked down for a while and raised her head with pain showing in her eyes.

"It's a long story! I will narrate it when we meet in India! Suffice to say, a woman who has suffered can only understand and help another woman who is in the same plight!" She said and got up.

"Wish you all the best, have a safe journey to your destination. God bless you!" She said and shook Hina's hand.

"Thank you! God bless you Chesa!" Hina said in a chortled voice with tears coming out from her eyes.

In the evening Hina boarded the train and settled down comfortably in the deluxe coupe. The train left Myitkyina station at 1030 pm.

Next day Khoula and his friend met Chesa in the hospital and accosted her, pressing her to fulfil her promise to them.

"Oh yes! The girl was the same one whose picture you had shown me, I found her in a room in the medical ward," Chesa told them.

"What is her name in the register?" He asked.

"Anton," she replied.

"Thank you," Khoula said and started to walk away from her.

"Oh, I went to the medical ward and checked this morning. She was discharged from the hospital last evening and she has left," Chesa called out loudly.

"Do they know where she will be going?' Khoula stopped walking, came near and asked her.

"Let me think! My colleague informed me that the girl had told her that she was going to take a taxi and head for India on the Ledo road!" Chesa replied.

□

18

Sazo sat in the office reading the latest transcripts of the messages intercepted over the radio and phones from across the international border, through Flexispy for voice and Copy9 for text messages.

"Thank you. Normal routine stuff nothing very interesting. In case you hear or read about an Indian girl dead or alive in Myanmar or our area, come to me immediately," he told Zumo, handing over the paper to him. Zumo was the IT expert who worked in the office.

"Yes Sir I will," Zumo said and left.

Sazo had reasons to be worried, his plan was sinking before it could take off. He entered the next room where Kiyanelie was in conversation with Loheleniyu. He sat down in the vacant chair and listened to them.

"You have no idea where the girl will be?" Kiyanelie asked Lohelniyu.

"So far we have no idea, and it is getting more difficult everyday to find her. We have very few men searching her," he replied.

"Loheleniyu, you must take more men. Get her quickly! She should not be allowed to return to her country or contact any Indian official in Myanmar!" Kiiyanelie ordered, showing his dismay and frustration. Loheleniyu nodded and got up to leave.

"Just a minute! I think we should think more before sending our men on a witch hunt! She would be close to or across the border by now! How she has covered the distance is a mystery but my reading is that we will not find her in Myanmar any more. Moreover, you should now plan to shift Brijesh from where he is, as his location is compromised," Sazo said and looked at Kiyanelie.

"OK, do not do anything about the girl now, but bring Brijesh to the camp and keep him next to the armory, where he will be guarded twenty-four hours. Speak to me later after you have completed the task," Kiyanelie told Loheleniyu, who nodded and left them.

"Now here is what we could do to ensure that the girl never communicates with the Indian authorities," Sazo said and pulled his chair closer to the table.

Resting his elbows on the table he spoke uninterrupted. Kiyanelie listened to him attentively, not missing out a single word.

"So pick up the phone and call up your friend now, without any further delay," Sazo concluded.

Kiyanelie got up from the pitcher, filled two glasses of water and handed one to Sazo; they emptied their glasses quickly.

"I hope he is not busy," he said, dialing the number on the mobile. He heard it ring and heard a voice after a few seconds.

"Hullo Kiyanelie how are you?" Shashi Damodar Kulkarni DG NSG asked.

"I am fine but we have a major problem here," Kiyanelie replied.

"What is the problem?" Shashi asked after a long pause.

"The girl has escaped," he said.

"You mean Hina, has escaped?" he suggested.

"Yes, the same person. We cannot find her and we think she will soon enter India. It is extremely difficult for us to stop her and we cannot allow her to meet you or any other Indian authority. We need your help immediately," Kiyanelie said.

"My help? How can I help you? I will have to listen to her when she contacts me and inform the higher authorities! I have no other choice!," Shashi raised his voice and spoke.

"Yes, you have a choice and a very effective one!" Kiyanelie spoke emphatically.

"What is that?" Shashi asked.

"You will arrange to kill her!" Kiyanelie told him, and looked at Sazo who nodded.

"What the hell are you talking about? Are you out of your

mind? I am not an assassin nor do I know any!" Shashi said raising his voice further.

"Calm down Shashi? You have a full night to make up your mind! Tomorrow morning at 8 o'clock an old friend we both know very well will meet you. Have your answer ready by then," Kiyanelie said in a friendly voice.

"Listen Kiyanelie you are crossing all limits! Why do you want to kill a girl who wants nothing else but to find her father?" he pleaded.

"I too had a father, mother, brother and sister once! What happened to them? They were killed by your army! My entire village was razed to the ground by your valiant soldiers. You have no memory, but I have? I wept and did not sleep for a week wandering through the jungle like an animal! I told you all this when you were here with your Battalion! How can you forget it so soon?" Kiyanelie spoke with feelings and at length.

"It has been over fifteen years since all this happened! Things are changing and you too have offered to surrender! Why then, do you want this girl to be killed?" Shashi asked him.

"There are issues which are beyond your comprehension and I cannot share them with you! You meet your old friend tomorrow morning and listen to him carefully," Kiyanelie said and hung up.

Shashi had received the call sitting in the rear seat of his car on his way to his home after finishing his work in the office. He was not concerned at the risk of being overheard by the driver, who was with him for over two years and had heard many such phone conversations. Kiyanelie had become a major cause for worry and concern to him, he was using him as a pliable tool.

The fear from his threats to him and his family's safety was becoming real now. Even though he was chief of the elite Paramilitary Force, he was vulnerable to multiple dangers to himself and his family, especially from the insurgents who could strike at any place at any time.

Money was a minor lure for him now, he had sufficient liquidity in his accounts in various banks in India and in Cayman Island. It was the physical fear from Kiyanelie who was degenerating into a vicious ruthless animal, which haunted him now. The very consideration of assassination repulsed him and he resolved that he will in no way make arrangements to kill anyone, especially an innocent girl. He contemplated feigning sickness and to send in an application for long leave for treatment in a hospital in London. His wife and daughter could accompany him. He was determined to distance himself from Kiyanelie forever.

The car reached his residence, he got out of it and taking firm strides he reached the door and rang the bell!

"Bindu has crossed all limits," Usha told him when he entered the room.

"What has my daughter done now?" He asked her.

"She has booked a room in the Oberoi hotel and is having a party with her friends," she complained.

"What is wrong with that?" He asked her.

"Her friends include men!" she replied. He looked at her and held up his hands.

"Don't worry! Dial her number and I will speak to her," he said, handing his cellphone to her.

She dialed and gave the phone to him. Keeping his voice low and affectionate he spoke at length to his daughter until he was satisfied with her response.

"See, she has agreed that she is not inviting men. Only her close girl friends will be with her and the party will finish well before midnight after which she will return home immediately," he consoled her and said.

"It is you who has spoiled our only child! You always permit her and agree to everything that she says or does. She has left her husband and is now partying in a hotel. It's too much!" Usha cried out.

"Calm down! She is having a party in the hotel because she does not want to disturb us by having it in the house. Relax, she will be here before midnight," Shashi said and held her affectionately.

They had an early dinner and after watching the television for sometime they hit the bed. The problems created by Kiyanelie disturbed his sleep. His mind kept evaluating the options he had before him. Would Kiyanelie leave him alone if he left the country without implementing his instructions? Will he take revenge? His thoughts kept examining and wavering with various speculations. He finally decided that his next step would depend on the meeting with Kiyanalie's man in the morning. He caught up on sleep late in the morning and kept on sleeping beyond his normal hours.

"There is someone who wants to speak to you. He is waiting outside," Usha shook him and said.

"Oh! Tell him to come after three hours. Please let me sleep a bit more," he said and turned away from her.

"I told him to come later as you were sleeping. He said his name was Soni and he has to speak to you now," she shook him again and spoke.

"Soni?" he said out loud and sat up, "Ok, ask him to sit in the living room and wait. I will be with him in five minutes."

He left the bed and hurried up with his immediate morning chores. He was keen to meet Soni to get rid of him.

"Good morning Soni, how are you? I will speak to Kiyanelie tomorrow, please convey it to him. You need not come here again," Shashi said on meeting him.

"Good morning Sir! I am fine! I will do as you have mentioned! May I request you to view this pen drive in your laptop?" Soni said with a humble smile.

"What is in it?" Shashi asked.

"I do not know Sir. I am only a courier" Please open the file and see it yourself." Soni replied and handed the pen drive.

Shashi nodded, picked up the laptop from the shelf and plugged the pen drive in it. The moment he opened the file and saw its contents, he felt his heart sink and the earth move under his feet. He felt dizzy, sat down and closed his eyes. After a while he lowered the laptop screen and pulled out the pen drive.

The video on the screen had devastated and broke him into pieces. His daughter, his loving daughter and her friends were dancing totally nude in the room. They appeared to be intoxicated and enjoying prancing around to the beats from the background music. The pictures were pretty clear, the acts shown in them were graphic.

"Is this Kiyanele's idea of blackmail? I am hurt! Deeply hurt, but certainly not scared! I will have it removed from every social media site that you post! I will have it blocked and have you arrested!" Shashi spoke angrily.

"Calm down Sir! We do not intend to spoil the reputation of your family. Not yet, this is just a trailer! Please view the contents in this pen drive!" Soni said and handed it to him.

"Now what more filth you have with you?" Shashi said and plugged the stick to the laptop.

A series of numbers appeared on the screen against various banks in his and his wife's names, followed by the last quarter bank statements, which showed details of balances in each account. After examining the bank statements he saw another set of videos which startled him.

They showed him wining and dining in restaurants and in the residences with two persons whom he recognised clearly, they were Rajat Saxena and Akram Bhat. The last three videos had him exchanging packages with Rajat Saxena, while Akram Bhat and Kiyanelie were looking. With a deep audible sigh he got up and faced Soni who looked at him with a blank face.

"Tell Kiyanelie, I will speak to him in an hour," he said and sighed.

"Yes certainly, I will do as you said. Good day Sir!" Soni replied, took the pen drive from him and left.

Shashi sat down with his head held in his hands; his malefaction had finally caught up with him! Rajat Saxena and Akram Bhat were drug smugglers who smuggled heroin from Myanmar into Nagaland and Manipur. As the Commandant of the CRPF Battalion he had ensured a safe passage to their heroin packages by transporting them in his vehicle. The video showed the drug packages being loaded in his jeep under his directions, while others watched.

After he had left his Battalion both Saxena and Bhat were caught and were now lodged in a jail in Imphal undergoing twenty years rigorous imprisonment.

With a heavy heart he got up and entered the toilet to perform the rest of the morning schedule. The bath was refreshing though a mild piercing chest pain continued to bother him. He dressed quickly and sat down to eat his breakfast served by his wife.

"What did Soni want?" Usha asked him. She had been busy with her prayers and supervising the cooking.

"Oh, nothing special. A small office matter," Shashi told her.

He left the house in the car and asked the driver to take him to his friend Basu Bhattacharyas house which was in Defence Colony and on the route to his office. Sitting in the car he dialled Kiyanelies number from his mobile.

"Yes Shashi, Have you made up your mind?" He heard Kiyanelie asking him.

"Yes, I will do whatever you say," he replied.

"Good! Don't forget we have the original video clips," Kiyanelie said and laughed. Shashi disconnected the call and put the cellphone in his coat pocket.

The traffic had reduced considerably, the road was open which gave the driver free space to speed up. They reached the house in quick time and he noticed his friend's car parked in front of the house. He got out of his car, walked towards the entrance door, pressed the bell and waited. His eyes fell on the nameplate on which was painted 'Shri Basu Bhattacharya Editor in Chief Freedom Express'. He entered the house and spent half an hour with the editor.

After leaving him he reached his office and dialed a number on his mobile.

"Good morning Shashi, how are you?" He heard Suresh Mathur NSA at the other end.

"Good morning Sir, I am fine. I rang up with a request for an urgent meeting. I want to brief you the RAW and IB chiefs on a very critical and dangerous development," Shashi told him.

"Give me a minute, let me see my engagements for the day, OK, I am cutting out my 3 pm meeting. Be here on time. I will inform Bhupender and Unni," Suresh said and hung up.

Shashi's thoughts remained in turmoil all through the period he was in his office; his daughter's picture hurt him much more than the pictures showing him with the drug smugglers. He knew that he was caught in a tight vise with no room for maneuvering. He had to save himself and his family at any cost; fabrication, distortion, deceit and lies were the only options left to him, to achieve it.

He reached NSA's office in time and found that the three members were already present. He wished them and occupied his seat next to Unni.

"OK Shashi, without wasting any time tell us what you have for us," Suresh addressed him.

"Sir! I have bad news all round! Agent Hina from SAG who was sent to meet our RAW mole in Kiyanelis camp has been captured and the mole killed!" Shashi said. A stunned pin drop silence followed for quite some time, after he had spoken.

"How did you get this information?" Bhupinder asked.

Shashi looked down on the table, his mind turned blank as he had not anticipated this question.

"Sorry Bhupinder, I am not in a position to disclose my source," he said in a soft voice, after some time.

"What? Not to us! We are the highest intelligence officials in the country who carry top most National secrets in our pockets all the time? Don't be foolish, spill it out Shashi!" Bhupinder cried out.

Shashi shook his head, remained silent and looked at Suresh.

"Fine with me. Keep the name of your source secret. But is he reliable? Is he telling the truth?" Suresh asked him.

"Yes, he is extremely reliable. It happened yesterday, and Hina has not returned. We do not know if she is even alive," Shashi spoke out.

"Do you have any information?" Suresh asked looking towards Bhupinder and Unni who shook their heads.

"What do we do then?" He queried.

"We could send an army patrol to the camp to find out. Or use the local agents," Unni suggested

"Do we have any local agents in Myanmar?" Suresh asked

"We have many but our experience has been that you cannot trust them completely," Bhupinder replied.

"Can we try to find out through satellites and drones?" Bhupinder queried.

"We can try, I will put ISRO on the task. However, considering that only four days are left for the meeting with the rebel leader and the PM, I do not think we are likely to get any information before that from ISRO," Suresh replied.

"It seems we are stuck. My suggestion is that we recommend that the proposed meeting be postponed for the time being. In the meanwhile let us find out what Kiyanelie is doing with the Pakistani and Chinese? Why was our agent killed? Who has captured Hina and where is she now? Sir, we need answers to these before proceeding any further," Bhupinder spoke emphatically at length.

"I agree with Bhupinder. The situation has become very fluid now. We cannot take chances with PMs safety and security. Let us be a hundred percent sure only then allow the meeting between them," Unni said agreeing with Bhupinder.

"What is your suggestion Shashi?" Suresh asked him.

"I suggest that the meeting should take place on the date that we have accepted. So far everything is calm and quiet in that area. I spoke to Kiyanelie before coming here. He has no knowledge regarding the meeting between our agent and Hina in his camp. In fact, he was surprised to learn that there was a mole.

I also asked him about his meeting with the Chinese and the Pakistani. He replied that, as he was surrendering he wanted to close all their earlier deals with them amicably. My reading is that he may not agree with postponing the meeting. We then have lost an opportunity for peace and prosperity in Nagaland," Shashi spoke out with confidence, in a firm tone.

"But as you say Hina is missing and the mole is dead. Are these not signs of insecurity in that area?" Bhupinder asked.

"I do not consider that the meeting place is insecure. We have relied excessively on Hina to obtain information. I know Hina well. She is my officer and she came to Nagaland taking part of her annual leave in search for her father. Right from day one her only concern is to find her father. Apparently she is engaged in it now at the cost of her duty. Her father is far more important to her than her country! With due apologies to Bhupinder, it was wrong to send her to meet the mole in Kiyanelie's camp. Someone else should have been sent," Shashi spoke out.

"What about the mole? Who killed him?" Unni interjected.

"It is not clear whether the mole was killed before or after meeting Hina," Shashi replied.

Suresh had listened to them patiently; it was up to him to determine the next step.

"Let the status quo remain. We continue to plan, the meeting will be held on the scheduled date," he said and got up.

□

19

"There is no trace of her! She has vanished in thin air?" Kiyanelie queried as he paced the room with worry and anxiety reflecting on his face.

Those sitting in the room kept looking at him without speaking, aware that the issue was compelling and needed instant answers, and they were clueless.

"If the staff of Myitkyina General Hospital had not played dirty she would have been in lock up by now," Khoula said

"Instead you have brought her father here, and are holding him a prisoner!" Yang said with a smirk.

"His location was compromised. She is hell bent on rescuing him. The Burmese would get alerted if she brings in a rescue force, which I think she would personally lead. The Burmese are going all out to improve relations with India. Any incident involving shooting and killing would hurt us, if they learn that we are harming Indians on their soil," Kiyanelie said.

"So what are you going to do with the prisoner?" Chou asked. Kiyanelie smiled and sat down in his chair.

"You tell me why you want him so badly? What is this about Op Indradhanush which you keep on asking him," Kiyanelie queried.

"Knowing about Operation Indradhanush is very important to the Chinese Government. From our sources we have learnt that this Operation deals with destruction of nuclear weapons in the sky, preventing them from reaching the ground by intercepting them in the air. I will show you the video on my laptop which will make it more clear," Choi said, switched on his laptop and played the video which showed a nuclear blast in the sky on account of a land rocket hitting the oncoming missile in the atmosphere.

"If you know so much, what else do you want from the Indian?" Sazo queried.

"This is just basics known to most countries threatened by nuclear weapons. We are interested in the technology details, the performance results of any tests that have been carried out, their tactical deployment for intercepting rockets and many other technical issues, which we are certain that the Indian can give us," Choi said.

"Why, here in Nagaland? Sazo asked.

"That is exactly what we are extremely keen to find out from him," Choi smiled and replied.

"I cannot understand how a nuclear explosion high in the sky affects the people down below?" Kiyanelie interposed.

"It can be from the debris falling on the ground. This is a very important aspect we want to know from him," Chou replied.

"So what do you suggest we do with Brijesh?" Sazo asked him.

"I suggest we give him some medical treatment now, and when he is in a condition to travel, we will take him with us to China," Choi replied.

"Yes, you can do that provided you carry our package too!" Sazo told Choi, who sat up and shook his head.

"The one you mentioned in the last meeting?" Yang asked him.

"Yes, the same one. If you do not take it and keep it with you, then Brijesh does not go with you," Kiyanelie told him in a serious tone.

"Why are you involving us in a very dangerous game? It will have major worldwide repercussions. We will have to answer to the UNO! We are not interested in your package at all! After getting the information from Brijesh, we will return him to you," Choi said.

"You know Mr Choi, for the past fifteen years I have been waiting for this day! To bring the Indian Government on its knees! To show to the world how a small person like me can shake the roots of an entire nation! I want revenge for all the atrocities committed by the Indians on my people by bombing our villages, destroying our property, raping our women and killing innocent people! You Mr Choi are going to help me to achieve it!" Kiyanelie exhorted emotionally. Choi remained silent and looked out through the window

"I will have to speak to my Government. It is they who will decide. You will know soon," Choi said and got up.

"Don't you think that you should postpone your surrender ceremony? The girl may upset your plans by revealing her experience to her bosses. Your life may be endangered, Kiyanelie," Yang said.

Kiyanelie looked at Sazo and both smiled.

"Do not worry, friend! Our man in Delhi will take care of us," Kiyanelie said and got up.

□

20

She was now on her way to the Island Peak, the highest of the Three Peaks referred to by the local Sherpas, as Imja Tse, an Island in a glacial sea. It was the last exciting and popular peak which had snow and ice on the upper sections. She hurried up to be behind the leading Sherpa.

Take it easy Hina, conserve your energy, she heard her father as she passed him. She looked back, smiled and slowed down.

You want to climb it but you have to be careful, as the ascent is at a steep angle on long snowy and icy slopes, the Sherpa told her when she took a step forward in the direction of the peak. I want to give it a try, she requested. Gradually with deep concentration and body control taking small steps she reached the top of the peak. A sudden strong gust of wind hit her, making her lose her balance. She found herself plunging down into the deep gorge. For a moment the rope tied to her held her as she swirled in the air. The knot suddenly untangled, and she went down in a free fall. She looked down and felt fear gripping her as the ground was nowhere in sight. She knew that she was going to die. Holding up her hand she looked up to pray. To her horror she saw her father coming towards her with his arms open beckoning her!

She shrieked out loudly! Papa! You stay there I love you very much I do not want you to die!

She opened her eyes with a start, sat up and kept sobbing.

"What happened to you my dear? Did you have a nightmare? Please calm down!" Said the old lady from the lower berth. She stood up and held Hina's hand.

"Yes I had a very frightening nightmare! I am sorry I disturbed you," Hina told her.

"Never mind, everyone has it! But I am glad that you slept throughout the journey. You needed the rest, you looked very tired when you boarded the train. Shwebo is the next station and we will reach there in the next fifteen minutes, so tidy up and get ready," she told her.

The journey between Myitkyina to Shwebo by train was over thirteen hours and now she had to travel to Tamu by car. Chesa's brother Hita picked her up from the railway station, drove the car and reached Tamu in six hours. The dark streets with an odd light from a concrete building greeted them as they drove along the near deserted road to the modest brick house in a side street of the town. Hina silently thanked the Almighty for safely entering the Myanmar border town without any untoward incident.

They got down from the car, reached the house and Hita knocked at the door. After a few minutes it was opened by a middle aged lady, who looked at him and smiled.

'Welcome we have been waiting ever since you spoke to Abhijeet on the phone,' she said.

"Thank you Binsa, meet Bennu," Hita said, introducing Hina.

They shook hands and entered the room which had assorted numbers of chairs and a center table.

"Hina urgently requires a bed where she can lie down and rest," Hita said.

Binsa looked at Hina with compassion and held her hand.

"Come with me I have a bed ready where you can rest as long as you want," she said, leading her to the next room. Hina followed her and without changing her clothes lay on the bed.

"Abhijeet has gone to Moreh to meet Chanitin, my daughter, whose husband has the papers for crossing the border. He will be here tomorrow morning with the documents," Binsa told Hina.

"Thank you, I am extremely grateful! Do mobile phones work here?" Hina asked as she got up from the bed.

"Yes, mobile phones work here! Hita has sent your pictures and details through his cell phone to Abhijeet for getting the papers prepared," she said.

"Can I speak to anyone in India from here?" She queried

"Yes of course. You can do it on my phone," Binsa said and handed the mobile phone to her.

Hina dialled Kashif's number which she had memorised. After a few rings she heard a voice saying that the number was out of coverage and could not be reached. She tried it a number of times and received the same reply.

She rang up her home number in Hyderabad and after a few rings heard Dada's voice clearly.

"Namaste Dada! Hina speaking, Dada!" she called out in a calm voice.

"Hina! Bitya, extremely glad to hear your voice! Your Dadi and I are very worried! How are you?" Her Dada was quite excited as he called out to her.

"I am fine, Dada! I saw Papa! Soon he will be with you. Please do not worry anymore!" She assured him.

"That is great news beti! Thank God! When are you both returning?" Dada asked.

"Very soon Dada! I have to leave you now as my friends are calling me. Give my love to Dadi. I love you both very much!" She said and hung up without waiting for a reply.

"Thank you, the person I wanted to speak, cannot be reached, his number is out of the coverage area. I spoke to my grandfather," she said, returning the phone to Binsa.

"The food is ready. I can bring it here," Binsa said. Hina smiled and nodded.

She finished her dinner and hit the bed after taking the medicine kept by Chesa in a handbag. After the long journey, at last she had found a bed where she could lie down in comfort and relax her sore and tired body. Her wounds were not troubling her any more and she prayed that they would heal soon.

Next morning Binsa made no effort to wake her and let her sleep. She dispensed with breakfast and kept herself busy preparing the midday meal. Hina got up late and joined her after her chores.

"I hope you have slept well?" Binsa asked her, offering her a cup of tea with a smile.

"Oh my God! Never slept better in my life! The bed was very comfortable. I was very tired, closed my eyes and was on cloud nine, in another world! Thank you very much!" Hina told her, sipping her tea.

"It is a normal bed! You were so tired after a long journey that any bed would be comfortable," Binsa said.

"This is delicious, it has a taste different from the meals I had in Myanmar! Where did you learn to cook like this?" Hina asked after tasting the dish. Binsa giggled loudly and looked at her.

"The taste is different because it is a Nepali dish! We are from Nepal, my grandfather migrated here fifty years back. Abhijeet my husband lived in Moreh with his parents before we got married. My daughter is working in a store in Moreh and stays with her grandparents. We own a clothing shop in Tamu, which was handed over to me by my father and Abhijeet looks after it," Binsa said.

Hita joined them on the table, complimenting Binsa on her cooking while enjoying the dishes.

"I am waiting for Abhijeet. I have to get some cloth for my shop from him. The festival season is beginning and the demand will go up," he said.

"He will be here any minute. I got a call from him," Binsa assured him.

Soon a fairly tall man with a thick tuft of hair entered the room, hugged Binsa and shook hands with Hita.

"Good morning!" I am Benna, you must be Abhijeet," Hina said.

"Good morning. I am Abhijeet, nice to meet you," he said and shook her hand.

"I am sorry, I am causing so much trouble for you and Binsa," she said.

"Hita is my business partner and a very dear friend. We always help one another, which is very routine for us," Abhijeet said looking at Hita.

"You are safe and in good hands. I have to leave now, it was very nice meeting you. My prayers are always for your safe journey," Hita told Hina, shaking her hands. He shook hands with Binsa and told her that Chesa would come with him in the next visit.

Abhijeet accompanied him to the car and asked him to collect the cloth from his assistant who was in the shop. Hita started the car and sped away.

"Hita and her sister are very close friends of mine and I have full faith in their judgement! Therefore, when I saw this news item in the newspaper and in the fliers pasted on walls in Moreh, I did not panic," Abhijeet said, handing over a page from a newspaper and a flier.

She looked at the newspaper page and saw her picture on it. The article under the picture mentioned her name and described her as a drug peddler who had escaped from Myanmar police custody and was heading for India. It mentioned that she was the keep and close associate of the Kingpin, who traded in drugs regularly. As per rough police estimates she had transported over two tons of heroin and hashish to various border towns of India. The drug dealer was financed and backed by the Chinese. A sum of 10 lac rupees would be awarded to anyone who could give information about her.

She finished reading, her mind in total confusion and in a quandary. She was at a loss to decide whether to laugh or cry! With a deep frown on her brows she looked at Abhijeet.

"Take me to the Indian Army Post, I will explain everything to them and you can claim the reward," she said.

"And get you killed!" Abhijeet remarked with a smile.

"What do you mean?" She looked up with a jerk and asked.

"This has happened earlier. The newspaper item and fliers have been published by people who do not want you to live. This is their way to flush you out from your hideout. The moment you expose yourself and are in the army or police custody, you become vulnerable and easy targets to your enemies. Please let me know about your enemies, who are desperate to kill you?" He asked.

"It's a long story! Come sit down and hear," she said and narrated the events from her capture by Kiyanelie's men to her present situation. He and Binsa listened to her without interruption. When she had finished Binsa got up, hugged and patted her.

"You have been through a very difficult period. The danger has increased further," Abhijeet said.

"All I want is to immediately free my father, and this is possible only when I reach my people in my country," Hina said.

"We will take you to Moreh, from there you can go to any place by hiring a taxi. The drug trafficking charge has complicated the issue, we have to take extra precaution while crossing the border. I did some thinking after reading the article and have come up with a fairly good solution," Abhijeet said.

He dialed a number on his mobile phone and gave directions of his residence to the person he had called up.

"A taxi is arriving here in another 15 minutes, which will take Binsa and you to Moreh. You will travel as daughter and mother; Binsa will carry the papers and produce them at the two border gates and army check posts. You are traveling as her daughter and will have to change your hairstyle a bit to appear like her as in the picture in her passport," Abhijeet told them. Hina nodded and smiled with relief showing on her face.

"Please be ready to move at short notice and please let Binsa do all the talking with the officials. The three Km drive from Tamu crossing gate to Moreh will normally take fifteen minutes. Binsa will take you to my daughter's house where they are waiting for us," Abhijeet told her.

The taxi arrived within the stipulated time, Hina and Binsa boarded it and left the house, Abhijeet followed them in another taxi. Their journey to Moreh was smooth, they passed through the gates and check points without any hassles. A large population of Indians and Nepalis cross the border daily and for the authorities examining their documents was very routine; in most cases they allow them to cross over without checking them.

"It will take you three hours to reach Imphal from here. You can leave within the next half an hour and you will be in Imphal well before sundown," Abhijeet told them as they sat in the living room of his house in Moreh.

"I know someone who works in Imphal Hospital. He will get you admitted for treatment immediately. You need not worry about the payments now, it can be settled later. Chanitin and you should travel together to Imphal, that is safer," Abhijeet said.

"Abhijeet, thank you for your offer, but now I have to get to my father to free him from the insurgents immediately. I have seen his plight and my grief is inconsolable. I have to rescue him at all costs," Hina spoke to him in a soft tone.

"But your condition is not good enough. Get well and then do as you want," Abhijeet said.

"I am OK Abhijeet! I have been in worse conditions earlier. But how can I thank you and Binsa? Someday, when the conditions are better, God will give me an opportunity. Please do not refuse to accept the money to cover the expense towards my papers and the bus fare," she spoke emotionally, and handed Binsa the amount she had received from Chesa.

"Please do not embarrass us! We cannot accept it," Binsa said.

"Please keep it and give it to Chesa! It was she who had given the money to me," Hina said and left the money on the table.

After obtaining the details of her journey's route from Abhijeet, she boarded the night bus to Tuensang which also halted for a short period at Imphal. The bus was fully occupied with passengers and had an armed escort occupying the front seats. Hina sat in her window seat and wrapped a cotton sheet around her! She slid down and closed her legs to avoid touching her co-passenger, a lady sitting in the adjacent seat. She closed her eyes as the bus raced on the National Highway. The cool fresh air through the open window relaxed her mind and body prompting her to relax and sleep. Her last thoughts before shutting her eyes were to find the person responsible for the newspaper article, expose Kyanelie and free her father. She slept throughout the journey, unaware of the number of times the bus stopped and the cities it passed through.

"Madam, we are in Tuensang! Time to get down," she heard a voice call out to her close to her ears. She got up with a start and removed the sheet from her body, stepped sideways into the aisle, to get down from the bus.

It was fairly dark, only the bus terminal lights were on. She looked at the clock on the tower, which showed 6 pm. She moved towards the exit gate where the taxis had lined up and were waiting.

Getting into a taxi she spoke to the driver at length, struggling to recollect the route which she had used only twice recently. Finally, she asked the driver to start the car and drive. With his assistance, after half an hour of cruising in the car she found the street which looked familiar. She guided him along, made him stop the car at the end of the lane, got down and paid the fare from the money Binsa had given her for the journey.

She rang the bell, the door was opened by the old lady, who recognised her and stepped aside and allowed her to enter the room. Leaving her, she strode along the corridor and entered the room with the stuffed animals. Wrapping the free end of the sheet around her nose to block the stench, she lifted the trap door cover from the floor. Got down, closed the trap door from inside and walked down the steps in darkness. Spreading her hand along the wall, she found the switch and pressed it. The room lit up giving her an opportunity to locate the bed room. Before making herself comfortable on the bed, she switched off the lights and slept undisturbed throughout the night.

The noise from the trap door and the sound of feet coming down the stairs were sufficient to wake her up. Soon the room lit up and a man with his back towards her stepped towards the tables on which the communication equipment and computers were kept.

"Good morning Keshoho! How are you?" She said coming out from the bedroom.

□

21

After leaving Hina with her captors, Sano ran as fast as she could towards HPakang village. She felt helpless and exposed! Hina was more than a friend, she was a very loving and dear person who inspired her emotionally! She was a precious icon for her to emulate and follow. Her mind was in complete turmoil, and her heart was filled with agony and remorse!

Though it was fairly late in the night, she decided to go to Sitni, without meeting Thila and Rangamutil. She set forth on the three hours long journey alone on foot. For most of the journey she proceeded unhindered and covered the distance in good time. As she approached the border, she left the beaten track and entered the thick undergrowth pushing herself through the tall bushes.

She felt the swish of a bullet pass her ear followed by the cracking sound of a rifle fire. Zig zagging her steps, she ran through the bushes and headed towards the line of trees away from the shooter. The bullets kept on following her closely, missing her by a few inches. As she entered the tree line, the firing stopped and she could hear footsteps approaching. Keeping her nerve intact, with grit and determination she jumped up, and hung on to the branch of a tree above her. Heaving upwards, she clung on to the strong and thick bough, gradually crawled up and hid behind the bushel of leaves.

"Where the hell did the animal go? I am sure I hit it!" She heard a man mutter.

"Never mind, we will find it tomorrow, let us go back to our post," the other man replied.

She heard the footsteps fading away and heaved a sigh of relief; so far she was safe, what next? Getting down from the tree, she cupped her hand to her mouth and cried out loud, imitating the sound of an injured wild boar! Soon she heard footsteps approaching her at a quick pace. Keeping her head down, she ran retracing her steps towards the beaten track she had left and on reaching it kept running towards the border. The Post was deserted, she detoured slightly from it, and headed towards Indian Territory. The open space of no man's land provided her observation as far as she could see. Finding the area free of border patrol, she ran as fast as she could in the general direction of her destination.

Choosing to keep away from the village, she headed for the Army Camp where she was stopped at the gate by the sentry who refused to disturb Kashif at this early hour of the morning. Hearing the commotion caused by the loud conversation the guard commander got up and met them. Sano with moist eyes entreated him in a very persuasive voice and emphasised the urgent necessity for her to meet Kashif. The guard commander relented, asking her to wait near the gate and entered Kashif's tent and woke him.

"What are you doing so early in the morning? Where is Hina," Kashif asked Sano when she entered his tent escorted by the guard commander.

"Can I have a glass of water?" She asked.

Kashif looked at her tired face, drooping body and felt alarmed. Quickly he helped her to sit on the chair. He poured water from the flask into a glass and gave it to her.

"You seem to have had a terrible time! Take a rest in Hina's tent, we can discuss later in the day," he said.

"No, it is very urgent! I must tell you immediately! Hina has been kidnapped by Kiyanelies men! The agent has been killed by them!" she said with tears in her eyes.

"What? Hina kidnapped?" Kashif said, raising his voice in astonishment, "I cannot believe my ears!" He came and sat close to her looking into her eyes, hoping that she was mistaken.

"I saw it with my own eyes! It happened right in front of me, and I stood helpless!" She spoke in anger, clutching her fists.

"Tell me everything, from the beginning," he said, consoling her.

Clearing her throat and wiping her tears, she narrated the events of the night leading up to her encounter en route while crossing the international border.

"Oh my God! We have to do something immediately!" He said and got up. She too got up from her chair and stood next to him.

"Leave it to me now, you should go and rest and do not wake up unless you have slept enough. You can use Hina's sleeping suits, she would not mind," he said and escorted her to her tent.

His office was a makeshift arrangement in a tent where he had positioned the communications network. Although it was 3 am, he asked the NCO on duty to connect him to Col Atul Dutta on the UHF secure radio. He soon heard the ruffling of a blanket at the other end and a sleepy voice speak out.

"Yes, Kashif, what is it?" Atul asked.

"Sir Hina has been kidnapped by Kiyanelies men and the RAW agent killed," he told him. Atul remained silent for a while allowing the news to sink in.

"Is it confirmed news?" He asked.

"Yes Sir, the girl Sano who accompanied her saw it happen from a hidden location," he replied.

"Is she reliable?" Atul asked.

"Yes Sir, she accompanied Hina to the meeting place," Kashif replied.

"Fine, I will do the rest. Remain alert," Atul said.

"Sir, I want to take a section out there immediately to rescue her," Kashif proposed.

"Give me some time to get permission to cross the border. Keep your men ready," Atul told him.

"Sir, can I speak to the GOC?" Kashif requested. Atul paused for sometime and replied.

"Go ahead, but be careful, you will be violating the chain of command," Atul cautioned him.

"Thank you Sir! I am doing it without your knowledge. This conversation never took place," Kashif said.

"All the best and keep me informed," Atul said and hung up.

Having witnessed at close quarters, he was aware of the daily routine adhered to by Maj Gen Ranbir Singh GOC of the Division. He decided to wait for another two hours before calling him up. He utilised the interim period to issue orders to his second in command to pick ten men fully armed for action and have them ready to move out immediately. Told his sewadar to get his personal belongings ready for the journey.

At 6 am he called up the GOC on his direct line. He waited as he was aware that the GOC was presently enjoying his cup of herbal tea after his yoga regimen, prior to his bath.

"Sir Kashif here! Extremely sorry to trouble you so early in the morning," he said on hearing Ranbir's voice at the other end.

"Go ahead tell me, I am fully awake," Ranbir told him.

"Sir Hina Rathore has been kidnapped by the rebels," Kashif told him. After a long pause he heard Ranbir's voice.

"Tell me everything," Ranbir said, sighing audibly. Kashif divulged to him all that he had heard from Sano without leaving out any details.

"We were planning to send a force across the border to rescue Brijesh, but were asked to stand down by DG NSG, who is handling all matters relating to Kiyanelie. He is convinced that the rebel leader is not involved in the kidnapping. Now, in light of your briefing, I will have to go back to the Army Commander with this fresh information. In the meanwhile, have your men ready. I will also send our Para commandos," Ranbir said. Kashif felt relieved and thanked him.

For the next two days Kashif anxiously waited for the arrival of Para Commandos and orders for him to commence the operation, for which he had rehearsed the plan with his men. Sano provided him with the information of the terrain, the camp layout the approximate strength and location of the rebels.

"Let me go ahead. I can gather further information for you and give it when you meet me near the rebel camp," she said.

Kashif did not agree with her request as he felt that if she was captured it would comprise the operation.

It was after the third day of his conversation with the GOC that he received the much delayed call from him.

"Stand down Kashif! It appears that your source is confused. Kiyanelie has personally confirmed to DG NSG that he has no part in the kidnapping of Hina. Our IB and RAW are further verifying, let us hope they come up with something," Ranbir explained.

"Sir, I can assure you that the Naga girl is not lying. She has seen everything and is telling the truth," Kashif reiterated forcefully.

"She may or may not be lying. But the fact is that Kyanelie has offered to peacefully surrender with his men and this will happen very soon in Sitni village. Therefore, there is no reason to believe that he would kidnap Hina," Ranbir said.

The surrender news was new to him and unprecedented, he was taken aback totally unaware. He thanked the GOC and assured him that he would take no further action. Feeling dejected and downhearted he sought out Sano and gave her the news who was bewildered and dazed at the insinuations against her. It was getting dark, so they moved to sit in the office tent which was lit up by the lone bulb hanging from the roof.

"Kiyanelie is telling a blatant lie. It was his men who killed the agent and captured Hina! I saw it with my eyes!" She said in an agitated voice.

"I believe you, Sano. My hands are tied. I am totally impotent! I want to rescue her but now I just can't," he said, shaking his head.

"I can and I will! I am leaving for HPakang early tomorrow morning," she said emphatically.

"I do not think that would be necessary!" They heard a voice coming through the tent entrance.

A figure emerged and stood facing them in the bright light.

"Good evening Kashif! Good evening Sano!" Hina said with a wide smile on her face and sat down on the vacant chair!

□

22

"No, I have not mentioned it to Keshoho! You and Sano are the first to learn of my harrowing experience and the torture inflicted on my father by Kiyanelies men and the Chinese. Neither did I ring up my DG, for I have a feeling that he is involved," she told Kashif after disclosing the events that befell upon her subsequent to her capture by the rebels at their camp.

They had moved to Hina's tent and were having their meals served from the langar (cookhouse) by Kashif's sewadar. To Hina the hot chapatis, spicy mixed vegetables and the lacy daal were out of this world, she relished every bit!

"Do you want me to inform the GOC?" Kashif asked her.

"No! Tomorrow morning I am going to meet Keshoho and Ram in their safe house in Sitni. From there I will speak to my boss," she told him.

"I think that is a better idea. You should take a rest now. Sano will be with you sleeping in the next bed," Kashif said.

He left them after they finished their meal and within no time both retired to their respective beds. Hina, tired from her journey from Tuensang, slept the moment she hit the bed.

Admiring her from a distance, Sano silently watched Hina, with a longing to go over to her, caress her forehead and cheeks with her hands. She wanted to tell her that she was always there for her, whenever and wherever. She too, soon fell asleep dreaming she and Hina were walking holding hands and laughing in a crowded market!

In the morning Hina got up to find that Sano had finished her morning ablutions and was waiting for her.

"Good morning! I had a wonderful sleep, fatigue has left me, my wounds have healed more or less and my body is all spruced up and rested," Hina said.

"Good! I am coming with you to Sitni. My mother is there and I want to meet her," Sano smiled and said.

"Give me another ten minutes, let me freshen up, I will be with you soon," Hina said and entered the toilet.

She changed into a Naga dress and after a quick breakfast set off for the village with Sano keeping her company. The location of Ram's residence was indicated by Keshoho on the sketch she carried and they reached it with ease.

"Hello, welcome!" Keshoho greeted them as they entered the room and introduced Sano to Ram.

"What brings you here?" Ram asked her as she settled in her chair.

"A few issues that I wanted to discuss with the DG," she replied.

"I spoke with him only half an hour ago, and he inquired about you. I told him that you were in the Army camp at Sitni," Keshoho said.

"Did he say anything further about me?" Hina asked him

"Yes, he appeared to be very perturbed and asked me if you had intimated to me any recent happenings, to which I replied that you looked tired and fatigued but had not given any explanation for it. I could hear a sigh of relief coming out from him over the radio. He then said that your work was over, your leave cancelled and you were to leave immediately and join your unit in Delhi," Keshoho told her.

Hina thought for a moment deliberating whether she should risk speaking to Shashi and if she did speak to him, should she spill out everything or play safe and not tell him about her father's condition and location. Going with her intuition and listening to her sixth sense she decided that she had to tread very carefully. She sat next to Ram in front of the table with Keshoho and Sano occupying the chairs behind her.

"Please connect me to the DG. I will be back after I visit the toilet," Hina said and left them. Ram picked up the phone connected it to the secret communication satellite and whispered the coded password in the receiver. Soon he was connected to Shashi in his office in Delhi.

"Sir I am Ram from RAW, your officer Capt Hina Rathore is here and would like to speak to you. Please hold on Sir, she will be here any minute," he said waited until Hina returned and handed the phone receiver to her.

"Good morning Sir! Capt Hina Rathore speaking," she said.

"Hello, Hina! I hope Keshoho has conveyed my instructions to you. You are no longer required there. Return to your unit immediately." Shashi ordered her.

"Sir please hold a minute. I want to speak to you privately," she said and looked at Keshoho and Ram, who took the hint and left the room closing the door.

"Sir I was kidnapped by Kiyanelies men taken prisoner and moved to Bhamo near Chinese border, where they were torturing my father in an isolated house." Hina said raising her voice in frustration.

"Where is your father now?" Shashi inquired, breaking his silence after a lengthy pause.

"I have no idea Sir! I do not know what they have done to him," she replied immediately.

"How did you escape and cross the border?" He asked her.

"I shot the interrogators and crossed the border at Saramadi, hitchhiking along the Ledo road in a vehicle and on foot. Kiyanelies men followed me throughout but I kept ahead of them and reached Tuensang yesterday," she answered, making false statements as she did not want to mention those who had helped her to escape.

"Can anyone corroborate your story?" Shashi queried.

"No Sir, but I have a local newspaper which has my picture with a write up, that I am the keep of a drug trafficker and absconding from the Myanmar police. Rupees ten lac is the award, for the informant who helps to get me captured," she replied.

"Impossible! You are lying," Shashi scolded her.

"I am not lying Sir! I have the paper and I will read it out," she said and started ruffling the paper in front of the receiver.

"There is no need to do it. You have lied to me all along! Freedom Express does not send its paper to an obscure village called Saramandi!" Shashi said and suddenly he realised that he had committed a faux pas. He quickly spoke again and in an attempt to hide his mistake, he turned loud, emphasising every word in an authoritarian tone in a firm and decisive voice.

"Listen Hina, you are trying to be extra clever, but you cannot fool me! I have dealt with more cunning, ingenious and smart people than you! All along you have been lying to me! I do not understand the reason for your loathing Kiyanelie! The rebel leader is surrendering very peacefully to the PM three days from today and you are trying to obstruct this historic event with your silly unsubstantiated story! I order you to immediately return to your unit and if you disobey I will take strict disciplinary action," Shashi instructed her.

Hina remained silent, put the phone receiver aside, and kept looking at the newspaper masthead written in bold, 'Freedom Express'! She sighed and picked up the receiver.

"Yes Sir! I will leave this place and will join my unit in a few days," she said meekly. She understood the futility of further discussions with him as she was convinced of his complicity with Kiyaneli.

"I am glad that good sense has prevailed. Forget about Kiyanelie and the stories that you have twisted around him. I assure you that you will meet your father very soon. That is my firm commitment," Shashi told her in a confident voice.

"Thank you Sir!" she said and placed the receiver on the table. She looked at Sano and shrugged; she had not expected the unmitigated arrogance and the brazen falsehood from her boss. Sano got up, opened the door and asked the others to come in.

"Conversation over with Shinto," Ram spoke into the speaker and pressed the off button on the receiver.

The name 'Shinto' hit Hina hard as she suddenly remembered the last words of the dead agent Afzal Beg.

"Who is Shinto?" She asked him.

"Shinto is the code name of your DG Shashi Damodar Kulkarni," Ram said.

For a moment Hina felt a bayonet had gored her stomach, she felt dizzy but soon recovered. Her conviction on Shashi's complicity was finally confirmed now.

"Thank you Ram and Keshoho, you both have been very helpful. As per my Boss orders I will be leaving you all and heading for my unit. I may not meet you both again. Goodbye and good luck. It was my pleasure working with you," she said, shook hands with both and left them, with Sano following her.

"I have to meet Kashif immediately. You can go to your mother and see me later," Hina told Sano.

"I will come with you and meet my mother later," Sano replied.

Kashif, who was eagerly waiting for her, was shocked on hearing her conversation with her boss.

"Now I understand why he was against sending a patrol to rescue your father," Kashif said.

"It is apparent that the peaceful surrender by Kiyanelie is more important than the life of my father," Hina said.

"Why did he say that Freedom Express does not send its paper to obscure villages when you had not even mentioned the name of the paper in which your picture was published?" Kashif asked her.

"I am absolutely certain now that he and Kiyanelie are in it together and they are into some diabolical plan," Hina uttered.

"Let me talk to the GOC about it," Kashif said.

"It is futile speaking to anyone as long as Shashi is incharge! He will always reiterate that such unsubstantiated information is false and any action on it will thwart the peaceful surrender by the rebels. People in Delhi will support him. All I am interested now is to rescue my father without any delay," Hina said.

"Let me give it a try," Kashif said and dialed a number on his scrambler phone. He was soon connected with the GOC with whom he spoke at length intimating the entire details connected with Hina's travails upto Shashi's lies, false accusations and intransigence behavior.

"The GOC endorses your views on Shahi's posture and conduct. He has agreed to send a Para commando patrol to rescue your father. The commandos will be here within three days," Kashif said.

The news uplifted her spirits! After a long period of misery and anguish a ray of hope appeared!

"I will go with the patrol," she said.

"You must go with the patrol. However, we have a lot of planning to do before embarking on the mission. First and foremost we have to get the confirmation of the location of your father's confinement. I am certain by now they have shifted him to a more secure place. We can only get this information at this short notice by sending someone inside the camp. Someone who can mix around easily and is familiar with the men there," Kashif told her.

"Impossible to have detailed information so quickly. I have a fairly good idea where my father is held and I can lead the patrol there," Hina said.

"Sorry, that will not do! We do not want any encounter en route, especially with the Burmese, our mission to fail prematurely. The enemy too will reinforce the area once he learns that we are on a rescue mission. We have to send someone immediately inside the camp to get as much information as soon as possible, especially about your father. Let me see if I can find anyone from my local sources," Kashif said and picked up the phone to dial.

"I will go and I will get the information! I have worked there," Sano told them with confidence and conviction.

Both looked at her and then looked at one another, Hina nodded and Kashif kept the receiver down on the cradle.

□

23

"Where were you all these days? I was scared that Kiyanelies men had done something bad to you. They searched the village looking for a girl who they said was Indian but wearing Naga clothes," Thila informed Sano.

"Did they find her?" Sano asked with a straight face.

"No, I do not think so, but they burnt Rangmutil's house, when they did not find him there," Thila said. Taken aback and alarmed, Sano decided not to ask any further questions.

"Has Monalisa left?" Thila asked.

"Yes. I went with her and spent a few days but she insisted I return to help you, therefore, I left Sitni village," Sano replied.

"Spend the night with me here, tomorrow we will go to the camp," Thila smiled and said.

Sano kept awake for most of the night, her mind restive and disquiet, striving to cipher the dangers ahead and feasible ways to overcome them. Fear lingered in her heart but she decided to face it with determination and confidence.

When Thila woke her up early in the morning she got up feeling groggy and grouchy, having slept for only few hours. She took her time to freshen up, dress and have breakfast.

Later in the day when she reached the camp, she was surprised to notice the tents and temporary structures dismantled, stacked and ready for transportation. The young boys and girls known to her were busy helping the men in striking down the camp.

"What is happening?" Sano went up to Luikham and asked.

"I do not know, but it seems that the camp is likely to be

shifted to some other place. I will find out and let you know later," Luikham said and continued with his work.

Her inquisitiveness awakened, she was eager to pick up as much information as she could. She joined Thila who was busy adding yeast to the powdered rice and helped her to pour the ingredients in the container for fermenting at the right temperature. They worked throughout the day to fill the pitchers with wine to meet the evening's requirement. When Thila left, Sano remained in the camp and joined the girls in carrying the wine to the storage points.

"For most of the days you were missing, where have you been?" The supervisor Pelikutoli asked her, when she was pouring the wine from her pitcher into the storage container.

"I have this problem in my stomach which keeps on recurring at regular intervals," she said, pressing her tummy and bending a little.

"How are you now?" She asked Sano.

"A little better. The pain has reduced, but I need a rest after I work for an hour or so," she replied, with a painful expression.

"John is dead and you are no longer required in the office. You can do some light work with Thila throughout the day. But at seven o'clock every evening you carry two bottles of wine to the Communication Office. Can you do that?" She asked.

Sano looked at her, nodded her head slowly and left immediately. She felt elated and thanked God for giving her a wonderful opportunity to get close to Kiyanelie and his associates.

The next day Sano helped Thila throughout the day and later in the afternoon after finishing her work she met Luikham in a secluded spot.

"You are lucky that none of the girls informed the guards and the supervisor that you were helping the enemy," he said.

"Yes, I am very grateful to them and have thanked them personally. I am not helping the enemy but friends who will get you out of this place," Sano told him. Luikham looked at her in surprise.

"When will that be?" he said, showing his excitement.

"I do not know, but you should also be ready to help at short notice," She said.

"We will help in any way we can," Luikham replied.

"Keep your eyes and ears alert, see and listen to all conversations, especially when Sazo and Kiyanelie meet. I want you to tell me everything that you see and hear. Have you noticed any new, different and strange activity in the camp recently?" She asked him.

Luikham thought for a while and remembered the new task given to him to carry meals for a prisoner.

"Yes there is a prisoner kept in a room next to the armory. I take cooked food for him everyday," he said. The information excited and alerted Sano, she held him by the shoulders and shook him.

"Have you seen the prisoner?" She asked.

"Yes, only once very briefly, when the doctor took him out to examine him in daylight. But I was asked to hand over the food and leave immediately," Luikham told her.

Sano stopped questioning him about the patient further as she felt that for Luikham to identify the prisoner would be exacting and her questions may embarrass him.

"When is the doctor going to meet him next?" She asked him, changing the topic.

"The doctor sees the prisoner every second day. Yesterday I saw him returning from the room, so I presume tomorrow he may go there," Luikham said.

"Does he go alone or does someone accompany him?" She asked.

"You know Khaila, the short girl, the doctor takes her with him. She is good with massage and bandages," Luikham replied.

Sano knew Khaila, they were on friendly terms, she decided to contact her immediately. Thanking Luikham, whom she promised to meet again, she headed towards the women's dormitory.

As the sun set she took the two bottles of wine from the supervisor and proceeded towards the Communication Office tent. Finding no guards at the entrance she entered the tent and noticed two men busy working on the computer. She also observed the electronic equipment and telephone sets placed on the tables on the three sides of the tent. Hearing her footsteps both men turned around in their chairs.

"Put the bottles on the table. From the pitcher at the entrance get water in the two mugs and place them next to the bottles," a man said and got up. Sano followed his instructions.

"I am going to wash up and will be back within an hour," the man said and left the tent.

Sano turned to leave when she heard the other man call out to her.

"Stay, do not leave. Come here and sit down," the man said. Sano went over and sat in a chair next to him.

"What is your name?" He asked her.

"Sano," she replied.

"Which tribe?" He enquired.

"Chang," she replied.

"You were captured and brought from your village?" He looked at her and asked.

"Yes," she said.

She heard him sigh as he placed his hand on his forehead in frustration.

"My name is Zumo. I am from Rengma tribe and like you I too am a prisoner," he said lowering his voice.

She got up and placed her chair close to his and spoke in a whisper.

"What are you doing in this office?" She asked him.

"I am the IT person looking after their computers, passing messages through emails, arranging online chats, and so on," he replied.

"How can you do that? There are no telephone or internet facilities here," she asked.

"We communicate through the Chinese satellites. We have the most modern and very user friendly set up here," he said.

"How did you land up here?" She asked him showing her concern.

"Oh! That is a long story, I responded to an ad and was selected on the basis that I was a Naga and had a postgraduate degree in Computer Science from IIT Chennai! My first work place was in Shillong and after six months I was moved to Tuensang to work for THEM. I was kidnapped and brought here and forced to live this weird life," Zumo said and she noticed that his eyes had moistened.

"Do you want to escape from this place?" She whispered close to his ears.

"As much as you want!" He replied, looking at her more closely.

"I can help you. I am working with the people in the Indian secret service and they are investigating Kyanalie's motives and moves. If you help them you will soon be a free man," she said, coaxing him. He paused and looked up gazing at the tent roof.

"I will do it. There are many activities happening presently and more are going to take place in the next few days. You would have noticed them. But there are certain very dangerous and treacherous events that are planned and only those involved know about them," he said.

"What are these? She asked. She saw him looking towards a telephone receiver which was flashing a red light.

"Shinto and Kyanelie are talking with each other," he said.

"Shinto? Is that an Indian name?" She asked.

"It is a code name for a high police official in Delhi," he replied.

"OK. Tell me about the dangerous events that are now planned?" She asked. They heard voices outside the tent and looked at one another questioningly.

"Write down everything in detail not leaving out anything. I will collect the printout at the same time tomorrow," she said and walked towards the exit and left the tent.

Outside it was dark, orienting herself she headed for the brewery with soft steps avoiding the men chatting at some distance from the tent.

The next day she stood in front of the armory waiting for the doctor who on noticing her stopped and looked around.

"Where is Khaila?" He asked Sano.

"Sir I am Sano, Khaila has sent me, she is not feeling well, I think she has stomach flu," Sano said. The doctor looked at her with quizzical eyes.

"How can you make out that she has stomach flu?" The doctor inquired.

"Last night she vomited and visited the toilet many times. I checked this morning that she has a mild fever, pain in the stomach and her muscles are aching. She is feeling very tired and weary," Sano told him.

"Come with me, you seem to know quite a bit. Did you do any course or practice medicine?" He asked Sano.

"No Sir. I did some first aid training with Father Rebello, our village priest. He told me about common diseases and their symptoms." she said.

"Good now help me bandage this patient," the doctor told her as he examined the patient's feet.

Sano looked closely as the patient turned his face towards her. Recognition soon dawned on her. Through the thick beard outcrop, she saw the soft look in his eyes and a curved smile. He was Brijesh, Hina's father and her mother's friend! He too had recognised her. Shaking her head and finger she cautioned him to remain silent. He nodded and looked towards the doctor who was applying antiseptic over his buttocks.

"You do know your job! Come again the day after tomorrow. He can sit and walk now, though not comfortably. He will be normal soon," the doctor told her, looking at Brijesh. They came out of the room and after wishing him she left emotionally excited.

Sharp at 7 pm she was in the office tent with the wine bottles. She was surprised to find that Zumo was missing. She felt dismayed and betrayed and stood next to the table waiting after placing the bottles and mugs filled with water.

"You can go now," said the man, whom she had met yesterday.

She looked at him, hesitated and left the tent disheartened and in despair. She dragged her feet towards the dormitory, her journey seemed to her to be never ending. Her mission appeared slipping out of her reach. From behind a tree she heard her name called out in a soft voice.

She stopped in her tracks. The caller came out of concealment and beckoned her waving his hand. With strong and quick strides she reached him, stepped behind the tree and faced him.

"Here is the printout, it contains details of all the activities that KIyanelie is planning. We do not have much time. You must give this to your boss at the earliest," Zumo said, handing over the papers to Sano.

"Thank you I had given..."

"I must leave immediately! The man you met in the office is forever suspicious and I do not want to give him a chance to question me. Good bye and good luck!" He said and disappeared into the thick growth before she could respond.

Feeling cheerful and stimulated, she folded the papers and put it next to her breast under the shirt top and sped towards Thila's hut.

"I am leaving very early in the morning as I want to cross the border before the guards wake up," Sano told Thila.

"I hope all is well. The supervisor has been checking with me whenever you are absent. I suggest you do not take any chances now, she will take it on me if you are not here," Thila said.

"Everything will be fine. I will be back tomorrow evening. I want to see how well my mother is at Sitni," Sano said.

"It will be better if you go to your dormitory, show your face to the supervisor and sleep there," Thila told her.

She thought of pleading with her to let her sleep in her house but better sense prevailed. She thanked her and left for the camp. When she reached the dormitory, the Supervisor was on her rounds checking the presence of the inmates. As the supervisor's back was towards her, she quietly sidestepped behind her and lay down on her bed. Later on, during the round the supervisor found her fast asleep.

Early in the morning when her colleagues were still sleeping, Sano left the dormitory. Keeping herself away from the sentries, she left the camp and with springs in her strides raced towards Sitni. She ran for most of her journey passing through the thick undergrowth to avoid the border guards. Crossed the border carefully and headed for the Army camp. She met Hina who was in her tent sitting in her chair waiting for Kashif to call her.

"Welcome Sano!" Hina said with a smile and hugged her.

"Brijesh is held in a room next to the armory of the rebel camp!" She blurted out in excitement.

It took Hina a moment to understand her utterance and then some more time to sink in. She held Sano with her hands and squeezed her palm!

"Are you sure?" She said, holding back her tears.

"I met him and bandaged his feet," Sano replied.

"How is he? Can he walk, can he sit?" Hina asked.

"He can. The doctor said that he will become normal soon!" She replied.

"Oh my God! That is the best news I have heard after such a long time! What else have you gathered?" Hina asked.

Sano took out the paper from under her shirt top and handed it to Hina, who unfolded it and glanced over its contents.

"Have you read them?" Hina asked her in a somber voice.

"No I did not get the time," Sano replied.

Sano lay down and relaxed on the bed. Hina sat next to her to read the paper again. The change in Hina's facial expressions were not lost to Sano, which started with the frown on her forehead and ended in apathy and utter disgust in her countenance. After reading it, Hina slowly folded the paper and put it in her pocket.

"We need to have a meeting immediately!" She said and went out of the tent.

She saw Puran near Kashif's tent and called him. On her instructions Puran left promptly to call Kashif. Soon Kashif entered the tent, greeted them and settled down in the chair.

"I cannot sit for long, I have to leave for a meeting immediately. My second in command who is in charge of the troops positioned around the football ground called me on the radio and wanted me there. Please be quick," Kashif said, showing some impatience.

"Sano has obtained information from Zumo, the IT and communications manager working in the rebel leaders office. The information is contained in these papers. She has also confirmed that my father is lodged in the rebel's camp," she said holding the papers. He looked at Sano with admiration and smiled.

"I have read the papers and find the contents extremely disturbing and dangerous," Hina said, handing them to Kashif.

He read the papers twice, got up and in a disturbed mood and paced the small space within the tent.

"I am dumbfounded! I do not know what to say! If the contents of this paper are genuine hard facts then we are facing a disaster of a very high magnitude!" He said.

"We have to pass this on to the highest authorities immediately," Hina said.

"Too late to do that, the highest authority is already in the pit! The PM's chopper has landed a few minutes back, and he is on his way to the meeting," Kashif said, looking at his watch.

□

24

The preparations for the rescue mission were more or less complete, Hina had met and briefed Capt. Akhilesh Singh the team leader of the Para Commando patrol party, sent by the GOC. Their task was simplified considerably with the intelligence gathered by Sano from the rebel camp. The risk factor had reduced considerably as Brijesh was in the rebel camp and not near Myanmar, near the Chinese border.

They planned the raid on the day of the surrender ceremony, when the rebels were to lay down their weapons in front of the PM and 'That Day' happened to be today. It was likely that they would find the rebel camp deserted with only a few soldiers guarding Brijesh.

Hina looked at her watch, only fifteen minutes remained for the patrol to leave and cross the border. Her mind was in total turmoil and she felt lonely and vulnerable. She had witnessed her father in captivity where he was tortured mercilessly, his shrieks and wails kept reverberating in her ears even now. The death-like expression on his face haunted her every moment. She felt his pain, her eyes filled with tears recalling the horror. She felt her heartache for him, a childish yearning to be near him, hold him and caress him!

Her past flashed in her mind with various fond images of his concern, care and love for her. She was his darling and he was her idol, the superman she always loved and admired.

"We have to leave now, it is time for the patrol to move. Let us go and join them," Sano told her. Hina jerked her head and recovered from her reverie.

"Yes, let us go!" She sighed, and picking up her helmet she came out of the tent.

"Tell me Sano and be truthful! If you find yourself facing this dilemma that I am in today what would you do? The life of my father is in great danger and at that very instant I find that the honor and integrity of my country is at stake. Should I save my father or ignore him and put my might into saving the country's honor?" Hina asked her. Sano looked at her with pain in her eyes, troubled and pained with her predicament.

"I know what is going through your mind! You came to Nagaland in search of your father. You have been through hell ever since you landed! Keshoho told me everything, how you nearly lost your life not once but twice. No one has helped you so far on the other hand they have used you unmindful of your safety and protection. You have faced death in close encounters and your life was saved by those who cared for you and not by those who ordered you into actions of their choosing. You were captured and as a prisoner you found your father imprisoned in a terrible condition. You persevered against all odds and escaped from another country despite having suffered serious injuries. We are now on our way to rescue your father which we will!" Sano said and held Hina's hand.

"Concurrently, you face another very critical issue! From the information I gave you we learn that there is a diabolical plan of grave consequences to dishonor the dignity of your country. You are on the spot and in a position to act in thwarting the enemy's horrific design to harm the country. You have sworn to defend the honor and integrity of your country from any threat, even if you have to lay down your life in doing so. Your dilemma is to make the right choice!" Sano stated and shook her head. Hina sighed audibly and kept walking.

"Yes the choice before me is either to acquit myself as a loyal and faithful daughter or accomplish my duty as a soldier. I know under the present circumstances I cannot do both at the same time. But you have not answered my question Sano?" She asked.

"I lost my father at a young age, therefore I do not know what fatherly love is. But I know, for you Brijesh is everything in your life! So my sweet sister let us go and get him and forget about the rest!" Sano said, putting her hand on her shoulder.

"You just said that I am a soldier and I have to protect my countrymen whose honor is endangered and at stake. Should I not go to protect it?" Hina asked her.

"There are special commandos and the entire army to carry out this task! One Hina will not make much of a difference!" Sano replied.

They had reached the area where the Para Commandos were waiting. Hina met Akhilesh, who asked his men to get ready to move.

"Can I ask you a rather inane hypothetical question, Akhilesh?" Hina spoke as he was tightening his shoe laces.

"Go ahead, shoot!" He replied.

"Imagine if at any instant in your line of duty you find that someone whom you love more than your life is in grave danger and has to be rescued by you, and concurrently you also become aware that the honor and esteem of the country is also in danger and you can help to save it. What would you do?" She asked Akhilesh.

"Hina, the answer is simple. You have to go to save the one you love so much! The country has the entire force for its protection! You have no other choice but to save the dear one whom you love more than your life!" Akhilesh replied condescendingly and gave orders to his men to line up and commence walking. Hina and Sano followed and kept pace with him.

They traversed the thick undergrowth for fifteen minutes when Hina asked Akhilesh to stop and went over to him.

"I have to leave you now. I will join you later," she said.

"Why? What happened? "Akhilesh asked her, astonished.

"I have some unfinished business to settle!" She replied in a firm determined voice. Akhilesh looked at her, shook his head and refrained from asking further questions.

"Sano will guide you to the place," she said.

"Fine with me, no issues! Take care and all the best!" Akhilesh told her and shook her hand.

Wish you all the same, Hina said silently and left them, after hugging Sano.

□

25

On the advice of his NSA the Prime Minister had instructed his Home Minister (HM) to attend the Nagas surrender meeting. Ankush Patil the HM accompanied with Libba Kassasu, his Minister of Home, arrived at Sitni helipad in the helicopter dot at 10 am. They were received by the Chief Minister of Nagaland and a host of other dignitaries. The Engineer Regiment had worked for the past three days on the road from Tuensang to Sitni and had made it easy for the vehicles to move right up to the village. All the officials and other VIPs used it to attend the ceremony.

The Jongas steel body including the glass windows and the tyres were bulletproof. The HM sat in the seat next to the driver, the rear seats were occupied by two soldiers from the NSG. Outriders on motorcycles and the protection vehicle formed the cavalcade which moved slowly, allowing the HM to look through the window's glass and wave to the crowd lined up on either side, all along the road up to the football ground, where the sitting arrangements were made for them to watch the ceremony. The crowd cheered loudly and waved holding miniature national flags.

The HM was received by the Team Commander, Mohit Verma from NSG and was escorted to the dais. He waved at the crowd in front of him and sat in his designated chair with Kassasu occupying one behind him. The CM and other dignitaries were accommodated in the VIP enclosure, well away from them.

Soon a steady stream of Nagas commenced to arrive. The first group consisted of boys and girls led by Pelikutoli. They were guided to sit in front and close to the dais. The next to arrive were the armed Naga rebels who marched in disciplined lines and sat at some distance behind the first group. Soon Kiyanelie the rebel leader followed without much fanfare. A hush fell among the audience as he stepped on the podium and shook hands with the HM. Barring his bodyguard no other person accompanied him.

"Good morning Mr Kiyanelie, very nice to meet you on this fine sunny day!" Ankush said, extending his hand. Kiyanelie smiled held the HMs hand with a firm grip and shook it several times.

"Good morning! But where is Mr Prime Minister?" Kiyanelie said, looking around.

Kassassu came forward to shake his hands.

"Welcome my brother Kassasu, but where is the PM?" He raised his voice with anxiety showing on his face.

"I am sorry, the Prime Minister at the last moment asked me to attend. He is indisposed, and advised bed rest for the next three days by his doctors," the HM said.

"Why was I not informed? We could have held the meeting after he recovers," Kiyanelie retorted.

"As I said, it was at the very last moment the doctors advised him to avoid the journey due to his critical condition. I am here, let us get going with the ceremony," the HM appealed to him.

Kiyanelie stood on the dais in an agonised and desperate mood. He looked ahead towards his men who were seated at some distance, and noticed the person he wanted to see. He raised one hand and waved, beckoning him. Sazo got up from his chair and moved towards the dais. Kiyanelie stepped down and met him midway. They conversed for a few minutes and returned to their locations.

"OK! Let us start the proceedings!" Kiyanelie said on returning to the podium and sat down.

"Sir, the papers you agreed for signing the accord are ready," Kassasu said, removing the folders from his bag and placing them on the table.

"Kassasu, with due respect when the cameramen capture me signing the agreement with HM, I would appreciate that your security men are kept away from the dais. Their presence may indicate that I am a captive, and forced to put my signature under duress and threat. This will not go down well with my followers!" Kiyanelie said, and looked at Ankush, who turned and whispered to Mohit standing behind him.

"Sir, with due respect, I suggest we decline the request," Major Mohit Verma the NSG commando leader whispered back in HMs ears.

"I can understand your anxiety Commander! As per standard operating procedure, you are to provide physical protection by never leaving your HM unguarded. You can see that I have no security men with me. The man here is my lackey who is always with me and he is unarmed. All my men are sitting over there in front, ready to surrender and my close advisors are sitting with the rest in the visitors enclosure. There is no threat from anyone or anywhere," Kiyanelie smiled and addressed Mohit.

Ankush got up, took Mohit aside and spoke to him in whispers, asking him to leave the dais with his men. On Mohit's reluctance to leave him, Ankush sat down and looked at Kassasu, who got up and approached Mohit.

"Major, we are aware of your anxiety and appreciate your concern. You will be only a few yards away from the HM. Please listen to him and leave with your men," Kassasu pleaded.

Mohit on hearing his name being called, turned around and looked back and noticed Kashif, who had just arrived and was fervently gesturing with his hands wanting him to meet him immediately. He raised his hand and nodded. He and his men left the dais and Kiyanelies bodyguard followed them. Only the HM, Kassasu and Kiyanelie remained seated on the dais.

"Can we commence the ceremony now?" Ankush asked Kiyanelie.

"Before we start signing, can we both say a few words to the assembled congregation? With your permission may I start?" Kiyanelie asked Ankush.

"By all means please go ahead with your speech," he replied.

Kiyanelie got up, ignored the mike, looked ahead, raised both hands and waved.

His action, which appeared to be a planned signal, generated a chain reaction from the boys and girls sitting close to the podium.

With alacrity and swiftness they left their seats and headed towards dais.

Mohit who had walked a few steps away from the podium was caught unawares and exhorted them to sit down. He was promptly interrupted by the sound of a bullet fired in the air.

"Follow me!" Shouted Pelikutoli, the supervisor, running with them towards Kiyanelie.

The horde of boys and girls occupied the dais and formed a human shield in front and around those present. The HM, stunned by the turn of events, remained seated waiting for Kiyanelie to disperse the mob.

"Mr Home Minister you will now please do as I ask you! In case you refuse, I have no other option but to shoot you dead!" Kiyaneli said, removing a pistol from under his shirt and pointing it at Ankush, who was caught unawares, looked shocked and turned speechless.

"Oh my God! This is treachery!" He shouted out.

"Now get up and follow that girl," Kiyaneli said, pointing towards Pelikutoli.

Ankush got up and stepped behind the girl who started walking in the opposite direction towards the car park. Kassasu, stunned by the turn of events, stood up and stepped forward to stop Kiyaneli.

"Come on Kiyanelie, this is unacceptable! We are brothers, we both belong to Nagaland, you cannot do this!" He cried out.

"You are not my brother! Stay away, do not block me!" Kiyanelie shouted at him angrily.

"Listen Kiuanelie this is not proper. We both are Nagas, our tribes may be different but we have the same culture, social norms and identical heritage. After ages we now have the opportunity to unite as a community and as a race. Become our own masters through a democratic process, serve our people and make their life better. Join us in this great dream and make it happen! Be part of this new and vibrant era and let the past be forgotten as a dreadful nightmare!" He pleaded with folded hands. Kiyanelie kept moving and brushed him aside with his hand.

"The Bible tells us to, 'get rid of all bitterness, rage, anger, brawling and slander, along with every form of malice. Be kind and compassionate to one another, forgiving each other, just as Christ God forgave!' I know you are a good Christian!" Kassasu kept pleading and following Kiyanelie.

"I have heard your political crap earlier too! You want to remain a servant and grovel, so be it! Not me, I am leaving with your HM! The meeting is over," Kiyanelie said, turned around and shot Kassasu in his stomach.

The muffled sound from the pistol with the silencer was heard by Ankush, who stopped and looked back.

"What have you done! You have killed an innocent person who belongs to your own blood!" Ankush shouted at him.

"Shut up and move! He will survive if he gets proper medical attention in time!" Kiyanelie said and pressed on pointing his pistol at Ankush's spine.

Mohit as a helpless observer witnessed the flurry of activities from some distance. He could not see the HM as he was hidden, surrounded by boys and girls. Realising that there was something amiss and out of place he ran towards the dais with his men following him. They attempted to push through the horde but were met with stiff and fierce resistance from the bunch.

For a moment, he considered ordering his men to fire at the human shield in front of him. However, better sense prevailed, he stepped near the dais and fired a few rapid rounds in the air. The crowd bewildered, panicky, ran helter skelter and left the podium in a hurry. He stepped forward pushed away those near him and noticed Kassasu lying on the floor groaning with pain, with blood trickling out from his stomach. He called out to his men to carry him to the ambulance for immediate medical attention.

"Where is the HM?" He asked Kassasu as his men lifted him.

"Kiyaneli has kidnapped him at gunpoint," Kassasu replied pointing towards the car park enclosure. The men carried him away on their shoulders.

Mohit looked around and observed activities around the cars parked at some distance. As he moved forward he was pounced upon by two Nagas who tried to snatch his weapon. He raised his rifle and hit the nearer Naga on the head, who collapsed and lay down on the carpet. The second Naga held him from behind in a tight grip and hit his legs with his boot. Mohit sank down, bent his body and rolled over. The Naga flew over him and landed on his head. Mohit got up quickly and kept on hitting him until he fainted.

He ran towards the car park and took cover behind a parked truck. He saw the Naga girl, some distance ahead, pushing the HM with her rifle towards a Land Rover. As he raised his weapon to aim he noticed another girl in his view, diametrically opposite, hiding behind HMs Jonga which was parked at some distance in line and behind the Land Rover. She too was pointing her rifle at the persons moving towards the Land Rover. He was about to fire at Pelikutoli but paused when he noticed the girl behind the Jonga lift her face and look at him. She looked very familiar, and when she waved at him, his heart missed a beat.

"Oh my God! it is you Hina!" He cried out.

"Yes Sir! Back to our fun days! let us show these bastards!" Hina shouted and fired, missing Kiyanelie by inches.

"Keep firing, I am going ahead," Mohit called out.

He skirted a stone wall and approached the Land Rover which now was a few yards in front of him.

"Hold it! Do not move!" He shouted.

Pelikutoli, who had opened the vehicle's rear door stood still, her rifle hanging from her shoulder. Ankush retrieved his step from the Land Rover and blocked Kiyanelie, who with the pistol in his hand stood behind the HM, shielding himself from Mohit.

"Kiyanelie, leave the HM alone, let him go. You are a dead duck, look behind you," Hina called out from her location.

Kiyanelie, bent down, pushed Ankush inside the vehicle, shut the door with force and shouted at the driver to leave immediately. Finding Mohit distracted, he ran and took cover under another vehicle in the vicinity. Pelikutoli slung her rifle, fired at Hina and missed hitting her.

Hina on finding Ankush hauled away in the Land Rover, grabbed the Jonga keys from its driver, entered the bulletproof vehicle and pursued the fleeing car.

Mohit fired at the fuel tank of the vehicle behind which Kiyanelie was hiding and was firing at him. His bullet hit the tank and soon the vehicle was engulfed in flames. As he stood up to aim at Kiyanelie, who was visible now, he felt the bullet fired by Pelikutoli hit him in the chest. Before he could return the fire, he fell on the ground and blacked out momentarily.

The sound of approaching steps woke him and he thanked the Almighty and the bullet proof vest for saving his life. Looking up, he saw a figure looming over him with the rifle pointing at his head. As she paused to reload the magazine, in one action he grabbed the pistol from his ankle holster and fired at Pelikutoli, who fell over him; the bullet had pierced her head between her eyes. He pushed her aside, got up and approached the burning vehicle. He looked for Kiyanelie, who was nowhere in sight. He waved at the Jonga driver, who was watching them from a distance.

"Did you see Kiyanelie?" He asked him when he came over.

"I saw him running towards the football ground," he said pointing out with his finger.

□

26

Kashif was in two minds, whether to join Mohit, or to ensure that the surrendering rebels do not react and cause problems. From his position he had noticed that Mohit and men were dispersing the children who had formed a human shield at the podium. He left them and came towards the line of his troops who were lying in firing position on the ground pointing their rifle towards the Naga rebels, who had also taken up positions and were ready to use their weapons. It was an eye to eye confrontation between his troops and the rebels ready to explode any moment!

The drama enacted on the dais had alarmed everyone and the sound of rifle fire had further aggravated the situation.

He took the megaphone from his second in command and addressed the gathering which had thinned out considerably; barring the Naga rebels most other civilians had left. Looking around he spoke in a deliberate and clear voice.

"There was a small incident. Nobody is hurt and none of you should worry about it. Your leader Kiyanelie is safe and is with our HM. Some miscreants tried to disturb the ceremony but they were unsuccessful and have been arrested. Our HM and your leader have signed the surrender agreement and now the weapons are required to be handed over by you all to our soldiers. So please stand up, get in straight lines and lay down your weapons on the ground," he instructed the rebels.

After a slight pause, he heard loud murmuring in the rank and file of the rebels. They did not get up but remained lying in the same position.

"Please keep quiet. Can the Commander come over here and explain the reason for disobeying my instructions?" Kashif told them.

A fully armed Naga holding his rifle in his hands walked towards him and stopped.

"Thank you for coming. What is your name?" Kashif asked him, putting down the megaphone.

"Loheleniyu," he said.

"Why are you and your men not surrendering their weapon?" Kashif asked him.

"Our leader gave us no instructions to surrender our weapons!" Loheleniyu said.

"Why are you here then?" Kashif asked.

"To protect our leader from your army," Loheleniyu replied.

"How many of you are here now?" Kashif asked.

"Two hundred and fifty men and fifty women and children," he replied.

"What about the rest! Why did they not come?" Kashif queried.

"The rest of our men and women are in various camps in Myanmar. My boss told me that your army can not harm him or any of us as we are going to kidnap your PM. But now it appears that everything has changed. You say that our leader has signed the peace agreement, can I meet him?" Loheleniyu requested.

Kashif was aware of the kidnapping ever since he had read the letter given to him by Hina. Zumo had provided very accurate information, which was of little use now.

"I will send a soldier to call your leader, but before that you will have to lay down your arms," he said.

"That is not possible! We will surrender our weapons only when our leader tells us," Loheleniyu replied.

Kashif felt the issue was leading to a stalemate, which could eventually become dangerous. He had to take a decisive step immediately.

"I am afraid that you leave me with no other options. Now listen carefully to what I will speak loudly and clearly and will not repeat myself!" Kashif said and picked up the megaphone.

"Your commander Loheleniyu has said that you have no instructions from Kiyanelie to surrender your weapons, and will only do so if he comes here and orders you to do so. Let me tell you that the situation has changed completely! From now on you will obey my orders! If you refuse to do so, you will have to pay with your lives! I am serious, and I am here to ensure that you will not leave this place without surrendering your weapons!" Kashif said and paused to feel the effect on the rebels who were now showing signs of restlessness.

"You are surrounded on all sides by our soldiers! You are 250 strong and have to face a strength of over 2000 men from my Battalion and the Assam rifles. You are in a bowl in a depression as sitting ducks to our marksmen, who are positioned on the high ground. Look around you, in front and rear, and to your right and left, you will notice machine guns, rocket launchers, and two inch mortars all aimed at you! Once the firing starts you have no route to escape and will find no one to kill to go out from here! Our sharpshooters will make mincemeat out of you fit only for dogs and vultures!" Kashif said and looked towards Loheleniyu.

"Are you going to surrender or not?" Kashif asked and handed over the megaphone to him. He took it, held it reluctantly, and looked around at the soldiers surrounding him on the high grounds.

"Friends, we have no other choice! Spread out in single files, put down all your weapons in front of you on the ground, and stand still!" Loheleniyu said to his men and laying down his rifle he handed over the megaphone to Kashif.

"Capt Avinash, please take your platoon to organise the surrendered men into parties of 20 and march them off to our camp. The weapons will be collected by Capt Mathur and his platoon and taken in the trucks. These will be deposited in our Battalion armory at Tuensang," Kashif ordered through the megaphone.

He picked up the weapon surrendered by the rebel's Commander, shook hands with him and asked him to join his men.

Mohit, who had arrived looking for Kiyanelie, witnessed the surrender spectacle from the edge of the playground. He searched around and noticed Kiyaneli and his bodyguard at the vacant VIP enclosure. As he ran towards them, he observed the bodyguard pick up his rifle to aim it at Kashif. He shouted out loud which distracted the shooter. The bullet from his rifle missed Kashif who dived on the ground upon hearing the shout. Before the bodyguard could fire again, Mohit shot and killed him. He pointed his pistol towards Kiyanelie and asked him to raise his hands.

"Oh! You are still alive! What a pity! You guys wear bullet proof jackets, she should have shot you in the head!" Kiyaneli said and laughed. Kashif who had joined them searched him and relieved him of the pistol hidden under his belt.

"So what are you going to do to me?" I came here to arouse my men to keep me safe and sound, sadly they have surrendered. You have taken my weapon, I too am surrendering!" Kiyanelie said and bowed down mockingly.

"Not so fast you bastard! Where is the HM?" Mohit asked.

"I do not know? And Major your language please! It hurts my ears!" Kiyanelie said and laughed.

"Let us take him to the camp and make him talk," Kashif said.

"That will not work! You see those cameramen and journalists sitting behind the trees and watching us? They will roast you if anything happens to me, and you do not find your HM!" Kiyaneli smiled and said.

"We will see to that, Let us go," Mohit said and prodded Kiyanelie with his rifle.

Kiyanelie with hands tied, surrounded by ten armed men arrived at the camp on foot and was taken to a tent where his legs too were tied with a rope. He sat on the chair with a smile on his face unmindful of the soldiers guarding him.

"Enough is enough! Let us cut out the bullshit! Where is HM?" Mohit questioned Kiyanelie, who smiled and kept quiet.

"It is fine with me if you do not answer now. You will soon face professional interrogators who will get the answer by torturing you! The choice is entirely yours," Mohit told him.

"Listen very carefully Major and tell it to your countrymen. If anything happens to me and if I am not allowed to go by tomorrow morning your country will have to appoint a new HM!" Kiyanelie said and smirked.

Mohit left the tent to meet Kashif in his office. He found him seriously listening on the phone and waited for him to hang up. After finishing the call Kashif looked up, raised his hands in a prayer and sat down.

"Hell has broken loose! The entire machinery in the country has been activated. High officials from most of the departments are on their way to meet us. Ugh! Everything looks so topsy turvy! We are saddled with a hell of a problem!" He groaned.

"Yes, we are looking like fools now! Only if the HM had listened to me! These politicians! God help us from them! We have no other option now but to wait for the professional interrogators to arrive," Mohit said and sighed.

"Did you notice where they have taken the HM?" Kashif inquired.

"No! I did not get a chance! The girl shot me and I fell down. Hina was there, I think she is pursuing the vehicle in which HM was pushed in by Kiyanelie," Mohit replied.

"Hina! Oh my God! She was supposed to go with the commando team to rescue her father, not to save the HM! May God save her!" Kashif cried out in desperation.

The earliest they estimated that the interrogators would arrive would be late next evening or early in the following morning. Every minute counted, especially when they had no clue of HMs whereabouts. Instructions were out to seal the border in the area and search the surrounding areas. So far there was no trace of the vehicle or its occupants. It was now left for the higher ups to speak to the Myanmar Government as in all probability the kidnappers had crossed the border.

By late afternoon, Brig Ravi Sharma Brigade (Bde Cdr) and Col Atul Dutta the Battalion commanders (Bn Cdr) arrived and huddled in discussion with Mohit and Kashif. After a while a soldier entered their tent and spoke to Kashif, who came out and greeted Longaya and Akai the chiefs of Yunsai and Sitni villages respectively. He took them inside the tent and introduced them to the two Commanders and Mohit.

"What brings you here?" Ravi asked them.

"We want Kiyenelie as our prisoner?" Akai said.

"That is not possible! Our HM has been kidnapped by his men! We want him to tell his men to free him or tell us his location so that we can rescue him," Ravi replied.

"Has he said anything so far?" Longaya asked.

"No, But he will tell it to our interrogators who will arrive soon," Ravi said.

"He will not tell anyone! You can torture him as much as you can! He is a Naga, he will prefer to die rather than betray his people!" Longaya advised them.

"So what do you suggest? How do we make him talk?" Ravi queried.

"Has he put forth any conditions for giving information?" Akai asked. Ravi looked towards Kashif and Mohit who shook their heads.

"No, not so far," Mohit said.

"He will! He will demand complete independence of Nagaland from India for the release of your HM!" Longaya said.

"If we do not agree?" Mohit asked.

"Your HM will be killed by Kiyanelies men. You will blame him and hold a long drawn out trial before you finally hang him. The media will play up and the entire world will come to know. He will become a martyr, not only for the people of Nagaland but also, a shining example for those inimical to you," Longaya said.

"I repeat so what do you suggest?" Ravi asked him.

"Give him to us and before midnight you will get the location of your HM," Akai said. The Bde Cdr sighed, and looked at the three present.

"Please wait in the other tent. We will call you as soon as we are ready with the answer," the Bde Cdr told them.

A soldier escorted the chiefs and took them to the adjacent tent. After waiting for a few minutes they were told to return.

"Fine, you can have him. Our interrogators are unlikely to arrive before tomorrow evening, until then he is useless to us. However, a platoon strength escort party will go with the prisoner and will remain with him," Ravi said. Both the Chiefs looked at each other and smiled.

"Thank you for handing over the prisoner," Akai said.

"You have to get the information from him before daybreak. He has told us that, if he is harmed or not released by tomorrow morning, his men will kill the HM," Ravi emphasised.

"Your HM will be found. We will get the location and rescue him," Longaya assured him.

Ravi looked at Kashif who left the tent and soon returned with Kiyanelie, escorted by soldiers. The moment he saw the chief's, Kiyanelie became angry and showed his annoyance.

"What are they doing here?" he shouted out loud.

"You are going with them. You are their prisoner now. They are free to do whatever they want with you," the Bde Cdr told him.

Kiyanelie looked shocked and agonised, sweat drops appearing on his forehead. He found it difficult to speak.

"I will not go with them!" he said in a loud voice after some time.

"You have a choice. Either you tell us where our HM is or they take you with them. Make up your mind quickly, we have very little time," the Bde Cdr said.

"I do not know where exactly he is presently. My guess is that he has crossed the border. You will have to speak with the Myanmar Government to allow you to rescue him," Kiyanelie said.

"Can you communicate on the mobile phone with your men who are with HM?" Kashif said handing his cellphone to Kiyaneli, who took it, dialed a number and put the speaker on.

"The person you are dialing is out of range," they all heard the message.

Ravi instructed the soldiers to take Kiyanelie out of the tent and to wait until further instructions. They discussed the information given by Kiyanelie and soon having reached unanimity asked the men to bring Kiyanelie back in the tent.

"Thank you for the information! Until the HM is not with us you will remain as a prisoner with Chiefs! Your fate will be decided by them, only after the HM joins us alive and safe," the Bde Cdr told Kiyanelie.

Crestfallen and downcast Kiyanelie collapsed and sat on the ground. Two soldiers lifted him and dragged him out of the tent.

□

27

"We will wait for five minutes for Shashi to turn up. He is not picking up the phone. I rang him several times," Suresh, the NSA, told the men assembled in his office for a meeting requested by Bhupinder.

"He will not come nor will he respond to any phone call!" Bhupinder remarked. Suresh looked at him with surprise.

"Why?" He asked him.

"He is with his family at the airport. They all are leaving the country," Bhupinder said.

"What! How do you know that, sitting here?" Suresh inquired.

"My men are with him now at the airport and closely watching him and his family. They are in touch with me on my mobile phone," Unni replied.

"What? How did you come into this Unni?" Suresh asked, showing his frustration. Bhupinder looked at him and intervened.

"Let me explain. We have been recording all conversations that Shashi had with his officer Hina who is Brijesh's daughter. She took leave to search for her missing father. She got involved in all this due to Shashi. I requested this meeting precisely to apprise you of the situation that Shashi has put us in. Unni has heard this audio CD and since then he has put his men to keep track of Shashi's movements. I am going to play the recording now," Bhupinder said and activated his laptop.

Suresh heard the conversations in silence and with deep consternation.

"Oh my God! This is terrible! Poor girl, she has suffered a lot!" Suresh cried out.

"Should we arrest Shashi Sir?" Unni asked.

"I will have to get the Home Minister's permission but unfortunately he is not here nor is the Minister of Home. They are in Nagaland," Suresh said.

"Let us get the PM's permission. If we wait any further it may be too late. He is going to board the plane in a few minutes," Bhupinder cautioned him, looking at Unni.

"Let me speak to the Home Secretary," Suresh said and moved towards the phone lying on the table.

Before he could reach it, he heard the phone ring and picked up the receiver. He listened to the caller, his heart racing away at a gallop. He sat down on the chair, put the receiver on the cradle, picked up the glass and sipped water from it.

"Gentlemen, we have failed miserably! The HM has been kidnapped," he said exhibiting immense distress, he looked at the two sitting in front of him. Bhupinder sighed and looked at Unni.

"We are aware of it. Our agent informed us ten minutes back and we have asked them to verify it further. We needed your permission to arrest Shashi immediately. He is possibly involved with the kidnapping. We want to use him to trace the HM and the kidnappers," Bhupinder contended.

"Let us move up to my office from where you can make your calls on your mobiles," Suresh said and moved towards the door.

On entering the office on the ground floor, Unni called up his agent on his mobile phone.

"Sir they are seated in the aircraft which will take off in a few minutes!" Unni said.

"Bhupinder, you ring up the Air Traffic Control Tower and tell them to delay the flight. Tell them you are speaking on behalf of the PM and it is an emergency!" Suresh said.

He called up his secretary and told him to get the airport security officer on the phone.

"Unni tell your boys to enter the aircraft and speak to the pilots. They should not let the aircraft to take off," Suresh told him after speaking to the airport security officer.

They waited holding their breath counting every minute. Suresh found his phone light flashing and picked it up immediately.

"Shashi is in our custody! Get our best operatives to work on him!" Suresh said, putting the receiver down. Both Unni and Bhupinder picked up their mobiles and got busy.

"Thank heavens the PM agreed to miss the surrender meeting! I need you both to remain 24 hours with me! This will be our operations room from now on until we find our HM!" Suresh told them.

□

28

Hina was surprised at the fairly wide level surfaced road passing through the thick undergrowth on which the Land Rover ahead was speeding well over 90 mph. She considered herself fortunate that she was pursuing the kidnappers in a Jonga, which could match the Land Rover in speed and robustness. She kept pace with the vehicle and was gradually catching up with it. The twists and turns did unsettle her initially, though gradually with alert anticipation and maneuvering she managed to hold the vehicle on the road.

She glanced at the map encased under a plastic cover lying next to her on the seat. The thick red lines indicated the International Border, which now was very close to her. She understood the reason for the absence of Indian Army presence in the area; the road on which she was travelling was not marked on the map and there was no habitation anywhere in sight. The entire area along the border was covered with dense forest on either side providing minimal access to men and vehicles.

As her vehicle crossed the border, the road became more bumpy due to the ditches and the protruding rocks. Looking ahead she observed a road crossing, and on approaching it she noticed a vehicle coming from the left towards her. She accelerated her vehicle and missed colliding with the speeding truck by a fraction of a second. The vehicle was loaded with fully armed men and after missing her vehicle it halted abruptly with a loud screech. The driver reversed the truck, brought it back on the main road and followed her Jonga.

In her rear view mirror she saw the men in the vehicle fire at her. Most of the bullets missed her, the few that hit it bounced off ineffectively. She pressed the accelerator pedal and increased the gap between her and the truck, while narrowing the distance with the Land Rover. When she looked again in the rear view mirror, her hair stood up and goose pimples covered her body! She noticed a rocket launcher held by a man on the truck, and he was aiming it at her vehicle. She zig zagged her jonga continuously in a bid to avoid the rocket and kept praying to her Deity. The rocket missed the vehicle by a few inches and hit the tree trunk on the right side of the road.

As she came near the end of the line of trees she noticed a bend in the road. Reducing the speed of the Jonga, she swung the steering to her right, drove it into the bushes and switched off the engine. She heard the pursuing truck head away on the road. Leaving the Jonga she stalked through the bushes until she reached the edge of the tree line. Ahead in the open field she saw the truck stop next to the Land Rover, where four persons stood near it. A man got down from the driver's cabin and met a person who appeared to be Sazo. Keeping herself within the bushes, she crept further until she was only a few yards from the Land Rover.

The man climbed back into the truck, which turned and sped in the direction it had come. She was about to leave her position to get further closer to the Land Rover, when she heard a faint noise probably of rotor blades of a helicopter. Soon the area ahead was engulfed by smoke from a cartridge fired as a signal for the chopper to land. Hina crept on her elbows and hid behind the vehicle. The smoke cleared and she saw the chopper hovering before it landed.

She noticed the HM walking towards the chopper with a person prodding him on his back with his rifle. Staying behind the Land Rover, she aimed her rifle and the bullet hit the man nearest to her, who fell instantly. Quickly, she aimed and killed the other two men who were attempting to fire at her. She saw the fourth man run away from her, and before she could aim he hid behind the HM, dragging him towards the helicopter. He fired a round from his pistol towards her, which missed her. Over the din of the chopper blades she heard his loud call.

"Listen carefully, I am Sazo, Kiyanelie's second in command and I have a pistol with me. I also have the Indian HM with me!" He said and fired at her.

She heard the bullet hit the Jonga which passed through its body and missed her closely.

"The next bullet will be in HM's heart! Whoever you are, throw your weapon towards the helicopter, raise your hands and come out! I am going to count up to three. If you do not come out after I finish counting, you will find HM dead!" Sazo called out and started counting.

Hina got up, threw the rifle towards the helicopter and walked towards Sazo, who kept moving closer to the Chopper using the HM as his shield.

"Ho ho! So it is our great Capt Hina Rathore! You indeed have nine lives! I am afraid you have outlived them," Sazo said and picked up her rifle.

"My life is in my God's hand and so is yours!" She said with scorn.

"Yes that is true, but God is with me now!" He shouted out. Hina approached him and stood facing him.

"You Mr Home Minister, get into the Chopper quickly before I put a bullet in your leg!" He ordered Ankush, who climbed into the Chopper with the assistance of the copilot and occupied the rear seat.

The pilot switched on the engine and the rotors swirled into action. Sazo went towards him and shouted out instructions, which he acknowledged by raising his thumb.

"Hold on for a minute for me. I will join you after I finish with her," Sazo called out to him.

When she saw Sazo turn to talk to the pilot, Hina lifted her leg slightly, removed the pistol from her ankle holster and put it in her pocket.

Sazo, after finishing his conversation with the pilot, came towards Hina with his revolver pointed at her.

"Kneel down and say your prayers!" He shouted. Hina knelt down on her knees facing him.

"I am sure you will give me my last wish!" She cried out, with fear showing in her eyes.

"Go ahead and ask!" He shouted back.

"My mother is the last person I want to see before I die! Her picture is in my wallet, which is in my pocket. Can I take it out, please?" She pleaded.

"Oh my! What a last wish! Go ahead and see the picture, but make it snappy!" Sazo said and smiled.

Hina dipped her hand in her pocket, held the pistol with her fingers, pointed it at Sazo's chest and pressed the trigger. The bullet passed through his heart killing him instantly. The pilot who was watching them from the cockpit, saw Sazo drop on the ground and Hina getting up. He immediately revved up the engine and the chopper started leaving the ground.

She jumped up, ran towards the helicopter and saw it rising up. Standing still for a moment, she leapt and managed to catch its landing skid. Heaving herself up, she stood on the skid and grabbed the door latch to steady herself. She held the pistol in the other hand and signaled the pilot to bring the chopper down on the ground. The pilot shook his head and raised it upwards.

Keeping her hand steady, she fired and the bullet broke open the door latch. She held the door with one hand, jerked it open and entered the chopper.

"Listen you dumb wits! If you do not do what I tell you, I will kill you both! I know a bit about flying, I can safely land the chopper here! Do you both want to die? Do you want to go where your friend Sazo has gone?" She asked pointing her pistol at them. They looked at one another and spoke in Chinese.

"Ok, where do you want to go?" The pilot said in English, handing over the map to her.

She examined the map and marked the location with the red pencil. Gave it to the pilot who turned the helicopter towards the new destination.

After crossing the thickly wooded area she sat next to Ankush and attempted to speak to him. Over the din of the noise from the chopper her voice remained unheard. She too could not hear him as he spoke. She tapped the copilot on his shoulder, took his headset from him and wore it.

"Look down!" The pilot shouted in his mouthpiece.

From the ground below she saw bullets fired from a truck which was moving in the same direction as the chopper. The bullets missed the chopper as it was flying at an altitude well beyond the weapons range. She shouted out to the pilot, when suddenly she saw a bright object speeding towards them.

"Look there! They are firing stinger missiles. Use the flares immediately!" She called out through the headset, pointing towards the oncoming object.

The pilot, taken aback, immediately changed the direction of the chopper and pressed the switch, releasing the flares. The missile hit the flares and fell harmlessly on the ground.

"There is another one on the way! Do we have flares left?" Hina yelled.

"Yes, the last ones," said the pilot and pressed the switch again. This missile too went the same way as the previous one, harmlessly dropping on the ground.

"Oh my God! What should we do now?" Hina called out loudly, as the flares were no longer available.

She looked down and noticed that the truck had halted, men had dismounted and were firing their rifles at random towards the chopper.

"It seems we have crossed the border and they do not have any more missiles!" Hina said and sat down with a sigh of relief. They were now in Indian Territory, she felt safe and hoped the nightmare would end soon. She looked at Ankush and gave him a thumbs up sign.

Her thoughts were disturbed when looking ahead she saw at some distance a speck in the sky, which was approaching them. As it came closer she felt relieved and stood up clapping her hand.

"It is our army armed helicopter sent to escort us! Thank God! We are safe now!" She cried out.

"She stood close to her chopper door, faced the pilot flying the armed helicopter and pantomimed, indicating that she was from India. She pointed to her army uniform, and gestured with her hands that they would not land but continue to proceed on their course.

A man opened the attack helicopter door, sat on the floor, aimed and fired his rifle. The bullets whizzed past very close to her chopper. The Chinese pilot, taken by surprise and alarmed, pushed the stick bringing it down, forcing the chopper to fly just above the trees. He continued flying at this dangerous height and took evasive action by maneuvering the chopper in a zig zag route. The attack helicopter kept hovering above them for some distance and then leveled with their chopper.

He noticed that the man in the armed helicopter was preparing to fire at them; without any warning, the pilot forced the chopper into a steep vertical climb, throwing Hina back on her seat. After rising more than two thousand feet the chopper leveled up and proceeded on its course. Hina heaved a sigh of relief and looked at the HM who sat with fear written all over his pale face, his hands trembling.

She heard the pilot speaking in Chinese over the radio to probably his counterpart on the ground in Myanmar. After completing his talk, he raised his hand beckoning her.

"Our traffic control tower is asking us to return to the nearest Myanmar helipad immediately. The Indian Government has objected to an unauthorised Myanmar helicopter flying in their territory," he said.

"Check up with them if they are communicating with Indian traffic control. If they are, then ask them to give us the frequency with which we can directly talk to the Indian traffic controller," Hina instructed him. The pilot conveyed it over the radio and shook his head.

"They say that they will not give the frequency, and are ordering us to return," he said.

Hena felt dismayed, the situation was getting critical, danger loomed from both sides. For her to return to Myanmar with the HM would be deja vu and extremely dangerous; she was quite certain that they would be sent to China immediately on landing. Sadly the Indian traffic controller was worried about the intrusion by a Myanmar chopper, totally ignoring the valuable asset, their HM who was flying in it. They were busy firing at their helicopter, not aware of his presence in the helicopter. She had to convey the message to them without any further delay.

"Tell them that the chopper has developed some snag and you want to land. You want the frequency to talk to the Indian traffic controllers. You will give them the location and seek protection from being arrested on landing," she instructed the pilot.

After much chat to and fro the pilot heaved a sigh and looked at Hina.

"I have the frequency you can speak to your traffic controller," he said, adjusting the instrument on the dashboard.

"What is your call sign code?" She asked.

"Papa Mike 1," he said.

"This is Papa Mike 1, calling the control tower, can you hear me?" She called out over the mike.

She heard a crackling sound and other static disturbances before a clear voice came over the radio.

"Papa Mike 1, control tower here, I can hear you loud and clear," the traffic controller said.

"I am Capt Hina Thakur of NSG. The Home Minister of India is with me in the helicopter. He had been kidnapped but now he is safe. Please allow us to land," Hina spoke.

After a long wait she heard the voice on the headset.

"We have no quick means to check up your concocted story! You are travelling in a Myanmar helicopter without any clearance. It is a violation of our air space. If you do not return to Myanmar immediately we have no other option but to shoot down the chopper. We will not allow you to land in our country," the Controller spoke in a stern and clear voice.

"Why do you not allow us to land? We can land in the next clearing in the forest," she suggested.

"No! We suspect you are carrying drugs or weapons which will disappear before our security persons reach you! Though you are on our radar screen it will take us sometime before we know your exact location. Presently we have learnt about you from the helicopter that fired warning shots on you, and is ready with missiles to hit you! Return immediately, or within the next three minutes you will be shot down," the Controller replied.

The Chinese pilot was listening to the conversation between Hina and the controller, he pulled the stick sideways to change the direction of the chopper.

"No, we are not going back! Keep on course!" Hina said, pushing her pistol on his temple.

The pilot quickly corrected the course to its original direction. The HM signaled to her if he could speak to the Control Tower. She signaled back indicating to him to relax, knowing fully well that the traffic controller will not recognise him.

"Let me try it my way," the pilot shouted out to her.

"OK, but do not do anything silly. I will shoot you if you play any tricks," Hina warned him.

The pilot nodded and adjusting the instrument on the panel, speaking in English.

"Papa Mike 1, this is Chang Li, the Chinese pilot. I have some good news for you. If you do not call off your helicopters and aircraft, the entire population in the village over which my chopper is hovering will be wiped out within minutes, and you will be held responsible," he said.

"What do you mean? I do not understand you!" The Controller replied with alarm in his voice.

"From Baoshan China, I am carrying mustard gas, a weapon of mass destruction, to deliver it to Kiyanelie. I got lost and strayed into your territory. My chopper has developed a serious snag, if you do not allow me to land, it will crash damaging the containers. The toxins from them will spill out, spread in the air, causing death and sickness to all living beings over many square miles," the pilot spoke emphatically.

"You are bluffing! I do not believe you," the Controller said.

"I am serious, and I request you to take me seriously too. I suggest that you have a word with your superiors," the pilot advised.

He kept the chopper hovering among the trees and waited for the Controller to respond.

"Papa Mike1, permission granted. Keep your communication lines open. Land at the nearest airfield or helipad and call me up," the Controller told him without consulting his superiors.

The pilot brought down the chopper to a reasonable height and directed it on its original route. Hina stood behind him with the pistol pointed over his head. They flew for another three minutes before she spotted the camp.

"You see the helipad ahead, land there immediately," Hina told the pilot looking through the windscreen.

As the pilot lowered the chopper, she noticed that the helipad was deserted with no signs of activity around it. She looked at Ankush who was smiling with his thumbs raised up!

"Papa Mike 1, to control tower, reached destination, preparing to land!" The pilot spoke out.

They were barely thirty feet above the ground when a bullet pierced through the windscreen killing the pilot. As the chopper wavered, the copilot in total shock and panic lost control, allowing the chopper to free fall and crash on the ground.

Hina plunged out through the open chopper door and fell on her head and blacked out. Ankush jolted, jarred and totally shaken by the impact remained in his seat with the seat belt holding him. The co pilot sat listless suffering from concussion from the blow on his head, which had hit the panel in front.

"Kilo Lima, to control the tower, mission accomplished as per your orders. Enemy chopper down! Returning to base!"

"Copy that," said the traffic controller, hearing the message from the attack helicopter pilot loud, and clear and heaved a sigh of relief!

□

29

The ten men strong Para Commando team, with Sano guiding them, reached the rebel camp before midday. It was not the fear of encountering the rebels en route that had prompted them to take circuitous route but to avoid a confrontation with the Burmese border guards and civilians. The soldiers wore civilian clothing and effectively camouflaged their personal weapons.

"The armory is 100 yards from the tree line." Sano told Akhilesh, as they halted at the edge of the opening.

"How many men are guarding Brijesh?" He asked Sano.

"I do not know. The camp appears to be nearly vacant. I can sneak in and find out," Sano suggested. Akhilesh heard her and contemplated for sometime.

'OK, go ahead. We will wait here for 10 minutes after which we move into action," he told her and gave her a walkie talkie for communicating with him.

Sano left them and walked at her normal pace towards the room where she had last seen Brijesh. She was 50 yards short of her objective when two Naga rebels hiding in a trench sprung up and faced her. Taken aback, her initial reaction was to turn and run.

"Stop, do not move!" She heard a rebel shout. She stopped and stood still.

"Why are you here? What do you want?" He asked her and came forward for a body search.

She was about to reply when looking over his head she noticed a familiar figure looking towards her. She jumped up and waved at that person. He waved back and in long strides reached her quickly.

"Sano you are late! You should have been here five minutes back. Never mind, let us go! You have to bandage the patient, maybe for the last time, as they are moving him out of the camp," the doctor told her, ignoring the rebel soldiers.

The soldiers stood aside and permitted them to walk towards the patient's room, where Sano found two men with weapons sitting outside on a bench. They got up as the doctor stopped to introduce her.

"She is Sano, who is helping me with the patient. He is Khoula and he is Yang, they are responsible for the safety of the patient," the doctor said pointing to the two men who nodded and sat down.

"Can I go to the toilet? I will be back in a minute," Sano asked the doctor, who nodded.

She headed for the ladies toilet, noting that no one was observing her, proceeded towards the side door and came out of the building. The laughter and chatting from close quarters alerted her and she bent and lay on the ground. Not very far from her she saw the heads of two men who were standing in a trench and facing away from the building. The source of the chatter was obvious, however to sneak past them posed a major problem for her.

It appeared to her that there were trenches all around the building and she would definitely invite attention if she attempted to leave from any of the sides. It was not possible within the time frame to meet Akhilesh. She had no other option but to speak to inform him on the walkie talkie, which again was risky in the open. She entered the building, sat in the toilet with the door closed, spoke to Akhilesh in whispers and updated him on the ground situation.

"Sano, please hurry up! I have to see a few more patients," she heard the doctor call out. Ending the conversation with Akhilesh, who cautioned her to be careful, she joined the doctor.

"Sorry Sir! I think I too will have the stomach flu soon!" She smiled and spoke to the doctor.

"Never mind! We will attend to you later. Let us get on with him," the doctor said, pointing towards Brijesh.

For the next half an hour both the doctor and Sano treated Brijesh's almost healed wounds. After Sano completed bandaging his wounds the doctor clapped his hands when he noticed Brijesh walk with ease wearing his shoes, and sit comfortably on the bench.

"Very good! Tomorrow you leave, my job is over," the doctor said and left the room with Sano following him. She looked back at Brijesh and gestured with her fingers that she would very soon be here to take him away. Brijesh smiled and waved back at her.

"Here take this, it is Ibuprofen. Take one tablet every six hours in case you have a fever. The flu will go away soon, if it is not viral. No other medicine is needed," the doctor said and handed the tablets to her after they had walked at some distance away from the building.

"Thank you very much! It is very kind of you Sir," Sano said, taking the tablets.

"No! I must thank you! You are a very good nurse! Meet me here tomorrow, I will take you to my clinic where you can work with me," he smiled and waved his hand. Sano left him and headed towards the tree line.

"It is too risky to go in now. We will wait until it gets dark," Akhilesh told her, handing her a cup of tea from his flask. Sano felt her nerves relax as she sipped it. Picking up a stick, she started to sketch the locations of the buildings on the bald ground patch. She marked the position of the trenches and the probable location of the guard room where the men lived.

"There are four trenches around the buildings and in each trench there are two armed men. Two men sit at the entrance of the building and probably there will be another eight men in the guard room to relieve those on duty. In all I would say we have 18 to 20 men here guarding Brijesh and what is left in the armory," Sano explained.

Akhilesh heard her with great attention and was impressed with the information she had submitted.

"Good going Sano! Now give me sometime to come up with a plan," he said.

Excluding himself, Akhilesh had 10 men which he considered as sufficient for the task at hand; Sano was also a very useful member. He sent two men on either side to reconnoiter the area around the buildings and took out his binoculars to look ahead and around the building.

The men returned after an hour and confirmed the information given by Sano. He gathered his men and in detail explained to each the task assigned to them. The men dispersed and positioned themselves in their respective locations waiting for Akhilesh's signal.

As the sun went down they started checking their weapons and ammunition. Brijesh gave Sano a pistol with a filled magazine. She hid it behind her back under her belt and covered it with her shirt top. She moved close to the fringe of the tree line and sat hidden behind a bush.

Soon she noticed a girl not very far from her going towards the building. The girl held a basket on her head with one hand and a bag with the other. She requested Akhilesh to allow her to join the girl. This will give her an opportunity to be inside the building, when they assault it. On getting his approval, she got up from her position ran towards the girl and joined her.

"Sano what are you doing here?" The girl stopped, and looked at her completely surprised.

"Oh, I am going to see the patient. What are you carrying Tierra?" Sano asked her.

"Dinner for the men and the patient," Tierra replied.

"Give me the patient's dinner packet, I will carry it," Sano said.

With her help Tierra lowered the basket from her head and put it on the ground. She removed a plastic carry bag filled with eatables and gave it to Sano. The men in the trench watched them as they continued walking towards the building where Tierra handed two bags to Khoula and left.

"What are you doing here?" Khoula asked Sano.

"I am here to see the patient. The doctor asked me to change his bandages as he is leaving tomorrow and to give him the medicine which I am carrying," she said pointing to her skirt pocket.

"What is in that bag?" He asked.

"It has his dinner," she replied. Khoula looked into the bag, gave it back to her and allowed her to enter the building.

The sun had set and lanterns were lit, as the generator was sent to another camp. From his position Akhilesh counted four locations from which the lights showed up. Each building had a lantern lit up inside a room and outside near the entrance door. He liked the darkness surrounding other areas especially around the trenches. On the walkie talkie he called up his men and ordered them to move in.

Three soldiers closed in on the building in which eight rebels not on guard duty, were having their dinner. Breaking open the windows on either side, the soldiers lobbed hand grenades inside the building. They then joined their colleagues who waited for the rebels at the entrance door. The grenades exploded killing three rebels instantly and injuring two others seriously. The remaining three who rushed through the exit door were shot down. The soldiers entered the building and killed the two alive and injured rebels.

Akhilesh, who had heard the sound of the simultaneous blasts all around when his men had closed in on the trenches, crawled close to a trench and lobbed the grenades in it. Escaping unhurt Nagas were shot down by a soldier waiting close to each trench. With no opposition nearby, he and the soldiers could now safely advance towards the building unhindered.

Suddenly to his surprise, a spurt of machine gun fire halted them, and made them run for cover. They turned, and hid behind the trees as the bullets continued to fly in their direction. From his night vision binoculars he located the machine gun and noticed that it was positioned at the entrance of the building in which Brijesh was held prisoner. He picked up his walkie talkie and called out.

"Sano, Akhilesh here, the machine gun in front of your building has to be silenced immediately!" He said.

"I will try," she said and switched off the walkie talkie, when she noticed the room door opening.

Yang entered the room with the pistol raised and without looking at her ran towards the side door. Sano left the room and came out of the building and found Khoula firing the machine gun with the bullets flying in front in an arc.

"Get inside, you will get killed. We are under siege," Khoula shouted out to her.

Ignoring his words she approached him, stood near him and removed her pistol from under her belt.

"Let me help you, I can fire the machine gun," she called out and approached him.

Khoula looked at her and found the pistol pointing at him. Before he could speak, the bullet from her pistol pierced his skull and he dropped dead, the machine gun became silent. She immediately rushed back and entered the room and found Yang pointing his rifle at Brijesh.

"This is the last opportunity for you! Spill it out or you die!" She heard Yang shouting. She heard Brijesh laugh out loud.

"Not me but, you are going to die my friend! Look behind you!" He said, looking at Khoula with pity and disdain.

With a jerk Yang turned his head, keeping the rifle pointed at Brijesh.

"You traitor..." before he could complete the sentence the bullet from Sano's pistol pierced his head and he dropped dead.

She went towards Brijesh and helped him to get up. He hugged her and planted kisses on her forehead.

"Thank you Sano for saving my life!" He said and put on his shoes.

She helped him as they ambled outside the building and lumbered ahead towards the treeline. Soldiers joined them from both the directions and lifted Brijesh on their shoulder carrying him towards Akhilesh, who met them at the predesignated RV.

"Let us get out of here quickly," Akhilesh told them.

He went towards Sano, held her shoulders tightly, encircled his arm around her and kissed her on her head.

"Thank you Sano! You are a true commando! May God bless you," He said emotionally.

The journey in darkness to the army camp was uneventful as they had carefully planned the exit route, avoiding the guard posts on both sides of the border. They reached in the early hours of the morning. Without disturbing anyone in the camp. Brijesh was taken to Kashif's tent who hugged Akhilesh, and congratulated him. Akhilesh left him, stating that he would brief everyone in the morning.

"You have had an extremely grueling and exhausting day. Please go to sleep now, we will meet everyone tomorrow," Kashif told Brijesh.

Removing his shoes Brijesh lay down, feeling a soft and a proper bed after a very long absence. From Sano he had learnt that he would soon meet Hina. With sweet anticipation and a light heart he closed his eyes and slept peacefully.

Sano left Brijesh and headed for Hina's tent which was in the opposite direction to Kashif's. It was dark inside, she found her bed lay down and closed her eyes.

□

30

Early next morning Kashif entered the tent and found Sano lying in her bed. As he turned to leave, he heard Sano calling him.

"How are you? That was a great job! I have heard everything from Akhilesh! He is full of praises for you!" Kashif told her and sat in the chair next to her bed.

"Thank you! We all did what Akhilesh told us. Everyone has done well," Sano commented.

"Where is Hina?" Kashif queried.

"I do not know," Sano replied.

"Here I am!" Hina said with a broad smile and entered the tent. Sano got up and ran up to her with open arms. She held Hina in a firm embrace kissing her cheeks several times.

"Oh my sister! What a relief! I am so happy!" Sano said.

"Where have you been?" Kashif asked Hina.

"Went to see my father! He is fast asleep! I will meet him when he gets up," she replied.

"Sano did a great job! Akhilesh and his team are all in love with her!" Kashif said with pride.

"Yes they should be! From the MI room tent, where I slept at night, I came to this tent early in the morning and found her sleeping peacefully! I knew instantly that my father was safely rescued!" Hina said, sat down with Sano on the bed and encircling her arms around her waist pulled her down. Sano rested her head on her lap.

"Tell me what happened to your head?" Sano asked her lovingly, looking up and touching her wound with soft fingers.

"Ask Kashif, he knows much more than me. I was brought here in a semi conscious condition," Hina said.

Sano looked towards Kashif, eagerly expecting him to shed light.

"I will narrate everything that I know. It was around 5 pm when I had returned from a meeting and was removing my shoes in the tent, I heard a loud sound from outside the tent. The noise appeared to be of something big hitting the ground and crashing. Putting on my shoes I ran and found my men heading towards the helipad. I followed them and on reaching the site, the spectacle on the ground shocked me. The wreckage from a helicopter was strewn all over; the cockpit with portions of the main body were intact but hung precariously on the cliff," Kashif said and left them. He went out and called out to the sentry and spoke to him.

"Sorry for the interruption, I have ordered tea for everyone," he told them when he returned.

"Please continue!" Sano said, showing her impatience.

"Where was I? Yes, the main body of the chopper! We pulled it out carefully and found three bodies in it. They were laid on the ground and the doctor examined them. One person was dead, and two were injured, one of them severely. The person who was not seriously injured was Ankush our HM, who soon opened his eyes but remained dazed. We removed them to our camp and the doctors got busy with them. It was getting dark, we could not evacuate them to our Base Hospital in Imphal. They spent the night in the camp under the watchful eyes of our doctors," Kashif said and paused.

"Where was Hina?" Sano asked impatiently.

"We found her lying on the ground some 15 yards away from the chopper debris. She was unconscious when we carried her to the camp. She was treated for nearly half an hour, only then she regained consciousness. The injury to her head is fairly deep, fortunately her skull is intact. The HM has been evacuated to our base hospital early this morning and Hina will be the next to go, as soon as the chopper returns or some other arrives. That's all! You know everything now!" Kashif said and smiled.

"Who were the two men?" Sano asked.

"Chinese pilots who were tasked to fly the HM to some place in China, where he would be held as a hostage along with my father," Hina told her.

"Oh my God! We had the information, and we could do nothing about it!" Sano said with a deep sigh.

"Yes, only if I had the opportunity to contact the HM before he attended the meeting! Well that is in the past now! Hina let us go and meet your father, see if he is awake," Kashif said. Hina got up and followed Kashif as they left.

"I will join you soon," Sano shouted out.

On reaching the tent Kashif learnt from the sentry that Brijesh was awake and had just finished his morning ablutions.

"You go ahead! I met him last night. I will meet him after sometime," Kashif said and left towards his office tent.

Her heart swelled with stored up sentiments when she entered the tent and found her father sitting on a chair with his face towards the tent entrance, perhaps expecting her arrival. She put the flap down and took a few steps forward for him to see her. He looked up with probing eyes and when she realised he had recognised her, she ran towards him and sat on her knees facing him.

"Papa!" She cried out putting her head on his lap.

"My darling! My doll!" Brijesh said, with tears flowing profusely and his hand caressing her hair.

"Papa! How are you Papa? Oh my God! At last you are with me! I am so happy! I feel so peaceful!" She said and broke down.

Her body shook as she wept uncontrollably and continuously. Her hysterical condition broke Brijesh's heart and he wailed loudly.

"My child! I am alright and will get better now! Please stop weeping!" He cried out, leaned forward and hugged her. She clung onto him, her weeping reduced but the sobbing continued!

"I missed you Papa! I really missed you very much!" She said between her sobs.

"Yes my child, I missed you too!" Brijesh sobbed.

"You know Papa! Dada and dadi are very very worried! They kept ringing me asking about you," Hina said.

"Yes, I too was very concerned about them! You tell them I am fine," he said.

"Here, drink some water and go wash your face!" Sano told her on entering the tent.

Hina gave the glass to her father and got up to go to the toilet. She returned after freshening up and sat on her father's bed. Both kept chatting, recounting their experiences, since he was kidnapped. He mentioned his days of torture and agony in captivity and showed no abhorrence or loathing towards his captors and torturers. Hina chronicled her efforts to find him and the help she received from various people. He appreciated her decision to help to thwart Kinayales attempt to kidnap the Home Minister rather than join the patrol to rescue him.

Sano joined them, narrated the adventure she had with her patrol which rescued Brijesh.

"How is Monalisa?" Brijesh asked her.

"She is fine. She is in Yunsi waiting for you to return," Sano told him.

"Yes we will go there soon. I do want to meet her," Brijesh said. Hina and Sano looked at one another and smiled.

A soldier entered the tent and spoke to Hina asking her if he could bring lunch for everyone now. Hina looked at her watch which indicated that it was 1230 pm and thought that it was a bit early for lunch.

"You can bring lunch after one hour. Tell Maj Kashif that my father wants to meet him," Hina told the soldier.

"Who is Kashif?" Brijesh asked Hina.

"Major Kashif Abidi is the leader of the team that provided security during the surrender meeting, and he has been a great help throughout. In fact he saved my life on several occasions. He told me he met you last night," Hina replied.

"Did he? Is he a tall and handsome young man?" Brijesh asked her.

"Yes. Hina likes him very much and he likes her too," Sano interjected with a mischievous smile.

"Oh! That's excellent! I would love to meet him again," Brijesh said looking at Hina.

"Papa, don't get carried away! We are just friends," Hina told him.

"Very close friends!" Sano spoke out quickly. Hina looked at her with menacing eyes and smiled when Sano too gave her a stare.

"Good afternoon Sir!" They heard Kashif say, as he entered the tent and stood facing Brijesh.

Brijesh returned the greeting and asked Kashif to sit in the vacant chair. He kept looking at him, feeling satisfied with his daughter's choice.

"Sorry Sir, I got delayed. I was in a meeting with Longayo and Akai. They are here and want to meet you. Can you walk up to my office?" Kashif asked Brijesh.

"Yes certainly, with a little help from my daughter," he said with a smile.

Hina helped him to stand and placed his hand on her shoulders. With her hands around his waist, she guided him towards the office. He was greeted by Ravi, Atul and the two chiefs and shook hands with them. They sat down in their chairs placed in a semicircle with Hina standing behind the one occupied by her father. Both Longayo and Akai got up from their chairs and faced them.

"On behalf of our people we wish to convey our happiness and joy over the successful rescue of our HM and my dear friend Brijesh! Our special congratulations and thanks to Hina, for her brave act in bringing back our HM safely! As a token of our affection please accept these shawls." Longayo said and picked up a bundle lying in front of him. Kashif came forward and received it from him.

"We have Kiyanelie as our prisoner. Before we hand him to you, our elders and we both have decided that we conduct an open trial against him in front of our people. This trial is necessary as it will tell our people of the treacherous criminal activities of Kiyanelie and his followers against us. We feel that this will expose Kiyanelie as an evil person so that he and his followers are shunned and ostracized by the community. I request you all to be present during this important trial at my village," Akai spoke out.

As the issue of the trial had been discussed and agreed to by the Bde Cdr earlier, the vehicles were already parked to take them to the venue. Brijesh sat in front in the Jonga and Hina and Sano occupied the rear seats. Kashif drove the vehicle and halted it near the village gate. They were escorted to the meeting area in front of the Morung where benches were placed for them to sit.

Ahead facing them they saw a large group of men, women and children waiting anxiously for the trial to commence. Longayo, the Chief of Yunsai village, came forward and addressed them.

"We have KIyanelie, the Konayak rebel leader as our prisoner. You all are aware of his activities in the past and have observed the chaos caused by him yesterday. We have assembled here to give an opportunity to our prisoner to defend himself before we pronounce our judgement. The defendant will be afforded ample opportunity to present his case. We all know that he is well educated and conversant with not only the Indian Penal code but also with our tribal laws.

This man may be an ordinary rebel in normal times but not today, when so much has taken place which could bring curse and dishonor to not only to our village but to the entire Nagaland. This man who is from among us, misguides our youth, our men and women to confront the might of our country India. Under the guise of surrendering peacefully he has staged a diabolical drama of horrendous proportions," Longayo said and looked around, noticing that he had drawn the attention of the crowd.

"My village Yunsai has suffered regularly at the hands of his men, who on his orders have forcibly stolen our rice and spices, kidnapped our young boys, abducted girls and women whom they molested and raped. He has taken our boys as prisoners, used them as gun fodder to attack Indian army soldiers and convoys regularly. In retaliation we have been humiliated and have suffered miserably at the hands of the Army during their search and cordon operations. His actions at Sitni today have brought dishonor and disgrace to all of us. I have much more to say, but I now request my friend Akai to narrate further misdeeds by the prisoner before he is afforded an opportunity to speak," Longayo finished speaking and stepped back.

Akai got up and addressed his people.

"The Chief has spoken well, and I have nothing more to add but to emphasize the gravity of the crime committed by Kiyanelie. He wants Nagaland to be a free country. Tell me everyone, are we not free?" He raised his voice, asking the crowd.

"We are free!" The crowd shouted in one voice.

"Did you hear that Kiyanelie? This is exactly what the people of Nagaland say, we are free! How many men do you have those who disagree and want freedom from India? 1000 or even say 5000? That's about all you can coerce and muster. Your excuse about the excesses, forced on us by the army will not hold water; the army is abiding by the Indian Constitution, where Nagaland is part and parcel of India and any threat internal or external to its integrity and safety will be protected by them at all costs!" Akai said, looked around and noticed that the men were listening to him very attentively.

"Let us hear you Kiyanelie? What is your argument in your defense?" Akai asked him and stepped back.

Kiyanelie, who was sitting on a bench surrounded by soldiers, got up, waited and looked around. He laughed out loudly and spat out on the ground in front of the two chiefs.

"I consider it below my dignity to talk to you traitors and subservient stooges! I am not afraid of you, I know the Konayaks will pay you back in kind if anything happens to me. Whatever you do to me, the Konayaks will repay in double. You are cowards, you have lost your fighting spirit and are servants of this stupid democratic system. Your masters are your politicians who grow rich every day while you remain poor beggars. For every little thing you want, you have to grease their palms. Your police and your judiciary do not take care of you as they are corrupt. The army killed my entire family without any reason and it kills your men and women without any reason! They destroy your villages and make you homeless.

Where are your tribal traditions and values? Where is your freedom and independence that we are so proud of? You have lost everything, you are totally impotent! I have nothing further to tell you, cowards!" Kiyanelie uttered every word loudly and emphatically and spat out again, as he sat down.

Akai looked at Longayo and together they approached a group of elders sitting on benches in the rear. They all huddled into a short conversation after which both the Chiefs returned.

"Kiyanelie has said that we have shed our tribal traditions. To let him know that we do follow our forefathers, it is the unanimous decision by both our village elders and the Chiefs that in keeping with our tribal tradition we award tribal justice to Kiyanelie," Akai told the gathering.

Hina was at a loss to understand the reason for the crowd to cheer and clap loudly.

"Kiyanelie please come forward, kneel down and lower your head." Akai told him.

Finding no sign from him of getting up, Akai looked towards his men, who stepped forward, lifted Kiyanelie by the shoulders and made him stand facing the crowd. They forced him to kneel, pulled his head down by his hair and kept holding it.

Alarmed and worried, Kashif jumped up from his seat and stepped forward towards the prisoner. He felt a hand hold his arm firmly and pull him back.

"Sit down before the crowd pounces on you!" He heard Ravi's stern warning. Retracing his steps, he sat down, lowered his head, and closed his eyes.

Raising the sharp dah, Longayo stuck Kiyanelies neck with a swift downward swing. The head sheared off from his body, spurts of blood gushed out from the headless neck. The body twirled and twisted until the blood had drained out completely. The head lay on the ground with the face towards the crowd.

Hina watched the spectacle in awe, with a mixture of sadistic pleasure and revulsion! The uproar from the crowd was deafening, everyone stood up, cheering and clapping.

Akai looked towards the Bde Cdr who was sitting rigid and emotionless in his chair.

"Sir, I want to hand over the prisoner to you. Please arrange to take away his body," he said.

"What about the head?" Kashif asked.

"That will remain with us. We will hang it at the Morung entrance," Akai replied.

"You can keep both the head and the body. But ensure that he is given a proper funeral," The Bde Cdr told him curtly and got up to leave.

"Please sit down Sir. We have another ceremony which will take only a few minutes," Akai said and looked at a wizened elder sitting in the group in the rear. The elder got up from his seat, came forward and stood in front of Hina, who was completely baffled, got up slowly and faced him.

"Child you are a true Naga warrior! You remind us of our men and women who endure insurmountable challenges and hardships but never give up! You are one of us from this day onwards! Your safety and honor is our responsibility! You are the one who deserves the honor of beheading the evil Kiyanelie! Please accept this symbolic token from us and wear it always!" The old man said. He held a silver chain with a miniature metallic human head hanging from it.

"Please bend down," he said and smiled.

Hina bent her knees and bowed her head towards him. He placed the chain around her neck and kissed her forehead.

The crowd in the audience went mad with whistling, yelling, clapping and dancing!